Grimgar of Fantasy and Ash

level.8 - And So We Wait For Tomorrow

Written by: Ao Jyumonji
Illustrations by: Eiri Shirai

Team Haruhiro gets split up?!

The giant wolf was coming.

Coming.

Closing in.

Grimgar of Fantasy and Ash

GRIMGAR OF FANTASY AND ASH, LEVEL. 8

Copyright © 2016 Ao Jyumonji
Illustrations by Eiri Shirai

First published in Japan in 2016 by
OVERLAP Inc., Ltd., Tokyo.
English translation rights arranged with
OVERLAP Inc., Ltd., Tokyo.

Seven Seas books may be purchased in bulk for promotional,
educational, or business use. Please contact your local
bookseller or the Macmillan Corporate and Premium Sales
Department at 1-800-221-7945, extension 5442, or by
e-mail at MacmillanSpecialMarkets@macmillan.com.

Follow Seven Seas Entertainment online at
sevenseasentertainment.com.
Experience J-Novel Club books online at j-novel.club.

TRANSLATION: Sean McCann
J-NOVEL EDITOR: Emily Sorensen
COVER DESIGN: Nicky Lim
INTERIOR LAYOUT & DESIGN: Clay Gardner
COPY EDITOR: Will Holcomb
PROOFREADER: Kris Swanson
LIGHT NOVEL EDITOR: Nibedita Sen
EDITOR-IN-CHIEF: Adam Arnold
PUBLISHER: Jason DeAngelis

ISBN: 978-1-626929-11-1
Printed in Canada
First Printing: October 2018
10 9 8 7 6 5 4 3 2 1

Grimgar of Fantasy and Ash

level. 8 — And So We Wait for Tomorrow

Presented by
AO JYUMONJI

Illustrated by
EIRI SHIRAI

Seven Seas

novel club

Table of Contents

Characters

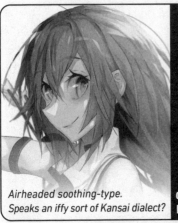

YUME

Airheaded soothing-type. Speaks an iffy sort of Kansai dialect?

CLASS: Hunter

HARUHIRO

Sleepy eyes. Passive-type. Provisional leader.

CLASS: Thief

SHIHORU

Shy and withdrawn. Hard worker with little presence.

CLASS: Mage

RANTA

Selfish, flaky joker. #1 most unpopular.

CLASS: Dread Knight

MERRY

Cool beauty. Has more experience as a volunteer soldier and is a little more of an adult.

CLASS: Priest

KUZAKU

The new guy. Hard to tell if he's motivated or not.

CLASS: Paladin

Other Characters

Soma's Comrades

Kemuri—CLASS: Paladin
Dreadlocks.

Pingo—CLASS: Necromancer
Age unknown.

Shima—CLASS: Shaman
Healer and big sister.

Lilia—CLASS: Sword Dancer
Tsundere elf.

Typhoon Rocks

Rock—CLASS: Warrior
Short and devoted.

Kajita—CLASS: Warrior
Skinhead.

Moyugi—CLASS: Dread Knight
Gentleman pervert.

Kuro—CLASS: Warrior
Former hunter and uses a bow.

Sakanami—CLASS: Thief
Biggest deviant in the Rocks.

Tsuga—CLASS: Priest
Man of common sense. Has important role of pointing out when things get silly.

MOGUZO

Bear-type. A somewhat slow, but reliable, bear. They relied on him too much.

CLASS:
Warrior

MANATO

Kept the party together. Was a good guy. (Past tense)

CLASS:
Priest

SOMA

Started the Day Breakers Clan. Seems to have some objective.

CLASS:
Samurai

CHOCO

Did Haruhiro know her? Fell at the orcish keep.

CLASS:
Thief

Grimgar of Fantasy and Ash

1 | Lost in the Fog

THE PATH WAS DARK AND TWISTED, and it sometimes grew so thin that it almost seemed like they hit a dead end, so the lantern's light only shone a foot or so ahead of them.

The rock walls he sometimes touched were hard and rough; so was the sensation of the ground under his feet. The further along they went, the more the fire of hope seemed to dim, and it felt like even the slightest breath could extinguish it. Even if they moved forward cautiously, step by step, was there even going to be a payoff for it at the end?

Was this the right choice?

Wasn't it a huge mistake instead?

It was hot when they first wandered in here, but sometime a while back the air took on a chill. The air was dry, but it still smelled like a bog for some reason.

"Hey, Parupiro..." Ranta began.

"What, Rantaronosuke?"

"Listen, pal, don't you dare add weird nonsense to the end of my great name. I'll kill you."

"If you stop messing with my name, I'll think about it."

"I've got rights, Parupyororin, and you'd better not infringe on them," Ranta said viciously. "Wait, hold on, is this really okay...?"

"It's fine," Haruhiro answered. He bit his lower lip.

Could he say that for sure? Was he confident about it?

No. There was no way he could be.

He didn't know whether it was fine or not. How could he?

This passageway connected Darunggar to Grimgar. Did he have any evidence? He had faith in Mr. Unjo's story, so that felt like something.

Mr. Unjo wandered into a foggy place on the border between the former kingdoms of Nananka and Ishmal, then reached Darunggar by passing through a cave he found there. He was a former volunteer soldier, with far more seniority than Haruhiro and the party. It was hard to imagine someone like that would lie to them. He was trustworthy.

Still, even if he wasn't lying, he could have misremembered. Even if Mr. Unjo had spoken the truth, what proof did they have that this passageway was the cave in question?

Was this even a passageway at all?

If it wasn't... No, how would they even decide that it wasn't?

If the path ahead was blocked, Haruhiro would have to admit this was a mistake.

That's right, he thought. *We have no choice but to go as far as it takes us.*

Was that really true?

What if they went as far as they possibly could, only to arrive at a dead end? Maybe it would be better for them to turn back while they still could, but how far was far enough to know for sure, and where precisely was that point of no return?

It started to bother him, so Haruhiro looked upward. He lifted his lantern. There was no visible roof; it was almost like they were in a deep, dark rift.

It's different, he thought.

This place wasn't like the passageway in Grimgar's Wonder Hole that connected to the Dusk Realm, or the one they had passed through on their way to Darunggar, either.

For starters, there were no gremlins.

Lala had talked about how gremlins could cross from one world to another, or at least find the places where worlds connected and flee through them.

But there were no gremlins in this passageway.

Didn't that mean this was the wrong place?

It might.

It also might not.

He didn't know.

How long had it been since they'd entered this passageway? His sense of time wasn't just dulled, it basically disappeared. The days they had spent in Darunggar were like a distant memory, and when it came to Grimgar, he had to question whether they'd ever been there at all.

Did Grimgar even exist? Wasn't he just imagining it did?

There was no way they could go back to a place he wasn't even sure existed.

Moving forward, turning back; it was all the same. They would never get out of here. They had no choice but to wander until the last of their strength gave out.

How was that fine? It wasn't. Haruhiro lied, to his comrades and himself.

He felt his regret, self-loathing, duty, weakness, and despair dragging him down, strangling him, binding him hand and foot. How could he move forward when he was suffering under their weight? Wasn't he going to stop?

Even with everyone here, he felt alone. The lantern lit the path ahead, but he saw nothing. He felt abandoned in an abject darkness.

Isn't this good enough? he thought in despair. *Time to stop. I mean, it's not fair. Why am I the only one going through this?*

Ranta can complain whenever he wants, so he's got it easy. If you don't like it, do it yourself, man. Take some responsibility. You try carrying this heavy burden. It's not like I ever wanted to. If I didn't have to, I wouldn't. I'm not kidding. I've had enough. I don't care who it is, I just want someone to take over.

"Is that really okay with you?" a voice said.

Haruhiro heard the voice, so he turned back. His eyes met Merry's.

"What's wrong?" she asked.

"Just now," he said, before he cut himself short.

No one had said anything. It was all in his head. He'd heard a voice when there was none. Of course. There was no way he could have heard that voice.

After all...it had been *Manato's voice.*

Manato was gone. He wasn't anywhere now, outside of Haruhiro and the others' memories.

But what if Manato was to ask him that?

Is that really okay with you?

If Manato hit him with that question, how would Haruhiro respond? If Manato *could* ask, Haruhiro might want to turn to him for help.

Please, he imagined saying. *I'm begging you, come back.*

Manato would probably give him a slightly troubled smile, then say, "Even if I wanted to take over for you, I can't. You know that, Haruhiro."

A ghostly voice spoke up again.

"I'm not one to talk," it said, "but I'll tell you what I think."

That was weird.

Really weird.

He could even hear Moguzo's voice.

"If you really don't want to—if it's hard on you—I think you can quit," Moguzo said. "If you talk to them, everyone will understand. But..."

"Haruhiro, would that be okay with you?" Manato asked again.

"If you're tired..."

When he heard Shihoru's voice, Haruhiro thought that maybe he was still sane. His feet were still moving.

"Nah, I'm not tired."

Haruhiro shook his head slightly, but then thought, *What about the others?* It looked like he was still thinking straight.

Is that okay with me? he wondered. *I dunno. Maybe not? What does everyone else think?*

Well, even if I suddenly said, "I'm done being the leader. Someone else do it," they wouldn't know what to do. Would it be like, "Come on, just do it?"

Well, I'll still do it. I know no one else wants to. So, for now, I'll do it. No matter what happens, don't come crying to me, though, okay?

If things went really bad, the rest of them would be just as much to blame for making a guy like him be the leader for so long. It wouldn't just be the leader's fault; Haruhiro wasn't alone. Even if Haruhiro screwed up as the leader, it would still be everyone's fault.

"Is that how you really feel?" Moguzo asked.

That's right, Moguzo, thought Haruhiro. *I'm sure I'm no better than this.*

Haruhiro had no resolve. In the time since Manato passed, he'd had more than enough time to make peace with being the leader, and he wasn't even aware of how unprepared he was. He went with the flow, pressed by necessity, and somehow he managed to deal with all the tasks that piled up in front of him up until now. That was all.

Manato was different. He was only with them for a short time, but it felt like if they followed Manato, they would get somewhere in the end. It felt like he'd pull them along to a better place. It felt like he'd lead them.

"We've become a good party," Manato had said once.

Thinking back on it now, Manato had seen something then, some sort of path toward the future they should follow. He stood up front, looking further ahead than anyone else, his eyes turned upward.

Haruhiro could see nothing. He wasn't even trying to look. He couldn't think about what was to come. What would things be like tomorrow... no, even later today? What was going to happen?

That was something Haruhiro didn't know. No, not just Haruhiro; nobody knew.

He didn't want to get his hopes up.

He didn't want to have hope.

He didn't want to be disappointed.

He didn't want to get hurt.

He always set his goals low. He only wished for the things he thought he could get. If it didn't work out, well, that was that. He could just abandon responsibility at the last second. What choice did he have? He wasn't cut out for this.

"Is that okay with you?" Manato asked again.

No.

No, that wasn't it.

Manato wasn't saying anything to him. He couldn't.

Manato wasn't going to show him where to go. Moguzo wouldn't stand up front and swing his sword for them. Those two wouldn't cheer Haruhiro on. They couldn't give him courage. Because neither of them were here.

Because they were dead.

Haruhiro came to a stop, and the party halted behind him. He took a deep breath. Things smelled a little different here, though it was hard to explain how. The air was damp.

"There are hurdles out there that are insurmountable," Haruhiro said aloud. "That's life. I'm sure there are things you just can't do anything about. I can't go and say that I'm sure it'll work out somehow."

Obviously, Haruhiro couldn't be like Manato. Even so, he wanted to see new things with everyone. He wanted to pull everyone along the way Manato had; not because he didn't have a choice, but because it was what he wanted to do. Haruhiro would find his own way to make it happen. For that, he had to take things on one at a time.

First, no matter what happened, he couldn't run away. He wouldn't abandon his role, his position. That was one thing he now resolved never to do.

"But still," Haruhiro said, "we can get over this one. I mean, we've been through a lot. Compared to some of the stuff we've been through, this isn't even that bad. If we're all together, I'm not worried in the least."

"There's some big talk. Like you're someone important," Ranta said before succumbing to a snorting laugh. "Well, when things get rough, you've got me. I can make anything work, man."

"If there's one thing we have to worry about..." Shihoru muttered.

"What was that?!" said Ranta. "I'll grope you! You and your damn squeezable tits!"

"Please rein in your libido some," Haruhiro said, sighing.

"Shut your face, Pyarupyororon! Listen, man! Let me tell you, I'm pent up, okay!"

"Too much information, Ranta-kun," Kuzaku said under his breath.

"Shut up! Fine, Kuzacky, Parupiro, what about the two of you?! If any healthy young man was living with women the way we are, it'd be perfectly natural for him to get so pent up he might explode! If anything, there'd be something wrong with him as a man if he wasn't, you know?!"

"Is that how it is?" said Merry. She glanced at Haruhiro and Kuzaku. The question demanded an answer that neither felt equipped to give.

"Well," said Haruhiro. He exchanged glances with Kuzaku.

Kuzaku shook his head, but it wasn't clear what the gesture meant.

Haruhiro looked down and twisted his head to the side.

"Not really," he said, "not for me. It's different for everyone; I mean, that's true for anything, but everyone handles it differently, you could say..."

"Hrm," said Yume.

She crossed her arms and puffed up one of her cheeks.

"Hey, hey, he was sayin' he's pent up, but what exactly's gettin' pent up anyway?"

"Er," said Haruhiro, "that's—"

"Oh, and if he's got somethin' pent up, and it's ready to burst, y'know, Yume was thinkin' maybe he should just let it out."

"Yume," said Shihoru, tugging on Yume's sleeve with an almost pitying look on her face.

The way Yume went "Huh?" like she wasn't just playing dumb was incredibly worrying.

Merry cast her eyes downward, apparently deep in thought. Haruhiro wondered if she was at a loss for what to do.

Kuzaku was looking up for some reason. He apparently wanted to pretend this had nothing to do with him.

No fair, thought Haruhiro.

"Heheheheh..." Ranta laughed creepily. "Heheheh. Gwahahahaha! That's right, Yume. You've got it. If I'm pent up, I should just let it out! That's the one true answer!"

"Uh-huh," Yume said. "That's why Yume said it."

"But! If I'm letting it out, the thing is, I can't just whip it out and go," Ranta declared.

"Wuh? You can't?"

"Yeah. Sorta. So, I'm gonna need you to put up with me for a bit. You were the one who suggested it, after all. Let me play with some tits. Let me play with *your* tits. While I play with your tits, I'm gonna—"

"Dark," Shihoru called.

The elemental appeared from nowhere and perched itself on Shihoru's shoulder. He looked like black string coiled into a human shape.

"H-hey," Ranta said as he backed away. "H-hold on. Okay? Lay off, Shihoru."

"Don't say my name. You're filthy. Dark—"

"Whoa, whoa, whoa, whoa, I-I get it, I mean, come on, you're misunderstanding, i-i-i-i-i-i-i-i-it was a joke, okay? A little joke! You ought to understand that much!"

"I don't understand, and I have no desire to."

"Sorry!" Ranta said, kowtowing so hard he slammed his head against the ground. "I reeeeeally mean it! Sorry! I was totally in the wrong! It won't happen again, I swear! Believe me! Please, I'm begging you!"

Ranta's overwrought kowtow seemed to be enough for Shihoru to let his behavior slide. Haruhiro hoped he'd learn the right lesson this time and rethink his priorities.

Not gonna happen? he thought. *Yeah. Probably not.*

Regardless, they probably had just a little farther to go.

The air was moist, and a faint breeze blew from the far end of the passage. Haruhiro didn't want to be overly optimistic, but there was no need to be too much of a pessimist, either. Whatever the case, the answer would soon be apparent.

Let's keep going, he thought. *We'll find out if we keep moving forward.*

"Fog," Merry whispered.

"Yeah," Ranta agreed, and then there was a long silence. "Heyyyyy?! Why's nobody saying anything?! Be like, 'Sure is,' or 'Hey, you're right,' or something! This is where you're supposed to say something like that, obviously! Are you bullying me?! My feelings can get hurt, too, y'know?!"

"Well, not really. I mean, they would get hurt, hypothetically, if I was that kind of guy."

"'Not really,' huh," Haruhiro said, sighing. He was a little jealous of how tough Ranta was.

Fog.

It was true; there was a thin fog, or haze or mist, of some sort hanging in the air of the passageway.

The name you use changes depending on the visibility, right? thought Haruhiro. *Maybe it was only called mist in the spring?*

Whatever the case, countless fine droplets floated in the air, making it look white. The further they went, the thicker it got, though only gradually.

Mr. Unjo, the super-senior volunteer soldier, had passed through a cave he found. Then, he reached the fire dragon's mountain in Darunggar.

The incline suddenly became a little steeper. At the top of the slope there was a bright white circle.

It's just like the moon, thought Haruhiro.

There was no sun or moon in Darunggar, and Grimgar's moon was red. This was a pale moon.

Where had he seen one of those? He didn't know, but he definitely remembered it. The white moon hanging in the pitch-black sky... That had to be...their original world, maybe?

"Isn't that the exit there?" Ranta said in an uncharacteristically subdued, even cautious, tone.

"Let's take it slowly," said Haruhiro.

He was aware he had incredibly sleepy-looking eyes. He wasn't tired, of course. If anything, his every sense felt heightened.

I want to get there quickly, thought Haruhiro. *But don't rush. I can't be hasty. Settle down, and move forward calmly.*

He looked to his comrades. Everyone was tense. Excited, too. Weren't they getting a little too stiff? Well, he couldn't blame them for that. Not this time. After all, they might get to go home. They might already be home.

He put out the lantern; they didn't need its light anymore.

White. The fog was so thick. Even so, it glowed bright enough that his eyes hurt.

He took a deep breath of the cold, wet wind. It was markedly different from the air in Darunggar; the taste, the scent, everything. Every cell in his body felt revitalized. Even though it wouldn't normally be his style, he wanted to do a happy little dance. He wouldn't, though. Now wasn't the time to celebrate.

The exit was right there. Only three more meters. Because of the slope, his stride was currently about forty centimeters. In seven or eight steps, he would be at the exit.

He took a deep breath on the sixth, then stopped.

Seven steps.

On his eighth step, he was finally outside.

It was all white. He could barely see a thing. That reminded him once again that it was too early to start celebrating. They had no idea what their current location was, or the lay of the land.

"Yume and everyone made it back, huh..." Yume said from behind him. From the tearful sound of her voice, the air wasn't the only thing around here that was a bit misty.

Shihoru let out a deep sigh.

Merry put an arm around Yume and Shihoru's shoulders.

The way Kuzaku thumped his chest once with a "Yeah!" then focused on the task at hand again was heartening to see.

Ranta was looking around this way and that.

Was the sky cloudy, or was it just the fog? It wasn't clear where the sun was, but with how bright it was here, it was probably still high in the sky.

"This is near the border of the former kingdoms of Nananka and Ishmal," Haruhiro said. "I think."

His legs felt ready to give out. Haruhiro clicked his tongue. He wished he could fix this weakness of his. He had to.

"I don't know the precise location," he added, "but the one thing I am clear on is that we need to head south. South is... Yume, help me out?"

"Meow? Oh. Well, if the sun were out, Yume'd be able to tell you. Mr. Moon or the stars would work, too. If there was a tree stump around, I could figure it out just goin' by the rings, more or less."

"Can't see the sun here," Kuzaku said as he looked up at the sky, then around the area. "There are stumps, though. Or trees, at least."

Just as Kuzaku noted, there were countless trees growing nearby. Some were straight, others were crooked, but none were especially thick or tall. There were fern-like plants on the ground, too. The soil was soft, turning almost to mud as they pressed on.

"It's hard to walk..." Shihoru complained.

"Pfeh," Ranta spat. "I dunno how heavy your tits are, but quit your moaning. This is no big deal."

Merry swung her staff at Ranta's head, stopping just short of hitting him. Her face was devoid of all expression.

"I don't think we made you kowtow enough last time," she said, "did we?"

"Eek! L-like I told you, it's a joke, okay, a joke! Jeez! You should never forget your sense of humor! It's a lubricant for relationships! Like me!"

Haruhiro could have come up with a witty retort, but there would be no end to it, and giving Ranta any attention would only make him worse.

Leaving Ranta alone and moving around a bit near the entrance to the passageway, there were many sudden rises and falls in elevation. Haruhiro didn't see any stumps, as it seemed there was no one doing any logging around here, human or otherwise. Should they try cutting one down themselves? If they were to use one of the blades they had on hand, it wouldn't be impossible, but Ranta's RIPer and Kuzaku's black blade were both weapons unsuited to felling trees. Yume's Wan-chan was like a machete, so it could probably hack off branches. Cutting down a whole tree, however, might be difficult.

"What, she can't magic down a tree real quick? She's useless for anything other than her tits," Ranta said under his breath.

Shihoru didn't seem to have heard him, but he clearly hadn't learned his lesson.

Were they going to go out of their way to cut down a tree? What were they going to do? It was a minor decision, but Haruhiro was surprisingly torn on it.

Yume noticed him wavering.

"Hmm, let's see," she said. "With tree rings, y'can more or less figure out the direction, but my master was sayin' the precision's low. When Yume asked him if he meant she should cut it down low, he told her, 'No, that's not it, it means it's not very accurate.'"

It was hard to be a decisive leader. Even so, he still had to aim on becoming one.

"First..." Haruhiro said, deciding to speak up. If he kept quiet, everyone would get nervous. *I'll just say something,* he thought. He'd sort out his thoughts on the matter as he spoke.

"...we head back to Alterna," he went on. "That's our primary goal, but it's pretty far. It's got to be six, maybe seven hundred kilometers."

Even having said it himself, it was dizzying to hear. It was supposed to be 300 kilometers just to cross the Quickwind Plains north of Alterna and reach the Shadow Forest, where the elves were said to live. North of the Shadow Forest was the former kingdom of Arabakia, and the former kingdoms of Nananka and Ishmal had to be even further than that.

In other words, this was five, six, or seven hundred kilometers from Alterna. Possibly even more.

How were they going to move around? They didn't know the roads. On top of that, they were in enemy territory. It felt pretty much impossible.

No, no, no. Stop that, Haruhiro told himself. *You can't give up.*

"If we assume it's 700 kilometers, that'll be thirty-five days if we walk twenty kilometers a day," Haruhiro told them. "I think twenty kilometers a day is fairly realistic, but we're looking at at least that long. We'll need water and food. It hurts that the fog makes visibility here so poor, but it helps, too, I guess. Even if there are enemies about, it'll be hard to be spotted. Even if we do get spotted, we can take advantage of it while running away. As for the direction... Well, the fog will clear eventually. If the fog was out year-round, there wouldn't be so many trees here. If we move around carelessly and find out it was the wrong direction later, it won't do us any good. For now, let's stay near the exit and wait for the fog to thin out. Once we know the direction, we'll all set out together. I'm going to go scout things out; I'll make sure I can find my way back. It's safest for me to move alone, so while I'm sure the rest of you are feeling high strung, do try to get some rest."

"Um, hey." Yume raised her hand. "Would it be okay if Yume came with you?"

"Don't do it," Ranta said in a whisper. "It could be dangerous."

"Why does Yume need you worryin' about her? You oughta mind your own pea patch," Yume retorted.

"I-I'm not worried! Wh-who'd be worried about you, you mo-ron?! A-a-also, it's beeswax, not pea patch, okay?"

"Ahh. Yume got it wrong. It's supposed to be beeswax, huh."

"W-w-well, be more careful!"

"What are you so shaken up over?" Shihoru said, shuddering. "It's creepy."

"I know," said Merry, casting a cold look Ranta's way. "It gives me nothing if not an ominous feeling."

"Give me some human rights!" Ranta yelled. "I'll cry, damn it! Wahhh, wahhh, wahhh, the women are bullying me! Let me squeeze your tits! Just enough to see what they feel like!"

Just how desperately did he want to squeeze them? There had to be limits to how sexually frustrated the guy could be. Was he going to be okay? It was a bit scary, but, well, it'd probably be fine. Ranta didn't have the guts to try and get his way by force.

Haruhiro reflected upon Yume's request. Yume was a hunter, so her knowledge and skills would be helpful. She had good eyes and ears, too. She was also light on her feet, so she wouldn't be a burden.

"Okay. Yume, you come along, too," Haruhiro decided. "Everyone else wait here."

"Meowger!" Yume declared.

The two of them left to scout. Just to be on the safe side, he marked the trees with his knife as they went. Even if they got turned around, they could follow the marks back to their comrades.

Still, the terrain was mind-bogglingly awful. It suddenly sloped up and down, and there were hardly any level spots. Even if the fog cleared, they probably wouldn't be able to see very far. In fact, even when the fog thinned slightly, the trees or some protuberance in the ground up ahead would pop up and block their line of vision.

"It's somewhere between noon and evenin', maybe," Yume offered. "That's just me playin' it by ear, though."

"I'd say that's about right," Haruhiro agreed. "Granted, I'm just going on a hunch, too."

Based on Haruhiro's senses, they had traveled around 500 meters in a mostly straight line away from the end of the passageway, and they'd found nothing. The sense that this wouldn't be easy deepened.

Even so, Yume was bright and cheerful, so for all the seriousness of their situation, it didn't feel as grave as it probably should have.

"You're always saving me," Haruhiro told her.

"Fwuh? What's this all of a sudden?"

"Well, I mean, without you here, we'd be a pretty gloomy party."

"Hmmm," Yume said. "Even without Yume, y'know, Ranta'd still be just as noisy, don'tcha think?"

"But the reason I don't have to butt heads with him quite so hard is because you're here."

"That Ranta," Yume said.

She came to a stop, tilting her head to the side. "Why do you think he wants to squeeze boobies so bad? Do all boys want to squeeze girls' boobies?"

"Well," said Haruhiro.

Looking at the group as a whole, that might not be untrue, but it would be a mistake to extend that into a general statement on the desires of all men. Or maybe it wouldn't. But he was pretty sure.

"It depends on the person," Haruhiro finished at last.

"How about you, Haru-kun?"

"Huh? Me? Nah, I'm..."

What is this? he thought, suddenly tense. *What do I do? Is it safest to deny it? But is that honest? If I did, would I be lying to*

Yume? I don't want to lie to a valued comrade. But what harm can a little white lie do? Still, given the few other redeeming qualities I've got, I may as well be honest with my comrades.

"I-If they belonged to someone I like, maybe?" Haruhiro hedged.

"Ohhh," said Yume. "Huh. So that's how it works. Yume loves squeezin' Shihoru and Merry's boobs, after all. Yume, she likes Shihoru and Merry.

There was a moment of dead silence.

"Hm?" said Yume.

"Huh?" said Haruhiro, flustered.

"In that case, does that mean Ranta's wantin' to squeeze Yume's boobies 'cause he likes her? If he hated Yume, he probably wouldn't want to squeeze her boobs."

Yume, Haruhiro thought, shuddering. *Damn, she's scary. She just went and opened Pandora's box like it was nothing.*

The truth was, Haruhiro couldn't deny the possibility. He'd thought about it before, but he'd also thought there was something kind of strange about Ranta's attitude toward Yume. It wasn't enough that he could be sure of it, and it was questionable whether Ranta himself realized it. With everything so iffy, Haruhiro figured it was probably best not to touch the subject—it'd be a hassle, after all—so he did his best to pretend he didn't notice.

But then, Haruhiro was probably the type who was a little dense about these things, so he may have misunderstood the situation.

"No, I don't think he hates you," Haruhiro said at last. "Obviously. He doesn't. Like, for someone to hate you, Yume, there'd have to be something wrong with them. Well, there *is* something wrong with him..."

"Why would there have to be somethin' wrong with a person if they hated Yume?" she asked.

"Ah, I mean, well, I dunno. It's just there's so little to hate about you."

"Y'think? Well then, do you like Yume, Haru-kun?"

"Sure. I like you," he said, then thought, *Oh, was that okay? Am I in trouble? Is she gonna misunderstand?*

Yume smiled.

"Oh," she said. "I see."

He was embarrassed by how impure he was.

Yes. Yes! That was right. It was right.

Feeling affection for a person depended on whether you liked them, not your romantic intentions, and you had to think of it as a separate thing entirely from sex. Thinking about it, Haruhiro certainly liked Yume. He could say that with pride. Of course he liked her. She was Yume, after all. That was a given. He had to like her. But still...

"Yume feels the same," she said with a goofy smile, and his heart raced just a little. "Yume likes you, too, Haru-kun."

"Th-thanks," said Haruhiro.

He scratched his head.

"Uh," he said, "is it weird for me to say that?"

"Dunno. But if you're feelin' thankful, Yume thinks it's okay to say so. When you do, it makes the person who said it feel good, too. Of course, that goes for Yume, too. She's feelin' super-duper happy now."

"I...guess so." He hesitated. "If you don't say what you feel, people may never know, after all. Yeah."

"So, if Ranta likes Yume, he should just say so, huh? He's always bullyin' her, or callin' her Tiny Tits, after all."

"He can have a pretty hard time being honest about how he feels," Haruhiro told her.

Or rather, the kind of liking someone Yume was talking about and the way Ranta liked her were different. Even if Ranta did come out and tell her honestly, Yume might take it differently from how he intended, and it could turn into a huge mess. There was a lot of room for worry in that scenario.

In the end, Haruhiro couldn't help but think preserving the status quo was for the best. Maybe there was room for improving his usual wait-and-see attitude.

He'd have to think about it. Not now, though. It looked like they had bigger concerns.

Haruhiro put a finger to his lips. He pressed himself against a nearby tree. Yume followed close behind him.

There was a noise. What was it?

Yume pointed up ahead to the left. Haruhiro followed her finger. He tried squinting, but he couldn't see anything through the fog. Still, if he focused in that direction, he could hear the sound more clearly than before. A noise? Voices? Fighting? Was it wild beasts? Or something worse?

It was time to make a decision. Naturally, he wanted to avoid danger. Would they hurriedly retreat? It wasn't clear if there was even any danger at this point, so maybe it was best to ascertain that much first? He felt the urge to run, but that was his cowardice talking.

He could still hear the sounds. Were they gradually getting closer? Hold on, this was—a voice.

Yes. It was a voice. Not screaming or shouting. Speaking in words. That was what it sounded like.

"Humans," Yume said in a hushed voice.

Haruhiro agreed. It was hard to believe, given the surroundings, but it was probably a man's voice. Naturally, he was surprised. Was he disoriented? No, it wasn't that bad. His pulse raced a little, but he was sure he was keeping his calm.

He motioned for Yume to follow him, then began walking. Then, less than thirty seconds later, he sensed a presence that seemed to stab into his back.

There was something behind him.

Yume didn't seem to notice. He was sure if he turned to look, it would strike. But he couldn't just stay as he was. The other party would definitely come at them eventually. He had to move first.

"Yume, get down!" Haruhiro shouted, pulling an about-face. Yume was already dropping to her hands and knees. Haruhiro switched his knife to his left hand, drawing his stiletto with his right and jumping over Yume.

"Wait, wait, wait!" someone shouted.

A person. It was a human, wearing what looked like a fur-lined coat and a knitted hat. There was a bow in their right hand, an arrow in their left. Both hands were in the air.

This bearded man had closed in thirty meters short of Haruhiro and Yume. It was unbelievable. Or rather, Haruhiro didn't want to believe it. To think he hadn't noticed until the man got that close!

Haruhiro still had his knife and stiletto at the ready, just in case, but he was more surprised than anything. He was feeling shaken, and his thoughts were a mess. He couldn't hope to fight like this.

"'Wait,' you said?"

A smile appeared on the man's chiseled features, and he tossed his bow and arrow to the side. "There. I won't do anything to you. It's okay. I never meant to kill you, after all. But you know you look suspicious right? Humans like you, in a place like this. You don't look like you're from the village, either. Then again neither am I, you know?"

"Hrmmm," said Yume.

She was still on the ground, covering her head with her hands as she looked into his eyes.

"You kiiiiinda sorta look like a hunter, huh?"

"Oh? You're a hunter, too, young miss? Well, it's 'former' for me. I'm a warrior now," the man said. "So that'd make you a volunteer soldier."

"You, too?" Haruhiro wanted to let out a long sigh, but he refrained and tried to keep to short, shallow breaths.

Don't get careless and let yourself feel relieved, he cautioned himself. *You can't let your guard down.*

"Are you also a volunteer soldier?" he asked.

"Been one for over ten years now," the man said. "Thanks to that, I've gotten old."

"Well, that would make you our senior, I guess," said Haruhiro.

"Well, about the only thing I can teach you is how to drink until you get a hangover." The bearded man shrugged his shoulders, giving them a smile that seemed awfully unguarded. "I'm Kuro."

"Kuro. Wait..." Haruhiro murmured.

Hold on, he thought. *Wait, wait, wait. I feel like I know that name. I've heard it somewhere. Is it just by chance? Pure coincidence? But maybe he actually is that person. This place being where it is, there can't be many volunteer soldiers who can come out this far.*

"You wouldn't happen to be Kuro-san of the Day Breakers, would you?" he said.

"Hm?" Kuro pointed at himself, his eyes wide. "Wait, am I famous?"

"No, um—I, or we, actually, we're sort of technically members of the Day Breakers ourselves."

"The way you're dressed; you're a thief," the man said. "Haruhiro?"

"Yes," he said. "Huh? Why do you know? Oh, is that it? You heard from Soma that—"

Kuro burst out laughing.

"You people were alive! Bwahahaha!"

"Wh-what are you laughing for?! Is it something to laugh about?!"

"How rude." Yume was still down on the ground. "It's a happy day, isn't it? Right?"

"Oh, happy day!" Kuro pointed at Yume and laughed out loud. "You're right, it is a happy day, bwahahaha! Well, I'm glad you're alive, yeah, real glad! This *is* a happy day! I'd figured you'd all bought it after all! Gwahahahaha!"

Haruhiro was dumbfounded. Kuro was clutching his belly, and there were even tears in his eyes. He was laughing way too hard. What was with this guy? He was creepy. Or rather, he was pissing Haruhiro off.

"Whew, sorry, sorry." Kuro wiped his tears away with his thumb and picked up his bow and arrow. "But it's certainly a co-incidence. Like, would we run into one another, normally? Well, I'm just glad you're not an enemy. Saves me the trouble of killing you. I'm busy enough as it is right now. On that note, I don't have time to look after you, but take care."

Returning his arrow to its quiver, Kuro waved to them with bow in hand and walked away. His steps looked slow and relaxed, but they were mysteriously quick; quiet, too. He barely made a sound. At a glance, he seemed to be wide open from behind, but if they attacked, he would easily dodge them. More than that, they'd likely receive a painful riposte. This guy was good.

"Wait, huh?" Haruhiro burst out. "Uh? Hold on, you're leaving? Huh? No way, h-hold on, please, where are you going?! H-hey! We're lost! We don't know the way back!"

"Huhhh?" Kuro said.

He turned back and started laughing again.

"Bwaha! Lost?! You're lost, wow, seriously, you're kidding, right? If you can't get back home, that's hilarious! You guys are great!"

"It's nothing to laugh about," Haruhiro muttered.

"Heee." Yume started giggling, too. She was still down on the ground, incidentally. "Somehow, y'know, even Yume's startin' to think it's funny. Heee, hehehehe..."

"Okay, got it," Kuro said.

He sniffed as he beckoned to them.

"You guys, come with me for a bit. I'll do something about the road back for you. Like I said before, I'm a busy man. I've got some things to sort out. You don't have to help; just watch. Okay?"

They couldn't refuse. Kuro was clearly a weirdo, but he *was* part of the Day Breakers. Probably. He was supposed to be.

This was an unexpected bit of good luck. What was it he needed to sort out? It wasn't dangerous, was it? There were things that left Haruhiro uncertain, but if they didn't take this opportunity, they might never make it back.

"W-we'll help!" Haruhiro said, grabbing Yume's hand and pulling her to her feet. "Well, assuming it's doable for us!"

"No need to push yourselves." Kuro grinned and began walking.

He was fast; keeping up with him was difficult. It wasn't just a matter of matching his pace; the footing was precarious. If they took one wrong step, they'd be liable to trip up or lose traction. If they weren't careful, they may even sprain an ankle. Haruhiro and Yume's skills meant they barely managed not to fall behind. That was the best they could do. Haruhiro couldn't afford to scope out the area.

He could hear the noises, though.

Beyond the fog, something—or someone—was there.

There was a place where the ground suddenly swelled up, and when they ducked around the side, they caught sight of a cluster of humanoid figures. It was hard to see them through the mist, but they may have not all been human.

No, not "may." They definitely weren't.

"Stop," Kuro hissed, raising his hand to stop Haruhiro and Yume.

"Well, well," he said. "Moyugi-kun's hard at work. Well, he's got Moira with him, after all."

"Moira," Haruhiro said slowly.

There was a name he didn't recognize. He did recognize "Moyugi," though. He was a member of the Day Breakers, like Kuro. He was part of a famous party: the Rocks, or Typhoon Rocks, named for their boss, Rock.

Which of them was Moyugi? Haruhiro counted six figures. One of them had to be—

"Oh," Haruhiro whispered.

Now there was one fewer.

That pale figure was most likely human. They backed away, thrusting out with some sort of weapon that caused another figure to collapse. In a blur, the pale figure delivered the *coup de grâce* to the one they dropped.

"Guess I'll get moving, too," said Kuro as he nocked an arrow to his bow. Or so Haruhiro thought, but he'd already let it loose.

Wasn't that shot kind of fast? he wondered. *Did he aim properly?*

Either way, it looked like he'd hit his mark. Yet another one of the figures collapsed.

"Would you kindly mind your own business?!" someone shouted. That was probably Moyugi's voice. He might have been saying it to Kuro.

Kuro said, "Yeah, yeah," and lowered his bow. It was probably none of Haruhiro's business to think this, but was it really okay for him to do that?

Yume, who was crouched down next to Haruhiro, let out an impressed sigh.

Excuse me? What are you crouching down and relaxing for? I know there's an atmosphere, or general flow of events here, like we don't need to do anything, though.

"I have this all planned out properly!" the person who seemed to be Moyugi declared.

The whitish figure moved smoothly. The remaining three figures tried to close in on the whitish figure that was likely Moyugi from three sides.

Moyugi ran away. Or rather, ran toward them. He was running this way.

But was Haruhiro imagining it?

That guy, he thought, *is he facing backward...?*

Moyugi looked like he was running backward.

He'll get caught like that, won't he? There's no way he can get away. None. Should we help him? But he got mad at Kuro for interfering when he tried. He said he had this planned out, or something like that.

"Funah!" Yume let out a weird cry, and Haruhiro gulped.

All of a sudden, Moyugi tripped. However, rather than

landing on his backside, it looked like maybe he'd sat down on his own...?

Naturally, sensing this was their chance, the three figures rushed at Moyugi.

That one's an orc, thought Haruhiro.

From its build, Haruhiro assumed the humanoid figure bringing its scimitar down on Moyugi's prone form had to be an orc. The other two looked human, but there was no telling.

Suddenly, a shape appeared from out of nowhere over the orc's head. Or that was what it looked like, but that was impossible; it must have been hiding somewhere. It mounted the orc's shoulders, wrapped both its legs around the orc's neck, and twisted. It drove a scissor-like blade into the crown of the orc's head and let out a cry that grated on the nerves of all who heard it.

"Nooooooooooooo!"

Having seen the orc's horrible end, the other two's morale broke. *Well, yeah,* thought Haruhiro, *of course they'd be shocked.* The two flinched and shouted something, then froze.

Moyugi stood up. He didn't trip after all; he sat down on his own. If he hadn't, he couldn't just stand back up like nothing had happened.

As an afterthought, Moyugi stabbed his thin blade into one of the enemies' faces, then tore it free. It didn't feel like an especially sharp move.

Haruhiro couldn't help but think, *What, it's going to go down to that?*

He thought, *Hurry, hurry. There's still another enemy, after all. Don't just take it easy, you need to hurry up and attack or—See.*

Maybe because it was enraged by the death of its comrades, the remaining enemy came at Moyugi with incredible vigor.

See, see, see! I told you so, thought Haruhiro. *Well, no, I didn't tell you, but I did think it. I knew you needed to hurry.*

Haruhiro was only noticing this now, but Moyugi was wearing glasses. He pushed them up with his left hand and greeted the incoming enemy with—nothing. He retreated.

He didn't really jump clear; it was more like he was drawing just out of reach. He pulled away from the enemy, snaking back and forth as he did.

The enemy was hot on Moyugi's heels.

Oh, no, Haruhiro thought. *Not good. He'll close in on him soon. Just one more step, and—*

At that point, for some reason, the enemy lost his balance. Had something tripped him up? That was what it looked like. It was a perfect chance for Moyugi. He didn't miss it, of course. If anything, it looked like he had predicted it would happen, and that thin blade of his flicked out, running them through. When he pulled the sword free, they collapsed to the ground.

The thing that had snapped the orc's neck with its legs was now fishing around inside the orc's skull with its scissors. Apparently finished with its job, it left the orc's corpse and went to stand beside Moyugi. It looked almost like a long-haired woman, but it probably wasn't human. Her shoulders were too square, her back too hunched, and her waist too thin. She was something else.

"Looks like it's over," Kuro said as he walked over to Moyugi.

Haruhiro exchanged glances with Yume, then followed after Kuro. Yume hopped along after them, too.

Moyugi was even more lightly equipped than Kuro. He wore a white top, little more than a shirt, really, and ordinary pants. His shoes were nothing special, his backpack wasn't especially big; a sheath hung at his hip; and he held a thin, straight sword in his hands. His minimal kit puzzled and intimidated Haruhiro.

What was more, Moyugi thrust out a hand to him.

"Greetings," he said. "I am the current strongest dread knight, Moyugi. I know not who you are, but it is a pleasure to meet you."

"N-n-nice..." Haruhiro said as he accepted the hand extended to him out of reflex, "...to meet...you. Um, I'm Haruhiro. From the Day Breakers."

"Indeed."

When Moyugi released Haruhiro's hand, he pressed on the bridge of his glasses with the middle finger of his right hand. The corners of his mouth turned upward.

"I thought that might be who you were. No matter how much of an incorrigible fool our Kuro is, he wouldn't go dragging around just anyone he happened to meet out here. From the looks of you, you're a young male thief. The young woman is a hunter. You must be Haruhiro-kun and Yume-kun, yes? I've heard about you from Soma. To think you actually made it back alive from the Dusk Realm! Is it just the two of you? What about Ranta-kun, Shihoru-kun, Merry-kun, and Kuzaku-kun? Did they die?"

"Of course they're alive!" Yume said. Her face distorted with anger, but, this being Yume, it wasn't all that intimidating.

Regardless, she still rounded on Moyugi, with her brow furrowed and her cheeks puffed up. She stood on her tiptoes and got her face as close up to Moyugi's as she could. She seemed convinced that it was threatening.

"I see," said Moyugi. Without so much as a change in his expression, he grabbed Yume by the chin.

"That is most wonderful. Now, would you mind if I suck your face?"

"My faaaace?" Yume said, blinking in confusion. "Suck it? Hmmm?"

"Wh-wh-whoa, whoa, whoa, what're you doing?!" Haruhiro said, hurriedly pulling Moyugi away from Yume. "What the hell are you doing?! Could you not?! You're not making any sense!"

"I'm not making sense, am I? You say some strange things." Moyugi said. He tilted his head to the side. "If you see a woman, the first thing you should do is take her, isn't it? You realize I *am* the strongest dread knight in active service."

"Well, yeah," Kuro said as he stroked his beard. "I dunno about you being the strongest dread knight, really, but if you think you can do her, you've gotta go for it. I'm not into kids, though."

"I limit my engagements to the fairer sex, but when it comes to women, I'll do just about anyone," Moyugi declared. "No matter how bizarre or unappealing, they each have their own unique flavor, you see."

What was with these people? Haruhiro wondered if they'd maybe run into a pair of crazies. No, not "maybe"—these guys were definitely unstable. It was probably best not to get involved with them.

If possible, Haruhiro didn't want to be anywhere near them; but even setting aside their connection through the Day Breakers, if he didn't get those two to tell him the route, their trip back to Alterna would become that much longer. Worse than that, it might not even be possible to get back without relying on them. He felt his head spin as he had Yume get behind him for protection.

What would he do? What could he do? What *should* he do?

"It can wait for now." Moyugi sheathed his thin sword. "We're a little busy at the moment, you see. Come along now, Kuro, Moira."

"Noooo." The being that looked like a long-haired woman gave him an unhappy-sounding reply. That was apparently Moira. Moyugi was a dread knight, so maybe she was his demon.

Moyugi walked off at a brisk pace with Moira in tow.

"You people come, too," Kuro said, nodding them over as he trailed behind Moyugi and Moira.

"Um, our comrades aren't with us yet," Haruhiro said, but Kuro turned back and scowled in irritation.

"They can wait until later," said Kuro. "We're sort of in a hurry. I'll leave you behind if I have to."

They really can't wait, and you guys don't seem like you're in that much of a rush, now do you? Haruhiro thought. He wanted to argue back, but he couldn't see it getting him anywhere, so he followed Kuro. Moyugi and Moira were already on the other side of the fog.

"Hey, Haru-kun," Yume said as she tugged on his cloak. "Yume's thinkin' it might be best if she went back. Can you find your way back on your own, maybe...?"

"Let's follow those people," Haruhiro replied, pulling Yume along by the hand as he followed Kuro.

Hearing what Yume had said, he realized he made a fatal mistake. But he preferred cooperating with his highly capable seniors in the Day Breakers, who were no doubt familiar with the area, to wandering alone in the fog.

Up until he noticed Kuro sneaking up on them, Haruhiro had been marking the trees as they went along. Ever since, he hadn't left a single mark. He had no choice but to follow and hope they'd guide him back eventually.

"Sorry, Yume," Haruhiro said. "I forgot to leave marks."

"Well, if you're gonna say that," Yume said, squeezing Haruhiro's hand tight, "Yume didn't do it, either. It's a bad habit of yours, the way you go takin' all the blame for things."

"I see," he said. "I'll try to be careful about it. But, while this may be our fault, I'm still in the wrong."

Because I'm the leader, he thought.

Was he unable to say that out loud because of embarrassment? Or was it because he wasn't able to fully shoulder the burden yet?

That aside, there wasn't any need for them to hold hands, was there? It felt even less necessary for them to stay this way.

However, Yume was gripping his hand pretty tight, so it was hard to worm his way out. He felt that if he could offer her even a little support, he had to.

Honestly, it was reassuring for Haruhiro, too, and it was tough to find the right time to let go.

2 | An Odd Couple

"**S**O SLOW!" Ranta snapped, his eyes wide open. "When are they getting back?! They said they were going scouting, damn it, scouting! They're taking too damn long! It's weird! Something must've happened! Hold on, could they be... Were they all alone together in the mist, and they felt a spark and just sort of s-started going at it?!"

"Nah." Kuzaku waved his hand dismissively. "That'd never happen. Not with Haruhiro. He's not you, Ranta-kun."

"Come on, don't go slogging me like it's an afterthought!"

"You mean 'slagging,' not 'slogging.'" Merry sighed. "How can you go around imagining things like that about your comrades? Unbelievable."

"You never know, right?!" Ranta yelled back. "They're a guy and a girl, after all! Besides, it was weird that Yume suggested she go with him! She coulda let Haruhiro go scouting on his own, like always! Y-yeah... I'll bet Yume secretly has a thing for—"

"Yume doesn't seem interested in that sort of stuff," said Shihoru, her tone as cold as ever. "But, even if she were, how would that be a problem?"

"I-It's a problem. You know! Of course it is. It affects the party's sense, of, uh, what was it again... Well, you know? It's not like it's against any rules, but they could be more open about it. If not, I mean, it's an affront to common decency, right? Hey, why are you all looking like you don't care? I'm talking about some important stuff here, you know?"

"Setting aside the question of whether or not it's actually important, do we really need to talk about it *now*?" Merry asked frigidly.

"Fine, I get it!" Ranta said as he crossed his arms and puffed up his chest. "In that case, let's talk about something really important. Haruhiro and Yume left to scout, but they haven't come back. It's taking way too long. I think something happened to them, so do we just sit here? Until sundown? For a night? Two nights? Three nights? Are you all okay with that?"

"What do you think we should do, Ranta-kun?" Shihoru asked.

"I'm glad you asked, Shihoru!" he hollered.

"The way you said that pisses me off," she said.

"Even if you do get pissy, I don't care one bit! So, anyway, in my opinion, we should go looking for them!"

"What if we miss each other?" Merry demanded.

"That's an excellent question, Merry-saaaan."

"I want to kill you..."

"Now, now, don't get so mad over such a little thing! It's a waste of that pretty face of yours, you know? You're beautiful, all right? Smile, okay?"

"Could you stop? I'm not sure I can put up with you any longer."

"Righto, righto. I think it's a bit much that you snap at me over a compliment, but I'll stop, I'll totally stop, I've done enough. So, about if we miss each other. The missing each other problem. I'm worried about that, too, but, well, can't we just leave half of the group here? Perfect solution."

"Hmmm," said Kuzaku. "Well, I am a little worried."

"That's—" Merry couldn't say she was unconcerned, and she thought they should just leave the two of them to handle themselves. "No, I feel the same way."

Shihoru hung her head and touched her lips. "But half of the group..."

"So, for a start, I'd be going, right?" Ranta gestured to himself with his thumb. "I mean, that's a given. Which means Kuzaku would be staying. He'd have to."

Merry glanced to Kuzaku. Kuzaku just so happened to be looking at Merry at the same time, so they ended up looking into each other's eyes. They both immediately looked away.

"I'll go," Merry sighed, shaking her head. "Left to your own devices, you'll cause trouble, and I don't want to put Shihoru in danger."

"The way you said that, isn't it like you're assuming that being with me guarantees she'll be in danger?" Ranta asked.

"Isn't it dangerous just being alone with you? Think back a little about how you behave, why don't you?"

"Okay, sure, I said I'd like to squeeze her tits, and I asked her to let me, but I'm not seriously going to try to squeeze them at a time like this, okay?! Use some common sense, would you?"

"Common sense?" said Shihoru, looking at him with utter disbelief. "This, coming from the guy with the least common sense in the world?"

"Anyway, I'll protect Shihoru-san," Kuzaku said with a sideways glance; not to Shihoru, but to Merry. "But still, Ranta-kun, don't go too far. It'd be pointless if you got lost."

"Be careful," Shihoru added, but it was clear that Merry was the only one she was actually concerned about.

"Yeah." Merry smiled, just at Shihoru. "You, too, Shihoru. Oh, and Kuzaku."

"The way you people play at being friends makes me sick. Bleh..." Ranta muttered, then stepped out into the fog.

Merry followed after him without a word.

Huh? he thought.

Wasn't she closer to him than usual? Maybe, for all her complaining, she actually didn't hate Ranta all that much? No, no, maybe she even kind of liked him?

Yeah, no. Not a chance. She was probably just sticking close because the fog was thick and she didn't want to get split up.

"She's not even subtle about it, seriously," Ranta muttered.

"Did you say something?"

"Not a word. Oh, yeah. This seems like the right time—O darkness, O lord of vice, Demon Call."

A dark purple cloud formed overhead, swirling into a vortex, and out it came. It was here.

It looked like a person with a purple sheet over its head, with two evil, hole-like eyes, and a vicious gash of a mouth underneath them. In its right hand it held an assassin's dagger, and in its left hand was a fearsome club. It had two proper legs, but it floated in the air. It was pretty close to a human in size.

"Zodiac-kun! You were so tiny in Darunggar!" Ranta, full of emotion, tried to hug the demon, but it dodged him. "Wait, what?!"

"Ehe... Ehehehe... Ranta... Honestly, you're annoying... Kehehehehe..."

"Hey, buddy, you're like an extension of me!"

"What a bother... Ehehehehe..."

"Poor Zodiac-kun," Merry sighed.

"Don't go pitying him, Merry! Z-Zodiac-kun's just, you know, awkward! Basically, he can't be honest with himself, with his feelings, but the truth is, he loves me."

"Ranta..." Zodiac-kun hissed.

"Wh-what, Zodiac-kun? Did you have something to say?"

"When it comes to you..."

"Y-Yeah?" Ranta asked.

"From the bottom of my heart, I..."

"Uh huh?"

"...feel nothing but disdain...and hate for you... Ehe..."

"Ouch!" Ranta complained.

Well, even though Zodiac-kun said that, the demon still came when summoned, and would stay at Ranta's side. Ranta knew there was no questioning it: Zodiac-kun loved him. He could tell, even if Zodiac-kun was the only one who did.

"I mean, that's all a dread knight really needs, am I right?"

"Ehe... Talking to yourself, Ranta? How pitiful... Kehehehe..."

"Shut up," Ranta snapped. "Just shut up! I'm your master, got it?! If you aren't more servile, I'll never use you again!"

"Kehe... Fine by me..."

On that note, with an understated *poof,* Zodiac-kun disappeared.

"Huh? Wait, Zodiac-kun? F-fine, then. I can just summon you again. O Darkness, O Lord of Vice, Demon Call."

Nothing happened.

"Huh? No response? Why...?"

"Even Zodiac-kun's finally given up on you now, don't you think?" Merry asked.

Merry's words stabbed into Ranta's chest. What did she mean, "finally"? What did she mean "even Zodiac-kun"?

Damn it, he thought.

Ranta hung his head.

The next moment, he puffed his chest out and held his head high. "Gahaha! Fine! Who needs Zodiac-kun?! I'm glad to be rid of him!"

"It looks to me like you're crying, though."

"You're imagining it," Ranta blustered. "Like I'd ever cry. I'd never cry. Not me."

"I'm sure Zodiac-kun will appear again eventually."

"Merryyyyy! Don't be so quick to console me! I'll fall for youuuu!"

"I won't console you again," Merry said. "Never again, no matter what happens."

"If something happens, I don't mind if you do, okay?! I won't fall for you! I swear! Please!"

But Merry was stubborn, and wouldn't give in to begging. Well, a dread knight didn't need anyone to console him, anyway, so it was fine. Now then, how would they search for Haruhiro and Yume?

There was a mark on one of the trees, carved with a knife or something similar, that caught his attention. When he found a second mark, it clicked for him.

"These weird marks," Ranta said. "I'm sure that moron Haruhiro left them. Seems like the sort of thing he'd come up with."

"You didn't need to call them weird, or call him a moron," Merry reproached. "But, yeah, I think so, too."

"He set it up so he could find his way back, so why isn't he back yet?" Ranta complained.

Merry said nothing, but seemed to agree with him. There must have been an accident or incident of some sort. That was all Ranta could think. He was getting mad.

"That loser," Ranta muttered. "Him and his sleepy eyes. He takes Yume along, and then lets this happen. This is why I can't trust him. He's trash."

"You're that worried about Yume?" Merry asked.

"O-of course I am. W-we're comrades, after all. No other feelings involved. Not for her and her tiny tits."

Anyway, they had no choice but to follow the marks left on the trees. It looked like Haruhiro and Yume had gone in a more or less straight direction, so it wasn't that hard.

It seemed the two of them had been doing a good job scouting.

But then something happened.

Thoughts of the worst sort crossed Ranta's mind, but he immediately dismissed them. It wasn't helpful to think of things he couldn't do anything about.

"I'm an efficient guy," Ranta said.

"The fog..." Merry suddenly interjected.

Ranta noticed it, too. The fog had suddenly begun to clear. He'd only been able to see five or six meters ahead before, but the area was getting noticeably brighter.

He could see...ten meters ahead. No, not just that. He could see much farther.

There were large swells in the ground, and the area was thick with trees. He couldn't tell what was going on too far away, but that bright white round thing floating in the milky white air... Could that be the sun?

"My eyes hurt," said Ranta, smiling wryly as he squinted. He'd been staring at the sun without meaning to.

Merry turned and looked back. "That's the direction we came. If the sun is there, then..."

"You can't tell what direction it is just from that. I think we'd have to make a sundial, or something like that. Damn it. If Yume were here, she'd know."

Ranta cocked his head to the side. "Huh?" he said.

"What?" said Merry.

"No, just now, it seemed like something moved," Ranta said, pointing over to his left. "Over that way. But it doesn't seem like anything's there. Am I seeing things?"

"Even if you are, we'd better be on our guard."

"Yeah." Ranta licked his lips. She didn't have to tell him; he already was. However, Ranta wasn't a chicken like Haruhiro. In a crisis, he showed even greater power than usual. He was a dread knight who thrived on adversity.

"If we get into a bit of a pinch," he said, "I can get us out easy as pie."

"Don't get carried away. If you screw up because you took things too easy, I can't save you."

"Fair enough," Ranta said. "If that happens, forget me and run for it. I won't hold it against you."

Merry didn't say a word. Ranta struggled to decide whether that was endearing or not.

Whatever. For now, they just had to follow the trail. The fog was starting to clear, so it was suddenly much easier to walk. Thanks to that, they picked up their pace. They were covering a lot of ground.

"Don't you think we're rushing too much?" Merry asked.

"Whaaaat? Can't keep up with my strong legs, Merry-san?"

"Whoever said that?"

"Hahaha," Ranta cackled as he looked back.

Merry was breathing a little heavily; Ranta's breathing was a bit uneven, too. Was he being hasty? He couldn't deny it. Ranta came to a halt.

"Hold on... Is that a cat?"

"Huh?" said Merry.

"That," said Ranta, pointing up and to the right. "Over there."

There was a swell in the ground, and there were trees growing out of it at an angle. A creature was sitting in one of the branches. It was...a cat? It had striped, brownish fur, and its face, or more accurately its head, was clearly that of a cat. It had a tail, too. The way it sat with its front paws together and its ears at attention was catlike, as well, but something was different about it.

"It's cute."

When Merry let that slip out, the cat's ears perked up. It turned quickly and was gone.

"Ah!" said Merry, reaching out in the direction the cat disappeared in, but stopped when she noticed Ranta looking at her. "I-It was cute, right? That animal just now. Like a cat."

"I don't care if it was cute or not. It was like a cat, but it wasn't, right?"

"I think so, now that you mention it," said Merry. "But that's not that strange, is it? It just means there're cute, catlike creatures living in this area."

"Is it that important that it's cute?" Ranta asked.

"I-It's not about it being important, it's just a matter of fact that it was cute, so I was—"

Merry's face went stiff. Did she find a monster instead of a not-cat this time? No, apparently that wasn't it.

"It's not just the one we saw a moment ago," she said. "There're others, too. Four of them. Lots, actually."

"Huh?" Ranta looked around, then gulped. "Seriously... Yeah, there are. Lots."

Over in the shade was a gray tabby. Up in a tree was a bicolor one with a black and white mask-and-mantle pattern.

There was a pure black one.

And a grayish one.

And a dirty white one, too.

Not all of them, but some of the cats had a glint in their eyes, and that was really creepy. The cats—no, they probably weren't cats. He finally figured it out.

Their heads were a little too big. They had fairly large bodies, but the heads were closer in relative size to what you'd expect on a kitten than what you'd expect on a full-grown cat. That was probably what made Merry think they were cute.

But their front legs... Oh, and their hind ones, too... The toes on their paws weren't cat toes. They were long, like they could probably grip things with them. Actually, some were doing exactly that and hanging from the branches.

It wasn't just two or three. They were all over the place. There were more than fourteen. No, there used to be.

They were all gone now.

All at once, *bam,* they'd vanished. Ranta got goosebumps.

"Did that seem natural to you?" Ranta asked.

"I can't say it did. Then again, Maybe not."

"I figured."

Ranta was struck by a strange feeling. Or rather, he couldn't do things the way he wanted to. He was strangely stiff. This had happened before in Darunggar.

When Haruhiro was out searching in Waluandin alone, two young orcs ambushed the party. Ranta was caught by surprise, and he couldn't move like he wanted to. No, in fact, it was worse than that. He was struck by sudden indecision, and in the end, everything he did was awkward. As a result Kuzaku was wounded, and even Yume got hurt.

He didn't want to admit it, but he knew the reason now. It was because Haruhiro hadn't been there.

If Ranta was alone, he could handle things and take care of himself somehow. The others were just nice to have around. He wasn't counting on them. Well, he did more or less have an idea of what each of them would do in certain situations. He took them into consideration before acting, but he was the main focus, and everyone else was secondary. If that guy was around, things worked best that way. But if he wasn't, things went a little differently.

For example, right this moment, Ranta was alone with Merry, and Haruhiro wasn't around. Merry was a priest, even if she could defend herself, combat wasn't her specialty. Besides, she was a woman. He had to protect her, and it was hard to fight while doing that. He wouldn't be able to fight to his full potential, and that might mean he couldn't defeat an enemy, and they'd lose.

He may have been better off not thinking about these things, but he couldn't help it. It wasn't like him, but Ranta was at a loss for what to do. It was that guy's fault for not being here.

Damn it, Haruhiro.

"Can't live with him, can't live without him," Ranta said as he drew RIPer. "Merry, get ready for combat. You know, just in case. Be on your guard."

"You think they're enemies?" Merry readied her head staff. "The catlike creatures?"

"Who knows. Here's hoping they're—"

Ranta shook his head. Why say something so timid?

"It's called not taking chances. I'll bet you don't want to be embraced by Skullhell just yet, you blind worshiper of Lumiaris."

"Don't let Skullhell trick you into rushing to your death either, okay?"

"Nice comeback," said Ranta, smirking.

Time to get back on his game. He could just handle it like usual.

"Do we continue? Or go back?" Merry asked in a whisper.

Don't ask me, Ranta nearly said, but he held it in. *What? Why am I so irritated?*

Would they continue or go back?

He just had to decide already. That was all. Besides, Haruhiro was always making decisions. If Haruhiro could do it, there was no way Ranta couldn't, either.

Yeah, he thought.

Make a decision.

Quickly.

Hurry it up.

Decide right now.

While he was struggling to come to an answer, Merry rushed him.

"Hey," she said. "What are we going to do?"

"Don't ask me! Use your own head! It's not like I'm the one who has to make the decision!"

"Don't shout at me all of a sudden. Okay, I'll decide, then. Let's turn back."

"We're going back empty handed?! My pride won't let me—"

He let out a hiccup.

He broke into a cold sweat.

He'd heard a voice; some sort of cry. It wasn't human or feline, it was like—a dog's barking? Or maybe a wolf?

Without either signaling the other, Ranta and Merry stood back to back.

The fog was getting thicker again.

Where? he thought. *Where did it come from?*

He heard footsteps.

Inside the mist, this way and that, from every direction, dark forms approached them.

Yeah, wolves. Black wolves, huh.

Though it was hard to imagine, a wolf appeared up and to their right, where they had first seen the catlike creature. Looking closer, it was too large to be a wolf; it was more like a bear. On top of that, there was something riding on its back.

Yellow-green skin. A hideous face. Ranta doubted his eyes, but there was no mistaking it.

"What, a gobliiiinnnnn?" he said.

3 | The Quiet Struggle Between Factions

"JUST NOW, did you hear something?" Kuzaku said. He stood half-inside the passage, listening closely. "Did I imagine it? No, I'm pretty sure I hear it."

"Really...?" said Shihoru.

She moved over and crouched down next to Kuzaku, turning her right ear toward the outside.

"Oh," she said. "You're right. It's...dogs howling?"

"Sounds more like wolves to me, if anything," said Kuzaku.

He leaned back, keeping as much distance from Shihoru as he could.

"Well," he said, "it's a forest, so I guess there being wolves isn't that strange, but..."

It wasn't because it was Shihoru; he just didn't really want to get close to anyone of the opposite sex right now. While he wasn't like Ranta, Kuzaku was aware he wasn't as disinterested as Haruhiro was. It'd be bad if he got into a weird frame of mind, and the girls were all a little unaware and unguarded, so he had to be the one to be careful.

"It does bother me," Kuzaku said. "You think they're all right? I mean, I think they are, but on the other hand I can't not worry."

"It's tough waiting," Shihoru agreed.

"Sure is. But that's what we've gotta do. Everyone's got their own role to play."

"Yeah," Shihoru said slowly. "I need to work out more."

"Huh? You, Shihoru? Like, you're gonna get all beefy?"

"I-I won't go that far. I have trouble building muscle. I can only put on weight where I don't need it."

"No, I don't think you don't need—er, not that I mean that in a weird way or anything. I dunno. It's best to be a healthy weight. Like, I don't think you need to be overly thin. Huh? Am I digging myself a hole here? Erm. Sorry? I was kind of rude there. I didn't offend you, did I?"

"It's okay. No need to walk on eggshells. I may not seem like it, but I've got a thick skin," Shihoru said, hanging her head with a wry smile. "It comes with being fat."

A self-deprecating gag? Should he laugh? Or tell her that she was wrong and compliment her? He wasn't sure which was better. Honestly, Kuzaku had trouble dealing with this side of Shihoru.

"But it's a pretty long way away, y'know," Kuzaku said. "To Alterna. Still, this is Grimgar, not Darunggar, so that's a step forward at least."

"Um..."

"Yes?"

"That was boring, right? Just now," Shihoru said. "I'm sorry. I meant it as a joke, but I can't come up with anything funny usually."

Whaaaa. You're bringing it back up now? Seriously? Normally you'd just let it go. That was definitely a thing Kuzaku thought, but if she was going to bring it up, he had to rise to the occasion. She wasn't a total stranger; she was his comrade, after all.

"Yeah," he said. "It was kind of hard to laugh at. I mean, our bodies can be a pretty delicate subject. Even if it was funny, I'd wonder, like, is it okay for me to laugh? You know? Also, you're not fat, obviously. Actually, you know, I think we all lost a lot of weight in that other world. It was harsh there..."

"Y-you might be right," said Shihoru.

She looked at Kuzaku with upturned eyes.

"Thanks for being straight with me. I'm really grate...*glad* that you did."

"Oh, you are? Well, good."

Kuzaku was relieved to hear it.

"It took some courage to say that," he said. "I was worried I'd offend you. But I shouldn't be so reserved, like you're a stranger."

"We're comrades, right?" Shihoru asked.

"We are, yeah."

"But...you're still overly polite sometimes?" she ventured.

"That's, well, mostly force of habit, I guess? You're all my seniors, so I think that's part of it."

"Not that we're very reliable seniors."

"That's not true," Kuzaku said. "I'm always relying on you guys.

It makes me feel like I must've had a big brother or big sister. I don't remember, though. That aspect of my personality, it's not a good thing. I'm the party's tank, after all. Really, I need to get to the point where you can rely on me."

"Well, at the very least, I can say that I rely on you, Kuzaku-kun. I think. I mean, you're protecting me."

"I wish I could cover for you better," Kuzaku said. "You know, I'm tall, and I've got pretty long arms, too. I think if I handle myself right, I should be able to draw all the enemies to me. I need to do that, or—"

"No!" Shihoru said.

She suddenly clung to Kuzaku's arm.

"You can't... Kuzaku-kun, don't stress yourself. It's not good to take everything on yourself like that."

"Is that what I'm doing? I don't think so."

"You definitely are, I think," she said. "You were open with me, so I'll be straight with you, too. Moguzo-kun was always trying too hard, thinking he had to do things, and that's how he ended up the way he did. I think you might be doing a bit of that. He tried too hard for the rest of us, because we were underdeveloped. We made him push himself. I don't want you to repeat that, Kuzaku-kun. I won't let you. We can't have someone wearing themselves down for the rest of us. One person can't sacrifice themselves for the rest of us, all of us have to work to make up for the others' shortcomings. That's what I think."

"Ohhhh," said Kuzaku. "That...makes sense. I mean, I don't mean to seem like I'm in a rush. I feel like I'm behind the rest of you. Well, I'm chasing after all of you—" Kuzaku started to say, and then realized what he was saying. "Haha... You're right, I may be rushing things. But it sure is tough, isn't it? I can't help but get ahead of myself, you could say. I mean, Haruhiro, he's amazing. He's very detached, but in a good way. He's calm."

"Haruhiro-kun... I think there's a lot going on inside his head," said Shihoru. "He just doesn't talk about it. I think, because he's the leader, he can't talk about it. If the leader was worried, and indecisive, everyone would feel uneasy. I'm sure that's what he's thinking."

"You think he's pushing himself too hard?" Kuzaku asked.

"I don't think it's easy on him. But there's not much we can do about it. Haruhiro was forced to become the leader because the rest of us are unreliable. It's not that we pushed it off onto him, but he's not the type who would normally volunteer for that sort of position."

"Well, yeah," Kuzaku said. "Haruhiro, he hates standing out. He's not really the leader type, I guess. I like his style, though. Easier to deal with than someone who's like, 'Shut up and follow me.'"

"I like his style, too." Shihoru smiled a bit.

Oh, she's cute, Kuzaku thought, and then immediately felt guilty about it.

"It's just," Shihoru said. She looked down. "I think we're causing a lot of trouble for him. No matter how you look at it, it's a job that hurts him. I wish I could at least do something to help, but I don't know how."

"Something to help, huh," Kuzaku said. "I'm not really the type for it...but, I mean, neither is Haruhiro, and he's trying his hardest. For all of us."

"If only there was some small thing we could do to take some of the burden off of him," Shihoru said.

Kuzaku crossed his arms and looked upward, closing his eyes. This seemed like something he really ought to think about. Or rather, he wanted to give it some serious thought. Even if he didn't have an immediate flash of inspiration, if he kept it in mind, he might come up with something eventually.

"Still," said Shihoru, "it's good for you to agonize over these things. Especially while you're young. Having more than enough time to pick a problem apart in your head is one of the privileges of youth."

"Oh, you think?" Kuzaku said. "Makes sense..."

"Huh...?" Shihoru gulped.

"Wait, what?" Kuzaku's eyes went wide.

"Hm?"

There's someone here...? thought Kuzaku.

It was obviously someone other than Kuzaku and Shihoru. Furthermore, that person wasn't Haruhiro, or Yume, or Ranta, or Merry.

That man was crouched just outside the exit Kuzaku and Shihoru were standing by, hugging his sheathed sword. He was wearing glasses, or goggles, rather, so it was hard to tell what his face was like. His hair was parted in the center, and his face was covered in stubble. He didn't look all that young.

Kuzaku figured he was probably human, but he didn't look like he was from Alterna. He wore a longish coat that was tied up at the waist, along with a pair of something like riding pants.

"Oh, pardon me," said the man in goggles, raising a hand and grinning. "I didn't mean to eavesdrop, but you folks hadn't noticed me. I thought it would be wrong of me to just keep quiet, so I took it upon myself to subtly insert myself into your little conversation."

"No..." said Kuzaku.

He hurriedly motioned Shihoru to get behind him, resting his free hand on the hilt of his black blade.

"That wasn't subtle at all, you know...? Clearly. I don't even know who you are."

"Indeed," said the man in goggles. "You speak the truth."

He scratched his head and frowned.

"Then allow me to say this: If I meant to do you harm, I would have already done so. I don't mean to mock you, but you were wide open. Even with my paltry skills, I could have easily dispatched you."

Kuzaku had to acknowledge that the man was right. Kuzaku had been absorbed in their conversation and wasn't paying enough attention. He was supposed to be here as Shihoru's bodyguard, too. How pathetic.

Even so, if they were to fight straight up, it was questionable whether he could win against this man. Kuzaku still hadn't drawn his sword. He couldn't. All reasoning aside, he could sense that if he drew his weapon, he'd be in serious trouble.

"We're volunteer soldiers from Alterna," Kuzaku said. "Does that mean anything to you as an explanation?"

"Indeed," said the man. "You are volunteer soldiers with the Arabakia Frontier Army, yes? I know them. I have acquaintances who are volunteer soldiers, too."

"I'm Kuzaku," Kuzaku said.

Shihoru followed suit.

"I'm Shihoru," she said in a quiet voice.

"I'm Katsuharu." The man raised his goggles up to his forehead, squinting. "If I say I'm from the village, would you understand what I mean? We simply call it 'the village,' but outsiders refer to it as the Hidden Village."

"The Hidden Village," Shihoru whispered. It seemed like she had some idea what he meant.

Kuzaku felt like he may or may not have heard of it. He wasn't really sure, but he could tell that it was a place where humans like Katsuharu lived, at least.

Which meant...what?

"Huh? What's that mean?" Kuzaku said, cocking his head to the side. "I don't really get it."

"It means we're not enemies," said Shihoru.

"Alterna's part of the Kingdom of Arabakia, and Arabakia and the Hidden Village aren't hostile to one another," she explained in a whisper. "Though we aren't exactly friendly with them, either. You might guess it from the name, but we don't know exactly where the Hidden Village is."

"So that's why it's a hidden village?" Kuzaku asked. "Huh. So, Katsuharu-san is from there, and... What does that mean? Uh..."

"You two are so easygoing. That's nice," Katsuharu said.

He sat down on the ground and rubbed his nose. He'd said Kuzaku and Shihoru were easygoing, but he was projecting a pretty easygoing attitude himself. Then again, it still felt like he might draw his weapon at any moment. He was a mysterious man.

"That said, I do find it a little odd coming across two volunteer soldiers in a place like this. Could it be that the two of you just returned from the world that lies beyond that hole?"

"You know about Darunggar?" Shihoru asked hesitantly.

"The name Darunggar isn't familiar to me," said Katsuharu. "However, some in the village are aware that that hole leads to another world. This place, Thousand Valley, is like our backyard, you see."

"Thousand Valley..." Kuzaku said.

He looked out into the fog hanging over the area. He had a sudden realization.

"Wait, if this is your backyard, you know the paths here? Right? The way to Alterna, too?"

"Indeed. I have made a number of trips to Alterna myself, after all."

"Then you could show us the way!" Kuzaku cried. "Oh, no, I know I shouldn't be asking you for a favor out of nowhere. You have no obligation to help us."

"As you say, I have no obligation to," Katsuharu said. "Not now, at least. We've just met, after all. However, I sense a certain kismet in our meeting here, and once we come to know one another better, I might feel obliged to."

"By which you mean...?" Kuzaku asked.

"Perhaps I was too indirect." Katsuharu hit himself in the head. "The truth is, I happen to be searching for someone. Could you help me, perhaps? When my business is finished, I'll show you to the village. You must be exhausted from your travels, no? Why not rest at the village?"

"I think he's a little suspicious," Shihoru whispered in Kuzaku's ear. "Isn't he being a little too generous when he doesn't owe us anything? Besides, if he shows us the way there, we'd find out where the village is."

"I can hear you," said Katsuharu. He pulled on his earlobe and smiled wryly at them. "I've got a good pair of ears on me, you see. Well, I suppose your caution is warranted. However, you've misunderstood one thing."

Could they trust him? Kuzaku couldn't decide.

"What are we misunderstanding?" he asked cautiously.

"It's outsiders that call it the Hidden Village, not us. I told you that, didn't I? We relocate the village every year, sometimes more than once in the same year. Most of the villagers are, well, not accepting of outsiders, you could say, but it's not as if the gates are closed to strangers. As a matter of fact, you people must have heard of the volunteer soldier called Soma, right? He was recognized as a samurai by the four samurai houses."

"Yeah," said Kuzaku. "We're technically Soma-san's comrades...? Well, we're in the same clan."

"Oh, are you indeed? Then you must be highly capable."

Kuzaku and Shihoru looked at one another despite themselves. How should they respond to that?

While Kuzaku was still confused about what to do, Shihoru spoke up.

"If only that were true. We still have a long way to go."

"How very humble of you to say that," Katsuharu said, grinning.

Somehow, he completely saw through their skill level, and he was teasing them based on that knowledge. That was what it felt like. But it didn't come across as nasty, and they really were inexperienced, so Kuzaku couldn't get mad at him for it. Kuzaku consulted with Shihoru in a whisper, knowing full well that Katsuharu would overhear, then decided to fill him in on their situation.

"Katsuharu-san, we've got other people with us, too," Kuzaku said. "Four of them. Two left scouting earlier, and the other two went out looking for them when they didn't come back. So, we were left here waiting."

"In that case..." Katsuharu's expression clouded slightly. "It may be that your friends have already gotten caught up in things."

"What's that supposed to mean?" Kuzaku asked.

"Where do I even begin? To make it simple, there's trouble going on. My adorable niece has been caught up in it, so I can't ignore it. She would be the one I'm looking for. Ahhh, this is such a hassle."

Katsuharu lowered his goggles, fixed their position, and then stood up.

"You two come with me. I'll explain more along the way. Or would you rather stay and wait for your companions? Either way, I'll be going."

"Maybe we should go with him," Shihoru said.

If she said so—well, it was really that Kuzaku couldn't make a decision, so he couldn't possibly object.

Katsuharu led the way, of course, with Shihoru and Kuzaku behind him as they advanced through the fog. It was strangely easy going; Katsuharu seemed to be choosing the spots with the best footing. He'd explained this was his backyard, and it was clear he hadn't just been saying that.

"Um, Katsuharu-san," Kuzaku said. "Now that I think of it, I heard what sounded like wolves howling."

"Forgan's beasts, no doubt."

Katsuharu wasn't looking around. He just walked straight ahead.

"Are they bad news?" Kuzaku asked.

"There's this guy called Jumbo, you see," Katsuharu said. "Forgan is the faction he leads."

"Huh? What do a faction of orcs and those beasts have to do with one another?" Kuzaku asked.

"Keep your voice down."

Katsuharu crouched and put his hand on the hilt of his sword.

Shihoru ducked her head and held her breath. It looked like Kuzaku would be best advised to ready himself and stay put, too.

For the next two or three minutes, he stayed there and didn't move a muscle. It got harder and harder. But, in Kuzaku's case, if he moved about carelessly, his equipment was guaranteed to make noise. Until someone told him it was okay, he had to put up with it.

Still, can we go yet? he wondered.

Instead of thinking things like that, he should have been scanning the area, thinking about what he'd do if something happened and what he was supposed to do until then.

I'm taking this too lightly, he thought. *I need to reflect on that. If I keep on going like this, I'll never catch up to Haruhiro and the others. But I can't see anything through the fog, and I don't really hear anything. If enemies attack, then protecting Shihoru is about all I can do, so...can we go yet?*

"There was a nyaa," Katsuharu said in a low voice.

"A nyaa?" Shihoru asked.

"Yeah. Have you people never heard of them? They're animals. A wild nyaa hardly ever shows itself to people. The village's onmitsu spies raise them, but that wasn't what that one was. That was likely one of Forgan's trained nyaas."

The more he listened, the funnier the word sounded. *Nyaa.* It was just too cute. Like, a pet nyaa. No, this was no time for laughing. It was probably a serious matter. Kuzaku cleared his throat.

"But I don't see anything that looks like that, and I don't sense it, either," he said.

"It was faint, but I heard a slight meowing earlier," Katsuharu told them. "It went 'nyaa'... It's gone now, though. It doesn't seem to have noticed us. Let's hurry onward."

If Katsuharu says so, that's probably how it is, thought Kuzaku. *It really is relaxing to just do as someone tells you. Obviously, it's easier, too. Having to think for yourself, now that's hard. Haruhiro is amazing, seriously.*

Honestly, by the time he noticed he was doing whatever Katsuhiro told him, he was a little exasperated with himself for getting used to that situation so quickly.

"It's like I'm a dog," Kuzaku murmured.

"True." Shihoru, who was ahead of him, giggled. "You do have a dog-like quality, Kuzaku-kun."

"Oh, you heard that? Huh. Am I really that doglike? Hrmmm. Well, I'm not catlike, I guess. Are you more of a dog person or a cat person, Shihoru-san?"

"I prefer dogs, I guess..."

"Oh? Really?"

"Huh...? Oh, i-it's not anything to do with you being so doglike."

"Nah, I'm not going to misunderstand you like that, don't worry," Kuzaku told her. "I'll bet you don't even see me as a man. I mean, I'm pretty sure all the girls in our group are that way."

"I wouldn't say that," Shihoru said.

"Nah, I'm sure of it. Like, considering how things went... No, no, I shouldn't talk like this."

"How what went? Now you've got me curious."

"Yeah, I guess you would be," Kuzaku said. "If I say this much, then try to keep it a secret, would you? You would, right? Well, you know how it is. I mean...I confessed to Merry, and got shot down hard."

"I thought so," Shihoru said.

"Urgh. You'd noticed?"

"Just vaguely, though."

"Well, that's embarrassing. But facts are facts, so what can you do? In the end, we decided to stay just comrades."

"It's tough, huh," Shihoru said, nodding. "Knowing how close you can get to people. Merry's the serious sort, and very well-organized, after all."

"I'm over it now, though. I'm trying to put it behind me. But I'm worried about Merry. I mean, she's with Ranta-kun."

"When I hear the two of you talk," Katsuharu said, laughing and pretending to scratch himself all over, "it makes me feel ticklish."

"S-sorry," said Shihoru. Her head shrunk into her body.

"It's nothing to apologize for," Katsuharu said. "I was like that, too, back in the day. It was a long time ago, but this brings the memories flooding back. That aside..."

Katsuharu came to a halt. He crouched, touching the ground.

"Looks like something happened here. These footprints are likely human. From two, maybe three people... Two, I'd say. These two people were probably surrounded by a pack of wolves, and then... There are no signs of a struggle. The two walked off on their own after that. They headed southwest. Hopefully we can follow the trail."

4 | Hard Work

THE PATH AHEAD dipped lower, and the fog swirled around them.

The sounds of fighting are coming from over there, thought Haruhiro.

Moyugi led the group, pressing through the fog with his demon Moira in tow.

"Huwuh?!" Yume let out a strange cry. "Where'd Kuroron go?!"

Haruhiro was taken aback. Kuro was gone; he'd vanished. He was right in front of them just a moment ago.

Haruhiro was surprised by that, but if they didn't hurry and catch up to Moyugi and Moira, they'd get left behind. If he was stuck alone with Yume in the middle of who-knew-where, that would be the worst.

He and Yume picked up the pace. For now, they were somehow managing to keep Moyugi in sight. But it also felt like they were maybe getting themselves in deeper and deeper?

Shihoru and the others must be getting worried, he thought. And Ranta... He just hoped Ranta wouldn't do anything stupid.

Damn it.

He only just firmed up his resolve to be leader, and was doing his best to be careful, then he made an awful mistake like this. Nothing ever went his way. It made him really, really resent how mediocre he was.

All that aside—they're here, he thought. *Going at it. It's a battle; they're fighting.*

Haruhiro could hear the sound of a man's husky voice cutting through the fog. It was human. There were a number of other voices, too.

Moyugi came to a stop. Moira went alone into the fog, vanishing out of sight. Haruhiro and Yume caught up to Moyugi, then stopped.

If he squinted Haruhiro could just vaguely make out a humanoid figure. The figure was swinging around a fairly large sword; he was likely the owner of the husky voice. Was the group that kept attacking him made up of orcs? Or were they some other race? Haruhiro couldn't tell that much, but it was one against many.

Despite his obvious numerical disadvantage, the man with the husky voice didn't take so much as a single step back. That said, it was clear he was fighting alone.

"Um, Moyugi-san?" Haruhiro asked hesitantly. "That guy's human, right? Don't we have to help him?"

"If it were necessary, I would, of course. That goes without saying. What are you, some kind of idiot?"

"I was just asking. No need to bite my head off."

"It's fine to ask questions, but think for yourself first," Moyugi snapped. "To put it simply, you look up to me as some sort of superior, and you were looking for me to give you orders, right? In other words, you're an idiot. They say an idiot is what you make of him, and it goes without saying that I could make good use of you. What do you say to that, Haruhiro-kun, the idiot?"

"I'll think before asking from now on."

"Please do. I hate having my thinking process disrupted by questions from idiots, you see."

"Moyugin's a real bully," Yume said, puffing up her cheeks in anger. But Moyugi just smiled faintly as if it didn't matter to him. Well, Moyugi made a fair argument, and he'd been right on the mark. He had been in this line of business longer than them. Without a doubt, he was more skilled, too. It would be hard to find anything they were better at than him. That was why Moyugi was way above Haruhiro, and why Haruhiro had decided to do as Moyugi said. He'd naturally accepted that relationship.

Moyugi, with his sharp tongue, had questioned that. *Are you okay with that?* he was asking.

Moyugi had clearly stated if Haruhiro and Yume acted like loyal little dogs who would just wag their tails and follow him, he'd be happy to use them as decoys or disposable pawns, and he wouldn't treat them any better than that. They were all members of the Day Breakers, but so what? If they thought that made them his comrades, they were massively wrong, and a massive nuisance to boot. They needed to do something to make him acknowledge them—that was what he was saying.

He worded it harshly, but he was being pretty considerate. Or at least, that was what Haruhiro decided to think. Haruhiro wasn't so earnest enough that he could get all worked up and think, *Fine, I'll make you acknowledge me,* but he certainly couldn't let himself be used as a decoy or pawn.

For now, even if they couldn't stand shoulder to shoulder with Moyugi and Kuro, they could still reflect upon things that needed reflecting on; they could learn what needed learning; work on the things they needed to improve. They could, little by little, narrow the distance, the gap, between them.

Is that too much for us? he wondered. *Well, even if it's difficult to accomplish, we can make the attempt.*

Think. Think hard... No, just thinking isn't enough. I need material to work with before I can think. I need information. Look for it with my eyes, hear it with my ears. Sense it with my skin.

What's going on here? What are Moyugi and the others doing? Fighting enemies. What kind of enemies? There were orcs. But it's probably more than just orcs. What about those enemies the guy with the husky voice is fighting? Are they just orcs? Or are there other races, too? I want to know. I need to learn more.

"Mind if I move up a little more?" Haruhiro began saying. "No, actually, I'm moving up."

Without waiting for a response, Haruhiro walked ahead of Moyugi. Yume came with him.

He could see it now: The man had an incredibly large sword with an unusual shape, and he was swinging it around left and right.

What a sword, thought Haruhiro. *I've never seen anything like it.*

Each sword had a center of gravity. That was the point where, if the sword was held and was allowed to balance itself like a scale, the weight on both sides would be equal. Generally, if it wasn't somewhere from ten to twenty-five or so centimeters from the point where the blade met the hilt, the sword became incredibly unwieldy. Unusable, even. And yet...

And yet, the man's sword had to be more than a meter-and-a-half long, which on its own was already enough to make it over-sized. And the tip was broad, too. It had a shape that might be described as looking like a thin slice of a giant mushroom. With a shape like that, the center of gravity had to be incredibly close to the tip. As a result, his swings were slower.

Because he was forced to use big, slow swings, he left many openings. The man resolved that issue by using something other than his sword—

His feet.

When an enemy got close to him, the man would let loose a kick. Those kicks had an incredible amount of force behind them. The man was built as strong as an orc, after all, maybe stronger.

If Haruhiro took a kick from one of those log-like legs, he'd probably never get back up. And it went without saying that, even if he tried to defend himself with a shield or armor, he wouldn't be able to stand up against the man's massive mushroom sword. If he tried to get in close, he'd be kicked; if he didn't, he'd be

GRIMGAR OF FANTASY AND ASH

bisected by that massive mushroom sword. If he found himself facing that man as an enemy, what exactly would he do?

Haruhiro only one had answer:

Run. What else?

The guy was terrifying even just to look at. He wore no helmet, showing off his bald head, and while the mustache might have been okay, why was he wearing sunglasses? He was nothing if not intimidating. No matter how you looked at it, this guy was crazy.

He shouted and swung his massive mushroom sword, turning an enemy into a corpse. He shouted three more times, and with each swing, there was another corpse. One enemy tried to charge him as he finished a swing, but he kicked them back, and then, with another shout, immediately bisected them.

The corpses were piling up as Haruhiro watched. Okay, that might have been overstating it, but the man's massive mushroom sword, the dynamic sword techniques, and the kicks that were quite agile for a man of his build all made Haruhiro want to describe it that way.

To add one more thing, he used the fog to his advantage, too. From his position, anyone who tried to get close to him was an enemy, but his enemies couldn't say the same thing. With visibility as bad as it was, it would be hard for the enemy to surround him with ten to twenty men on each side, pressing inward.

Haruhiro could see now why Moyugi didn't try to join the fray. If he carelessly approached and tried to lend a hand, he might only succeed in disturbing the man. That being the case, couldn't they just support him from a distance?

By no means was that something Haruhiro was actually thinking of doing.

But then he carelessly got himself noticed by the enemy. That was it.

"Yume!" Haruhiro readied his stiletto and the knife with the hand guard.

The enemies were closer than he had thought.

Incoming. Green skins. Orcs, two of them. One with blue hair, the other red. Wearing metal armor. Their swords are probably single-edged. They're curved. Katanas, maybe?

If they came at him together, he and Yume probably wouldn't be able to hold out, not even for a little while. First, they had to split up the orcs, Haruhiro and Yume each taking one.

Haruhiro charged at the blue-haired orc, showering it with a series of blows from his two blades. He focused on getting in every slash and thrust as quickly as he could. Even if they hit, they wouldn't be able to do much damage. Even so, he managed to take some of the wind out of the orc's sails.

He could hear Yume shouting as she used her machete to trade blows with the red-haired orc, too. While Haruhiro had the blue-haired orc on the defensive, he adjusted his position so that his back was facing Yume's. This way, even if new enemies came, they could at least avoid being attacked from behind.

Moyugi, Moira, Kuro, anyone, could you come save us, please? he thought desperately.

Don't get your hopes up, he warned himself. If he couldn't handle this by himself, how could he do anything?

In fact, it was because he had tried to rely on others that, the moment the blue-haired orc went on the offensive, he tried to pull back.

"Ah...!" Haruhiro shouted.

Whoa! Damn! He's fast!

As the blue-haired orc took a savage swing at his throat, Haruhiro used the knife in his left hand to Swat it away. With an immediate twist of his wrist, the orc moved into an overhead swing. The knife in Haruhiro's left hand wouldn't make it in time. He used Swat with the stiletto in his right. He couldn't fully deflect it.

The blue-haired orc stabbed at him. It looked like he'd be overpowered if he used his left, so Haruhiro used the stiletto in his right to Swat, Swat, Swat.

He's strong, this orc, he thought.

It was only to be expected that each blow would be heavy, but the orc's blows were skillful, too. He didn't rely on power alone; his technique was precise and accurate. If Haruhiro described it as being like fighting a human, was that taking orcs too lightly? Still, that was how Haruhiro felt. This guy looked different, but he was human.

Human...?

No, he wasn't. Not only was his body larger than a human's, he had greater strength. If he was smarter and more dexterous on top of that, that would mean, on the whole, he was greater than a human.

While cautiously using Swat to deflect the blue-haired orc's katana, Haruhiro shuddered. He may have misunderstood something all this time.

The No-Life King appeared around a century-and-a-half ago, giving birth to the undead and unifying the orcs, kobolds, goblins, and others into a single faction. They had destroyed the human kingdoms of Nananka and Ishmal and forced the Kingdom of Arabakia to retreat south of the Tenryu Mountain Range. As a result, the orcs and undead were now both powerful factions on Grimgar's frontier.

That just showed how incredible the No-Life King had been. Somehow, that was what Haruhiro had ended up thinking.

Orcs were clever, and stronger than humans, and that was why they were in a better position than humans on the frontier. Had Haruhiro even once considered that possibility?

To be frank, no, he hadn't.

Maybe Haruhiro hadn't known what the orcs were truly like.

"Yume!" Haruhiro said, narrowly managing to Swat the blue-haired orc's next attack, a two-strike combo of a horizontal attack chained to a low one, then glanced over to Yume. He only saw her for a brief moment, but it was clear she was struggling.

We can't hold out, he realized. *Not like this.*

The way things were going, Haruhiro and Yume would both go down sooner or later.

It was a fresh and clear reminder of how much more powerful Moyugi and his group were. Things were clearly hopeless, and they couldn't win anyway, so should he just give up? No, that wasn't an option... Clever. He had to get clever. Haruhiro may not have realized what a real orc was like, but their enemies didn't know a thing about them, either.

"Two, one...!" he called.

"Meow!" said Yume as she quickly turned. At the same time, Haruhiro did an about-face.

They switched places.

The blue-haired orc had been getting used to Haruhiro's fighting style, and the red-haired orc had probably been getting a handle on how Yume moved. If their opponents suddenly changed, that would confuse anyone. Human or orc, it made no difference.

Haruhiro pressed the attack now. Naturally, he didn't understand his opponent, so it was risky. Still, the way things were going, there had been little chance of them winning, so he would have to take the chance and attack.

Haruhiro committed to it, getting in close to the red-haired orc. He used Slap and Shatter, and made it look like he was trying to transition into Hitter. Instead, he feinted into a Cut and another Shatter. The blows were all shallow, but his combo bewildered the red-haired orc.

Now, thought Haruhiro.

He slipped past the orc, getting behind him. He performed a Backstab with his stiletto.

It wasn't just one shot, it was two, then three. He pierced the armor, but it wasn't a fatal strike.

The red-haired orc turned to face him.

Circling around to get behind the orc again, Haruhiro performed another triple Backstab combo.

The red-haired orc staggered, but with a cry of "Orrrsh!" it managed to stay on his feet.

Having anticipated this, Haruhiro immediately grappled him from behind. The red-haired orc was wearing a helmet; however, there were large openings for the eyes and mouth, and the orc's red hair was sticking out from inside it.

Haruhiro rammed his knife with the hand guard into the mouth hole, then stabbed his stiletto into the orc's right eyeball. He pulled both free in an instant, leaping away.

The red-haired orc groaned, dropping to one knee, but it didn't fall yet.

Just how tough is this guy? Haruhiro wondered. *Even if he's dying, there's no telling what he might do until he's completely dead. I have to think that way. Harden my heart.*

Haruhiro kicked the red-haired orc down, then immediately twisted his stiletto into the orc's right eye.

"Sorry about this!" he shouted.

Die. Die. die, die. Please, die.

Leaving the now-motionless red-haired orc lying where he was, Haruhiro looked over at Yume. She was using Wan-chan to deflect the blue-haired orc's sword, but he could see she was clearly tired. He wanted to get in there and help immediately—

But don't rush, he cautioned himself. Haruhiro had his own way of doing things.

First he had to relax his breathing, get it under control, release the excess tension from his body, and erase his presence. He couldn't make the fog go away, but he could clear his mind.

His field of vision quickly broadened. He could see. He could hear. He could feel. His mind was set loose from his flesh, and it felt like he was looking down on the area, himself included, at an angle. He felt this was a little different from the Stealth skill that Barbara-sensei had taught him, but Haruhiro was at his best like this.

Moyugi hadn't moved a step, and was just standing there, as if he was saying, *Show me what you've got.* Haruhiro had expected that, so it didn't piss him off. He wouldn't be able to wring even a grunt of approval from the man, but he'd do what he could.

Moving calmly, like he was one with the fog, Haruhiro circled around behind the blue-haired orc that Yume was trading blows with. Not only had the blue-haired orc not noticed him, Yume hadn't detected Haruhiro moving, either.

He couldn't see the line, but he moved without the slightest bit of indecision. Sheathing his knife, he went for a Backstab with his stiletto. It went in deep, and, for an instant, the blue-haired orc stopped.

Without missing a beat, Haruhiro used Arrest. He grabbed the blue-haired orc's left arm. Caught by surprise, and with Haruhiro having such a firm grip on his elbow, the size difference between them meant little; it was easy to throw him off balance and trip him. Haruhiro stabbed his stiletto into the fallen orc's right eye.

"Meow!" Yume jumped in, slamming her curved blade into the orc's right wrist. Though she didn't manage to cut off his hand, the sword he was holding went flying.

I'm finished, the blue-haired orc was probably thinking. His despair was palpable. Even so, he worked up the will to try and rise once more.

I won't let you, thought Haruhiro.

He straddled the orc, pulling his stiletto free and stabbing it back in, pulling it free and stabbing it back in. He cut up the blue-haired orc's face.

The stiletto was a weapon that specialized in stabbing, so its penetrative power and ability to inflict lethal wounds were frightening. It didn't take long for the blue-haired orc to die.

How do you like that? Haruhiro thought. It wasn't something he was going to say, but he turned to look at Moyugi.

He's not even there, he thought.

With a series of shouts and grunts, the bald man wearing sunglasses was still at it. The same as before, he was slashing at enemies with his massive mushroom sword, intimidating them into backing away, and knocking them back with kicks.

The orc he kicked to the ground tried to get up—and couldn't. Before he was able to, Moyugi, who had moved over there at some point, thrust his thin sword through the back of the orc's neck.

"Now, then," said Moyugi.

He pulled his sword free and adjusted the position of his glasses with the middle finger of his left hand.

"I'd say it's about time. We'll finish this by the time I count to eight. One..."

There was a visible shift in the tide of the battle. The enemies that had focused on the bald man in sunglasses until now decided to spread out. Maybe half of their force changed targets, closing in on Moyugi.

Soon, one of them went down.

An arrow, huh? thought Haruhiro.

That had to be Kuro's doing. But another enemy sprang at Moyugi.

He didn't dodge. Instead, he said, "Two," still adjusting his glasses and counting.

What does that guy think he's doing? Isn't that dangerous?

As if she was doing it to show that wasn't the case at all, Moira emerged from the fog, and with a cry of "Noooooo," she dragged down the enemy that was about to take a swing at Moyugi. At almost exactly the same time, two arrows fired in quick succession struck another enemy, and they collapsed.

While counting "Three," Moyugi crossed blades with yet another enemy, this one a white-haired orc. In that moment, Moyugi glanced at Haruhiro.

What? he thought, startled. *In the end, you're using us after all, huh? Well, not that I mind.*

Haruhiro swam through the fog using Stealth. When he got behind the white-haired orc, Moyugi counted "Four," then turned to the left as if he had lost interest in his opponent, walking off like he was taking a casual stroll. It caught the white-haired orc by surprise, probably enraging him; it prompted him to swing at Moyugi.

His back was wide open. Well, there was only one thing to do about that. With a disinterested glance at Haruhiro, who had gone in for a Spider and was trying hard to finish off the white-haired orc, Moyugi leisurely went about running the other enemies through.

"Five," he said. "Six."

Seriously, what was with that guy?

The number of enemies was quickly dropping.

Hidden in the fog, Kuro shot them to death. Moira used Moyugi as bait to attack the enemy. Moyugi was casually stabbing them to death, as well. It went without saying that the sunglasses-wearing bald man was still striking down enemies with his massive mushroom sword, too.

How they were killing enemies, that was something even Haruhiro could tell. But wasn't it weird for things to be going this smoothly? He felt like he was being shown a magic trick.

"Seven."

Moyugi backed away, looking like he might trip at any moment. That one wasn't an orc; a four-armed humanoid enemy was charging at Moyugi.

An arrow stabbed into his right flank, and then Moira tackled him from the opposite side with a "Nooooooo!"

Moira got on top of the enemy.

"Noooooo... Nooooooooo... Nooooooooooooooooooooooooo...!"

With a glance to Moria, who was murdering her enemy in an unspeakable manner, Moyugi returned his thin sword to its sheathe with an elegant gesture.

"Eight," he said. "Done. Just like I calculated."

"Whooo..." Yume said as she looked around the area.

Haruhiro could only sigh. He shook his head.

The orcs were gone. There had been so many of them, too. But, at least as far as he could see, not one of them was left standing.

It really ended by the time Moyugi had counted to eight.

Well, since Moyugi was doing the counting himself, and he could adjust the length of time as needed, it didn't seem entirely fair, but still.

"Hrmmm..."

The bald man wearing sunglasses let out a low groan, stabbed his massive mushroom sword into the ground, and then twisted his head side to side slowly.

"Indeed," he said.

"Good work," said Kuro as he appeared out of nowhere, slapping the bald man on the shoulder, "Kajita."

The man he called Kajita smiled and gave him a thumbs-up.

Moira slowly rose up. Her four-armed enemy didn't so much as twitch. Or rather, it was such an unrecognizable mess that it couldn't. Enemy or not, did she really need to mutilate the body that badly?

Or was that just how demons were? Would Ranta's Zodiac-kun act like that eventually?

Haruhiro grimaced at that unpleasant thought.

"Um..." Haruhiro said.

He shook his head.

"This—I don't know what it's called, the four-armed enemy... What is it?"

"What? You don't know?" Kuro said with an exaggerated look of exasperation. "It's an undead, of course. The ones with four arms are called double arms. Or, that's what they call themselves."

"This is an undead..." Haruhiro said, rubbing his throat.

The one Moira had killed was destroyed beyond recognition, so he looked through the other bodies to find one, and—there it was. Here, there, everywhere; all the non-orcs must have been undead.

The undead weren't unlike humans. They were more or less humanoid, but the ones called double arms had four arms, and there were others that had two arms that were oddly long; or they had extremely long torsos with short legs, really big butts, or strangely large heads. They also had very little exposed skin. Their bodies were covered in cloth, leather, or metal, and the rare bits of flesh that peeked through were horribly blackened, brown, gray, or pale blue.

And unlike the orcs, no blood flowed from their wounds. Instead, an unsettling green mucus seemed to be leaking out.

"Huh," said Yume as she hesitantly walked over and crouched next to the undead's corpse. "Listen, Yume, she's got this one thing she's been wonderin' about for a while now."

"Sure," said Kuro, walking over and crouching down next to Yume. "Ask away. Though, if I don't know the answer, all I can do is lie to you."

"If you're gonna lie, tell Yume it's a lie, okay, so she doesn't go believin' you, okay?"

"Wahaha!" Kuro laughed. "Sure, sure. You've got it. I'll do that."

"Listen, undead, they're dead that un, right?"

"Huh? What, what? 'Dead that un'? What's that supposed to mean?"

"Like, they're dead that are un, right? Un is un! Right?"

"Wahaha!" Kuro cackled. "That's a funny joke, but I have no

idea what you mean, okay? You know what, you're cute. Like some kind of animal."

"Murrrgh! Yume, she's an animal, but she's human, okay! Oh, but humans're animals, too."

"Haha! What are you, the pet every family wants? Wahahahaha!"

Kuro hugged Yume's head close to him and patted it like crazy. "Hey, Moyugi, Kajita, can I keep her?"

"When it comes time to feed her, be sure you do it yourself," said Moyugi. His eyes had a creepy glint in them.

Kajita grinned and gave him a thumbs-up.

"Indeed."

"Basically..." Since this was going nowhere, Haruhiro did his best to interpret for her. "...with 'dead' referring to death, and 'un-' being a negating prefix, I think she wants to say, aren't undead not supposed to die?"

"Haru-kun, that's it!" Yume said as she brushed Kuro's hand away. "Jeez! Now you've gone and fussed Yume's hair up!"

"Yume, I don't think fussed is the word you're looking for."

"Hoh? Tussed? Hussed? Oh, Yume doesn't know anymore."

"Heheheh..." Kuro wheezed. He was doubled over, holding his sides. "Oh, damn. My ribs. You're killing me here, seriously. Okay, okay. I get what you meant. I see. Sure. You're right. If you write it out in kanji, they're the 'race without death,' but these guys, they die pretty easily."

Kanji? Haruhiro thought, startled. *Oh, right, kanji. If you write it in kanji—wait, huh...?*

I know what kanji are. They're written characters. They're used here in Grimgar, too. But there's something... Yeah, that's right. Kanji?

I don't think anyone calls them kanji, do they?

They're one type of written character, and I've only heard them called ideographs. They might have a name, but I've never heard it. Even though they're definitely kanji.

"What's wrong, Junior?" Kuro asked him.

When Haruhiro looked up, he saw Kuro had a stupid grin on his face, but there was a sharp glint in his eye.

"Is something bothering you? Speak up."

"No..." Haruhiro shook his head. "It's nothing."

"Oh, yeah?" Kuro took a short breath, then gestured toward the felled undead bodies with his chin. "Well, whatever. So, back to the undead. They've got this thing called a core, and it's thought that they'll die if you bust it. The core is usually inside the head, so as long as they're intact from the neck up, they'll round up enough dead body parts to revive themselves. Weird, huh?"

"It's only speculated?" Haruhiro raised his eyebrows. "Has it not been properly confirmed? That this core, or whatever it is, exists?"

"Exactly. The core hasn't been discovered," Moyugi said smoothly. "The undead are said to be a race that was initially created by the No-Life King's curse. The fact of the matter is, even now, if a person is left lying around after their life functions are terminated, they'll eventually begin to move because of that curse. It's not limited to people, though. We know that not only elves, dwarves, orcs, goblins, kobolds, centaurs, and gnomes, but all the major sentient races turn into what we call zombies three to five days after their deaths. A number of other intelligent creatures do, too. However, though they can turn into zombies, they can't become undead. Why is that?

"There are those who theorize it has to do with the No-Life King being gone from this world; but whatever the case, his curse is still functioning. Furthermore, when the No-Life King was still around, the undead were born from that curse. Based on that, I theorize that the so-called core is not a thing inside the undead, but a thing that has come to reside inside them in some form. When that form breaks, they cease to be undead. In other words..."

"This is long," Kajita said. He gave a thumbs-up, then turned it into a thumbs-down. "Too damn long."

Moyugi clicked his tongue.

"Well, let's leave it at that, then. We've been talking too long. My operation, it goes without saying, is still ongoing. Come on, we're moving on to the next stage. Come on!"

"Huh...?" Haruhiro and Yume said, exchanging glances.

Yume had been spacing out. To tell the truth, so had Haruhiro.

"What do you mean, next?" he asked.

"Guess we should go." Kuro stood up, stretching and cracking his fingers. "Two more left. This is tough on an old man like me."

Kajita shouldered his massive mushroom sword as if it was light.

"Indeed."

"No, Kajita," said Kuro, "I know you don't look it, but you're waaaay younger than me, okay? This is easy for you, I'll bet. It's a piece of cake, right?"

Kajita gave him a silent thumbs-up.

Moyugi had already gone far ahead with Moira.

"Two more..." Haruhiro said, walking on unsteady legs. "I guess we'll have to finish them quickly?"

Was that okay? Or wasn't it? He didn't really know anymore.

The fog was still thick and deep.

5 | A Loss Too Great to Compensate For

THOUGH THEY FACED MANY—no, countless—crises of the sort that would make any other man abandon hope and give in to desperation, Ranta had carved his way through every one of them and made it his own.

Difficult situations are nothing to me, he'd always thought confidently. *I can get out of anything.*

That was what he believed; he was confident of it. Abso-total-lutely.

Ranta grinned to himself. That word just then was clever. "Abso-total-lutely." Should he have shouted it out loud? Who knew? It was hard to say. If he shouted, they might get mad, maybe? More than that, perhaps? Or maybe them just getting mad was the least of his concerns?

Fog.

He had been in the fog for some time now.

There was nothing but fog, and he couldn't help but be sick of it.

Good grief. Was there no way he could use the poor visibility provided by this fog to run for it?

Yeah, no. Great though he was, that was a little too tall of a task. He was tied up, after all.

Neatly bound, you could say?

The ropes bit into his upper body. This was that thing, you know, the turtle one. Turtle shell binding. Surprise of surprises, his legs were free, but his arms were cuffed together behind his back, so he couldn't move them the way he wanted to. The rope extending his handcuffs was tied tightly around the trunk of a nearby tree. It was tiring to stand, so he sat and crossed his legs.

Ranta's helmet had been taken off, but he was still wearing his armor. Before being tied up, his captors subjected him to a body search that was more violent than thorough, and they relieved him of all his possessions, weapons included.

Well, of course they had. It was a body search, after all. He went through it, and so did she.

He glanced to the side. Their shoulders were touching. She was next to him, kneeling with her head hung.

Hey, hey, hey, don't get so touchy-feely, he thought. *Do you have a thing for me, huh? Well? How about it?*

Ranta could have engaged in some light-hearted banter with her, but he didn't. He couldn't. They might get mad.

Just maybe, they might do more than get mad. If he was unlucky—maybe they might kill him...?

He couldn't see all that well through the fog, so he didn't know what kind of place this was, but they weren't on top of a hill, at least. There was a cave right nearby. Of course, it wasn't the exit they came out of before.

Ranta and Merry weren't the only ones here. There were others; lots of others.

First, there were those things: the catlike creatures with dexterous-looking hands and slightly oversized heads. There were tons of them around. It was fair to say they were surrounded by the catty critters. Up in the trees, on the ground, lying around, curled into balls; there were all sorts of them, but it felt like they were watching Ranta and Merry. Or, well, the creatures were definitely watching them. He already knew they weren't feral.

It wasn't just the catlike creatures; there were the deep black wolves by the mouth of the cave. They were all trained pets.

It was that goblin.

There was one black wolf lying down next to the cave that was larger than the rest, large enough to be called magnificent. The goblin that was sitting next to it, petting it lovingly, was apparently the keeper of the catlike creatures and the wolves. Based on what Ranta had observed, that was the only possible conclusion.

However, that goblin who was wearing tight-fitting leather or something... It had a goblin's face, a goblin's figure, and a goblin's physique—it was the gobliniest goblin ever—but there was something different about it. It was completely calm, like it was intelligent, and had an air of something like sorrow about it.

That's no ordinary goblin, Ranta thought. *Must be some kind of special goblin, huh?*

That was plain to see. Well, of course it would be.

"H-hey?" Ranta tried talking in the quietest voice he could manage. "Don't let it get you down. We're still alive, you know. So long as we're alive, we can do something. Okay?"

"You're right." Merry kept her head hung as she spat the words at him. "So long as you're alive, you can get down and kowtow."

"Urkh..."

Dark memories rushed back to him in an instant.

Kowtowing. It was true, yeah; he'd kowtowed! They were surrounded by wolves, and it seemed like things were about to get bad, okay?! It was on the spur of the moment! He did it reflexively, as the one viable option! It was a masterful choice anyway!

Yeah, he did it!

He did it, okay? He'd gone and done it, because of course he would, right? He kowtowed, okay, all right?! That was fine, right? It was the right choice, in the end.

"Th-thanks to that, we're still alive," Ranta said. "We managed to avoid getting killed there. Show a little gratitude, why don't you. My rapid and timely kowtow overwhelmed our opponents."

"More like it appalled them."

"Either way, we survived... Think positively, Merry."

"Positively? In this situation?" Merry said, letting out a strained sigh. "Quit joking around."

Ranta gave her another sideways look. Well, if she couldn't be positive, maybe he couldn't blame her. They were tied up, after all.

The ropes were digging in a bit, too. Wasn't that kind of erotic? No, not kind of—it was erotic, right?

Incidentally, that goblin had been the one to tie up both Ranta and Merry. It had done the body search, too. That meant it had gotten to feel Merry all over. Ranta hadn't thought of it at the time, but looking back on it now, he was jealous.

No! It was outrageous! How dare a lowly goblin do that? Ranta hadn't even touched her yet!

"What are you looking at?" said Merry, glaring at him.

"I-I wasn't looking," Ranta said as he turned to face forward. "Okay, so I was... I was looking, I was looking, I was totally looking. Is looking wrong? Hmph. You okay there? If they're tight, or it hurts..."

"You pervert."

"I... I was just concerned!"

"Your voice."

"Urkh..."

Ranta hurriedly shut his mouth and looked around. The cat-like creatures were all looking their way. The wolves were, too. And that goblin. There were others, too.

The truth was, in addition to the catlike creatures, the black wolves, and the goblin, there were several green-skinned orcs here, too. There were also a number of non-orcs hiding their skin. They went in and out of the cave or loitered around the area.

What was with those guys? Who were they? For starters, why weren't they trying to kill Ranta and Merry? If they'd wanted to do it, they could have. Even now, they still could. Weren't orcs the enemy of humanity? What were goblins that should have been in and around Damuro doing here?

Ranta peeked at Merry again. They wouldn't kill them quickly...was that it? Like, the fun was still to come? If there was something coming, was it *that*? Was it gonna be *that*? Like, *Gehehehe, everyone gets a turn, guys?* Like, *Merry's gonna be in trouble?* No, not like she was going to be in trouble, she already *was* in trouble.

Yeah, he thought. That's how it goes, huh.

If they were in a situation where their enemies could do them in at any moment, it meant they were in a situation where they could do her at any moment, too. Merry had to know that. She was definitely in for a bad time. She must be thinking it'd have been better if they'd killed her quickly and gotten it over with.

Which would come first? Would they kill Ranta, or would they get to Merry first? They might do it right in front of him while he was still alive... That would be hard on his psyche. He didn't want to see it, but he kind of did. No, no, he did not. There was no way he'd want to see that.

Ranta shut his eyes tight. *S-s-s-scaryyyyyyyyy,* he thought. *So damn scaryyyyyyyy. No, no, no, I don't want this. Save me, save me, save me, please, I'm begging you!*

He heard Merry gulp.

Ranta opened his eyes, opened them wide.

Someone had come out of the cave. Someone.

It was no orc, no goblin, no humanoid-like creature. It was humanoid, though. Because, well—it *was* a human.

He was coming, walking this way. A human. His long, stiff hair was tied up at the top of his head, and his face was covered in hair. His cheeks were sunken.

A kimono? He was wearing that sort of outfit, with an obi tied tightly around it, and his left hand was thrust inside his collar. He...had no right arm? Or was it just hidden inside his sleeve?

The long, thin object he held in his mouth seemed to be a pipe. He was smoking tobacco. The man was one-eyed. His left eye wasn't just closed, there was a scar there.

Was he in his forties, maybe? He was an old man. But...

What was going on?

There was a human, together with orcs and goblins? Were they comrades?

"Hmmm." The old man grunted as he stopped in front of Ranta and Merry, removing his hand from his collar to stroke his chin. It made a scratchy sound. He had a curved sword at his hip. It looked like a katana, maybe.

"What a fine woman," he said. "She looks delicious."

"What, you're going to eat her?!" Ranta couldn't help but poke fun at him.

The old man raised a bushy eyebrow and looked down at him.

"The brat's a feisty one, too."

"Freshness comes first, huh? Dammiiiiiiiit. W-we're gonna get eaten, huh?"

"I'm pretty sure that's not it," Merry said coolly.

"Shut up, Merry! And hold on, what are you so calm for?!"

"I wouldn't say I'm calm, exactly..."

"Well, settle down," said the old man. He yawned. "It's true, if we decide we want to boil you, or bake you, and eat our fill, we're free to do that. We can do whatever we want, whenever we want. If Onsa weren't so capricious, you two would already be wolf food. You managed to avoid that. Why not be happy about your good fortune? Hm?"

The goblin was petting the big black wolf fondly as it looked at them. Maybe Onsa was that goblin's name.

Ranta looked at Merry. Merry was looking down, her shoulders heaving up and down. Her breathing was ragged. Her entire body was shuddering.

Was she scared? Of course she was.

Ranta took a deep breath and fixed his eyes on the old man. He was scared silly, but he wasn't going to let anyone think he was a chicken. He had his pride as the most atrocious dread knight to consider, after all.

"Kill me," Ranta told him. "If you're gonna kill us, do it already. But, you know what? You guys aren't gonna do it. You've gotta have some reason, right?"

"It's not much of a reason." The old man blew a puff of smoke. "When we take captives, no matter what they're like, we don't just go and kill them. That's the law."

"The law? What kind of group are you guys?"

"What, you don't know about us?"

"Well, no," said Ranta. He licked his lips.

So that's how it is, he thought.

They wouldn't kill them right away; the old man had guaranteed that. In that case, what did he have to fear? He wasn't scared. He wasn't scared one bit.

"We just got back from a little trip to another world, you see," Ranta told him.

"Another world, huh?" The look in the old man's eyes changed a little. It looked like he had the guy's attention. Good, good.

"I may not seem it, but I'm kind of a well-known volunteer soldier," Ranta bragged. "So, after building a ton of experience in another world, I've come back to Grimgar, bigger and better than ever. If you wanna hear about it, I can tell you stories."

"Are you stupid?" Merry was whispering something in a low voice, but what did he care?

"It was an adventure that'd make your blood boil and your flesh dance!" Ranta declared. "No, it was a whole series of super adventures! Unknown lands, surprising creatures, our gold not worth a thing, our words not understood, our hard-earned experience irrelevant; we went through the ultimate survival experience in a place like that! How about it?! If you don't hear me out, I guarantee you'll regret it later, you know?! You want that?! To not hear this? If I were you, I'd listen, though!"

"Let me think."

The old man tilted his head to the side and blew another puff of smoke.

"I'll pass."

"No waaaaaay..."

"Let me ask you one thing."

"A-ask away! N-no! D-depends what it is?! I don't mind answering, I mean, I'm happy to cooperate... Really?"

"It's in your own best interest to answer," the old man said. "You two, what's your connection to the village?"

"Village...?" Ranta and Merry said, looking at one another.

Merry shook her head, not seeming to understand. Ranta had no clue either, but was it okay to answer truthfully?

"The village, huh?" Ranta said, looking up at the old man. He tried to read the guy's intentions from his face, but it was no good. He wasn't displaying anything that could be called an expression. The old man had a totally flat affect. He'd have to go with his gut here.

"Oh, the village," Ranta said. "Yes, I know what that is. I mean, I'm the most knowledgeable guy around. If anyone tells you otherwise, they're a liar. Why, I could stay up all night telling you all about villages! But let's save that for another time..."

"I see," said the old man. He frowned and scratched the back of his head. "I can't tell if you're trying to pretend you know, or desperately trying to hide the fact you do."

"Heh," said Ranta. He closed his eyes.

Yeah, I'll bet you can't, he thought. *That's exactly what I was going for.*

"Looks like it's safe to dispose of you."

"Whaaa?! Why is that?! Why's it sabe?! Sabe?! What's a sabe?!"

"You, you're a funny one, but shut up."

"Sh-shutting up...right now. Okay?" Ranta said.

"Woman." The old man crouched down, seeming to lick

Merry's body up and down with his eyes. "The thing about human women, strangely enough, is that it seems the other races don't mind them, either. We're an all-male group. If you don't put up any strange resistance, you may not die."

Merry said nothing. She looked down at the ground, gritting her teeth. Maybe imagining the horrifying fate that awaited her in the near future had left her unable to say anything.

Ranta didn't have time to feel sympathy for Merry. The way things were going, Merry was going to become a plaything for the orcs and goblins, and Ranta would get killed either before or after it happened.

Ranta-sama, the most fearsome of all dread knights, didn't think there was any way he could die here like that. Honestly, it just felt so unreal.

It had to be a scam where they make him think, *You're gonna die, you're gonna die,* or rather, *You're gonna get killed, you're gonna get killed.* They'd never actually kill him. Yeah. Of course he was gonna be fine.

Or maybe he just wanted to think he'd be fine...?

When you died for real, was it really just that easy...?

Die.

Was he going to die?

No way.

He couldn't die. Not yet.

He hadn't even done it with a woman yet!

No, well, he didn't remember anything from before he came to Grimgar, so he might already have had that experience, but if he didn't remember it, it was the same as if he hadn't. He wanted to at least do it before dying. No, no, he didn't want to die. He wanted to do it, screw around like crazy a whole lot more, and live. No matter what happened, he had to live.

If the most atrocious of all dread knights went down like this, it would be a great loss for humanity. He had to live, for the sake of all humankind.

But how?

"Don't make trouble," the old man said with a low-pitched laugh, then blew on his pipe and walked off in the direction of the cave.

Ranta clicked his tongue.

Damn it.

Before the old man left, he should have performed one last theatrical, brilliant, and powerful kowtow...

6 | Two Sides of the Same Coin

"**T**HEY JUST NEVER LEARN." The man with a buzz cut who was wearing a priest's uniform stuck his metal rod out.

An orc with its hair dyed many colors deliberately swung at the rod with its katana. That was all it looked like to Haruhiro, but that couldn't be right. The man with the buzz cut was relatively short, while the orc had to be at least 190 centimeters tall, even at a conservative estimate. It seemed like the orc should have been the stronger of the two, but obviously it couldn't cut the metal rod in half with a katana.

That had to be Buzz Cut's skill: to lure in his opponent, make them strike where he wanted them to, then use his opponent's own power to strike back at them.

Buzz Cut's metal rod spun around, striking the orc in the side of the face. But orcs were tough; even taking a solid blow to the face from a rod made of iron, or perhaps some other heavy material, the orc staggered, but didn't go down. Buzz Cut should have been more than capable of following up with another attack, but he didn't, instead backing away.

"I've got this!" Bursting out of the fog, a lanky man attacked the orc from behind. This man had a weapon in each hand. Based on that and his strategy of attacking from behind, the man was a thief. However, he didn't quite seem like the type.

"The reason I can't be happy, and the reason I'm haunted by sadness, and the reason my soul can't find salvation, and the reason people won't recognize my accomplishments, and the reason I don't have a harem, they're all your fault!" he shouted.

The thief moved in a way that seemed to challenge the limits of flexibility. He was fast, yes, but he bent and wriggled like crazy; it was kind of creepy. It was good that he'd pushed the orc down and stabbed the hell out of him, but did he have to seem so vengeful about it? Besides, it was pretty clear that none of that stuff was the orc's fault. He was just venting, right?

What was more, when the orc stopped moving, the man stood up slowly, soaked in his victim's blood.

"I've sinned again," he muttered. "My god, the god inside me, is dead!"

He made no sense. But whatever. He could do what he wanted. Well, not that he needed to be told that; he was apparently going to do it anyway, because the thief vanished into the fog once more using that bizarre walking style of his.

Meanwhile, Buzz Cut was using his metal rod to dodge another orc, and then strike back.

"We'll leave Tsuga and Sakanami to their own devices, as

planned," Moyugi said. He pressed on the bridge of his glasses with his middle finger, then immediately ambled away. "We'll move on to the next place."

It seemed natural that Moira followed him silently, because she was his demon, but why did Kuro say "Righto," and tag along, too? The priest with the buzz cut, Tsuga, and the strange thief, Sakanami, were their comrades, weren't they? They were members of the Typhoon Rocks. Despite that, was it okay that they just watched their comrades fighting from a distance, without lending a hand, then acted like it was none of their concern what happened afterward?

While Haruhiro was confused, a big hand came to rest on his shoulder. When he turned to look, Kajita, the big bald man wearing sunglasses, was giving him a thumbs-up, his mustache upturned in a smile.

What? What's that sign supposed to mean?

"Oh. Okay then," was the only response Haruhiro could give.

Kajita shouldered his massive mushroom sword and followed Kuro. He walked at an easy pace, with a swagger. He walked so boldly.

Did people like him not hesitate, or feel indecisive? Or did they? Which was it?

Yume poked Haruhiro in the back. "Haru-kun, should we be goin', too?"

"Oh...yeah."

She was right. They had to go.

I keep thinking that, don't I? Is this really okay?

He'd been thrown totally off his pace. Or rather, he couldn't keep pace with the others. It made him doubt that he even had his own pace to begin with. Haruhiro followed behind Kajita with Yume, thinking, *Man, I'm so fragile,* and feeling ashamed as he did.

In his usual group of six, he managed to lead them somehow, bringing them together in some form. But when other factors came into play, like now, he was suddenly hopeless. Everything fell apart before he knew it, and he had no idea what to do in response.

Why...? he wondered. *What's the problem? What am I lacking? What's missing?*

If he were to answer "everything" to that question, he felt like that would be running away from it. If he said that, it would be all over. He was frustrated, and hopelessly angry at himself. He didn't want to stay like this.

"Yume...hold on," Haruhiro said suddenly.

"Fwuh?"

"I want to talk to Moyugi-san."

"M'kay. While you do that, Yume's gonna stay next to Kajitan."

Kajita turned back and gave them a thumbs-up. He didn't speak much, and it was hard to figure out what he was like, but he was reassuring to have around.

Haruhiro began running, passing Kajita, then Kuro, before coming up beside Moira. Moira suddenly turned and fixed her pit-like eyes on Haruhiro.

"Nooooooooooooo..."

You're scaring me here, Haruhiro thought nervously.

No, he didn't have time to be scared. He had to absorb things. To beg for teachings, or whatever else he could, and take in everything he could. He'd make them his own.

"Um, Moyugi-san, Is this—"

"If your question is stupid, I'll ignore it."

The way Moyugi went out of his way to tell Haruhiro that, it showed he might be surprisingly considerate of others. Either that, or he just liked to talk.

"I've done some thinking, but... This plan, normally you'd want to concentrate your forces, but you're doing the opposite," Haruhiro said hesitantly. "By splitting up, are you trying to make the enemy divide their overwhelming larger force, and taking them out one group at a time, maybe?"

"If it were up to me," said Moyugi, "we'd never follow a stupid plan like that."

"Same here... Even if I thought of it, I don't think I could do it. It's too risky."

"However, when it comes to tactics, you can't plug your variables into some sort of formula and have them lead you to the answer. Based on countless conditions, your process will change. And your result, too, of course."

Haruhiro understood that. Even if his group had its own form, it depended on what they were up against. What kind of enemies; where they were fighting; whether they could launch a surprise attack; whether they were suddenly attacked themselves. Many factors came into play, and that changed their ideal plan. They had to change and adapt it.

"This time, it just so happened to be that the situation made you choose a plan you normally wouldn't. Is that it?" Haruhiro asked.

"To put it another way, we have no plan," Moyugi said, not answering Haruhiro's question directly. "We have the essence of one, of course. Like, this is the way things are, and this is what to do if this happens. But, even with that, there are exceptions. In the end, when it comes time to make a decision, plans are just another factor we take into consideration. What do you think strength is?"

"Huh?"

That came out of left field, thought Haruhiro. Or was it actually connected somehow?

"Well, the ability to win, I guess," Haruhiro said. "It may seem trite, but I'd say something like, 'The strong don't win; those who win are strong.'"

"There's truth in that. For instance, I, the strongest dread knight in active service, do not possess exceptional physical prowess, or a rare potential for dread magic."

While thinking, *He's not going to give up on that "strongest dread knight in active service" thing, huh?* Haruhiro nodded.

"*Right.*"

"Let us imagine there was a fierce warrior who could kill a dragon with a finger flick to the forehead. If they were attacked in their sleep, or were slipped poison, they'd die easily. The fact of the matter is, there have been no shortage of heroes who have met their end that way. I know that's true. Unfortunately, not being able to remember my original world, I can't offer any concrete examples. For someone from here, maybe the No-Life King would count?"

"Strength doesn't require power," Haruhiro said slowly. "Is that what you're saying?"

"Having it doesn't hurt. You use what you have available to you. However, even with training, not everyone is going to be able to run the 100-meter dash in under ten seconds, right? Though, in this world, for the moment, at least, it doesn't seem there's any way to accurately measure times that are less than a second. I think there was in our original world, though."

"You keep managing to slip in those mentions of our original world."

"Doesn't it concern you? If it doesn't, then you're a fool. Though I suppose most people are fools."

"I can't say for sure whether I'm a fool or not, but...honestly, it does concern me," Haruhiro said.

"You're a member of the Day Breakers, so I figured it would."

We're searching for a way back to our original world, Shima had told Haruhiro.

"Soma says there are signs of the No-Life King returning, and he formed the Day Breakers with the objective of entering Undead DC in the former Kingdom of Ishmal," said Moyugi. "Setting aside the issue of whether there are any signs of it happening, I'm sure that the No-Life King, said to lie sleeping in Ever Rest in Undead DC, will eventually rise again. His curse is still in effect, after all. When that happens, not just Alterna, but the entire Kingdom of Arabakia's mainland will not be left unscathed. I'm sure we'll be forced to fight for the survival of humanity, whether we like it or not, with each of us putting our lives on the line. If possible, I want to take care of things before it comes to that. To destroy the No-Life King as soon as possible. That's what Soma has been gathering the power to do. On the surface, at least."

"But his real objective is to return to our original world?" Haruhiro queried.

"There may come a point when we have to slay the No-Life King, so while that's the reason we give for public consumption, it's not just a front," Moyugi said. "I want to become strong, after all. To defend what needs defending, to seize what I desire, and to reclaim what I have no doubt lost."

Though Moyugi was by no means short, he wasn't especially tall, either. The reason he looked lanky was because he was thin. He had the bare minimum amount of muscle that he needed, but you couldn't exactly call him musclebound. His gestures lacked strength and power, he wasn't nimble, and he himself said he had no special gift for dread magic. In fact, if Haruhiro set his mind to it, he could probably get behind the man. When it came to strength, agility, and maybe even endurance, it was possible that Haruhiro was better than Moyugi.

But he couldn't beat him. Even if he could get behind him and prepare a one-shot kill, the tables would be turned on him. He couldn't help but feel that way.

There was Moira, for one thing. Besides, if Haruhiro aimed for Moyugi's back, there was no doubt Moyugi would predict it.

This was true of anything, but if he was expecting it, there were steps he could take. Moyugi would anticipate that Haruhiro was better than him, and lay traps.

What kind of traps?

He didn't know. He couldn't imagine.

If he fell into some unknown trap, would he come out of it alive?

He couldn't predict that. His legs cowered in fear. He couldn't think straight.

He was guaranteed to lose at this rate.

"Everyone plans a step ahead before they act," said Moyugi.

"So you plan even further ahead, right?" Haruhiro asked.

"I read one hundred steps ahead before I move. Well, that's what I'd like to say, but there are too many branches, so it's not realistically possible."

"Um... Well, do you plan something like ten steps in advance, then, Moyugi-san?"

"I'm always three steps ahead. Even for me, the strongest dread knight in active service, that's the best I can manage."

That's not very many, was what Haruhiro initially thought, but then he reconsidered. "Always," Moyugi had said. That meant he started each fight by predicting three steps in advance, but that wasn't the end of it. If he kept thinking three steps ahead with each turn that passed, that meant he needed to keep thinking at all times.

That'd be tiring. It'd wear him out. It'd be tough; so tough that it'd make your nose bleed.

Did he have to go that far in order to become stronger and win?

Yes. He wasn't a genius or some sort of chosen one, so if he didn't do at least that much, he wasn't going to be able to win. He couldn't become strong. That was probably what it meant.

In this line of business, defeat could very well mean death. If Moyugi didn't want to die, no matter how tough it was, no matter how exhausting, he had to do it. If he didn't, it'd be fine for as long as he kept pulling out victories somehow, but he'd eventually lose and die. If he didn't want that, he had to call it quits.

"Um, Moyugi-san," Haruhiro spoke up.

"What is it?"

"Thank you. That was helpful. I learned a lot."

Moyugi just snorted, not saying anything.

Thinking. Up until now, Haruhiro thought he had been doing that. But if you asked him whether he thought and thought and thought until he reached his limit, he wouldn't be able to puff up his chest proudly and say *Of course*.

Haruhiro felt like he thought pretty hard. But hadn't he always felt, somehow, that it was enough?

He hadn't pushed it to the limits, that was for sure. Sometimes he tried pretty hard, but in the end, after reaching a certain point, he tended to take a hands-off approach and let what would be, be. He figured he'd done enough, so it was probably fine. No one was going to complain to him.

It was only natural there would be a gap between a person like him, and a person who kept thinking and analyzing.

It wasn't simply a difference in ability. It was a question of who was doing everything they possibly could. That was the only difference, but it all piled up to create a huge gap between the two of them.

"By the way..." Haruhiro decided to ask a question, though he didn't expect an answer. "These enemies, who are they anyway? Why are you people fighting against them?"

"If I were to sum up our reason simply," Moyugi actually answered, to his surprise, "it's on a whim."

"On...a whim?" Haruhiro said, looking at him quizzically.

Before he had time to digest that, the next group came to attack them. The fog was still as dense as ever, and thanks to that, he couldn't see them. But he could hear the noise. He heard voices, too.

Haruhiro expected Moyugi to scope things out again, but he saw no signs of the man slowing his pace.

This area was comparatively flat, and it was thick with thin, dark trees. They had to slip between them, so walking wasn't easy.

"Kuro. Kajita."

Without stopping, Moyugi signaled something to the two of them with his hands.

Haruhiro came close to asking for orders, but he couldn't do that. He had to think first.

Turning back, Kuro was heading left, and Kajita was heading right. Yume was looking at him in anticipation. Kuro specialized in shooting enemies dead without them discovering his location, so it was best not to get in his way.

Let's support Kajita without getting too close or straying too far away, Haruhiro decided.

He headed back to where Yume was, and they followed Kajita together. Moyugi kept pressing ahead with Moira accompanying him.

Kajita turned his head toward Haruhiro and Yume and gave them a thumbs-up. It'd be rude to just ignore him. Haruhiro hesitated briefly, then gave him a thumbs-up in return.

Kajita looked satisfied, or at least that was how it seemed.

Haruhiro still couldn't see the enemy, but eventually he was able to more or less make out their voices. There were probably multiple orcs. There was a human man, and a woman, too. One of each, huh? But they weren't shouting, just letting out a sharp battle cry every once in a while.

"Rock!" Moyugi shouted, probably intentionally.

There was an immediate "Yeah!" from a man who seemed to be in high spirits in response.

"It's going just like we planned!" he said. "Kill 'em all!"

"Rarrrrrrrrrrrrrrrrrrgh!"

Kajita let loose a loud roar that seemed to make the heavens and earth shake. It wasn't just any ordinary shout; he used a special vocalization method to emit a sound it seemed like no person should be able to, intimidating all who heard it. It was a warrior's war cry. Even so, this was the most incredible one Haruhiro had ever heard.

Haruhiro covered his ears despite himself, and almost crouched down. Yume staggered and blinked in amazement.

Yeah, it hits you pretty hard, Haruhiro agreed.

The enemies were coming this way. Naturally, that was what the war cry was meant to make them do.

"Yume, get in front of me!" Haruhiro shouted.

"Meow!" Yume bobbed her head up and down vigorously, then drew Wan-chan and got in front of Haruhiro.

Haruhiro had his stiletto in his right hand, and the knife with a hand guard in his left. He steadied his breathing, erased his presence, and went into Stealth.

It was lame hiding in Yume's shadow, but he couldn't afford to be concerned about appearances. Instead of just reacting, he would think, then act on his own initiative. This was necessary for him to be able to do that.

At some point, a fighting style in which he used Swat to fend off his opponent's attacks, waiting for an opening to strike, had become second nature to him. But Haruhiro was a thief. Swat was only meant to get him out of a tight spot. Keeping an enemy busy wasn't a thief's job.

Thief skills could be divided into three categories: ambush tactics, thieving techniques, and lethal combat techniques. He was meant to be an attacker in combat.

An orc leapt out of the fog.

"Indeed!"

Kajita met him with his massive mushroom sword. He tried to cut through the orc along with the dark trees, but the orc dodged.

A second then third orc appeared, pressing in on Kajita.

Is he going to be okay? was one thing Haruhiro didn't have to worry about. He'd most likely planned for this possibility, and Kajita didn't need someone insignificant like Haruhiro worrying about him. Besides, Haruhiro and Yume had enemies coming their way, too, from up ahead, to the left.

It was—not an orc. An undead, huh? It wasn't one of the four-armed ones called double arms. Its neck was weirdly long, with uncanny sloping shoulders and long arms.

Haruhiro silently adjusted his position. He was on the straight line that connected Yume and the undead. This was the spot. Here, the undead couldn't see Haruhiro. It couldn't detect him.

Yume raced forward. The undead charged in.

Should I keep waiting? Haruhiro wondered. *No.*

Forcing aside his indecision, Haruhiro moved. He maintained his Stealth, taking a somewhat wide route around Yume's right side as he steadily approached the undead.

The undead still hadn't noticed Haruhiro. Soon Yume's curved blade and the undead's sword sent sparks flying. Just after that—no, before that—Haruhiro managed to circle around behind the undead. With his stiletto and knife, he slashed a cross shape into the thing's bizarrely long neck.

As it collapsed, unable to withstand the blow, Yume pounded Wan-chan down on the top of its head.

"Chowah!"

With its head smashed open, the undead lost its strength. It was almost like a broken doll. Without pausing for a breath, Haruhiro got behind Yume again.

Kajita was taking on three orcs at once. He hadn't defeated even one of them yet. It looked like they were tough ones.

"Yume, let's give Kajita-san one less enemy to deal with," Haruhiro said.

"Meowger."

Yume walked quickly toward one of the orcs.

Her shadow. Haruhiro had become the brave Yume's shadow.

The orcs noticed Yume. Here it came. Just one of them. The other two stayed pinned to Kajita. This one's hair was dyed gold and braided, and his weapon was a katana. He was about as tall as Kajita. Tall as he was, though, he was still light on his feet. The fact that his head didn't bob up and down was proof that he had a stable center of gravity.

At a glance, the orc seemed lightly equipped, but he was actually wearing armor that protected him from the neck down. He had guards on his knees, elbows, and shins, as well as armored gloves. Given he had been able to give Kajita trouble, there was no doubt he was skilled.

Haruhiro tried to move forward on Yume's left side while maintaining his Stealth, but the golden-haired orc immediately detected him. It was a sharp one. Haruhiro immediately hid himself behind Yume once more. Immediately after that, the golden-haired orc and Yume had an intense exchange of blows. Its katana was slightly longer than Yume's Wan-chan, and it was more muscular, too. It felt like Yume was just barely managing to fend off its attacks as she backed away.

The golden-haired orc was putting pressure on Yume, but he still had the presence of mind to watch out for Haruhiro.

I have to support Yume quickly, thought Haruhiro. *I can't just act randomly. Think. Hurry. Don't lose your head. Think.*

"Yume, pull back!" he called.

Yume quickly rolled back and to the left. It was Pit Rat.

Haruhiro immediately moved up. Now the golden-haired orc couldn't pursue Yume. Haruhiro acted as intimidating as he could, taking up the stance for Assault.

"Ohhhh!" he cried, realizing what was going on.

If he didn't hit the golden-haired orc with everything he had, he might be swept aside. He had to go all out from the beginning.

The golden-haired orc seemed to be saying, *I'll take you on.* He wouldn't underestimate Haruhiro. He'd be a nasty enemy to deal with.

And the enemy's weapon had a much longer reach, so if Haruhiro didn't get up close, it wasn't even going to be much of a fight. Haruhiro charged in as if he was going to tackle the orc.

That was what he made it look like, but then he used his right foot to kick up some of the almost mud-like dirt; it was Flinch. Basically, he was throwing dirt in his opponents' eyes. He hadn't used it much in actual combat, but the dirt flew toward the golden-haired orc's face like it was supposed to. The orc didn't even flinch, just raising up its arm to block it. During that time, Haruhiro—didn't charge in. He turned on his heel and raced the other way.

"Urga?!"

That surprised the orc. And so he hesitated, thinking it must be a trap. The truth was, it was a trap, in a way.

Haruhiro ran about four meters, then turned back to face the golden-haired orc. Walking sideways, he moved to a place where he could flank the orc with Yume. Haruhiro signaled to Yume with his eyes, but it wasn't necessary.

Yume returned Wan-chan to its sheath, pulling out a throwing knife and immediately tossing it. "Star Piercer, meow!"

The orc quickly reacted, twisting to dodge the throwing knife. Haruhiro tried to close in on the orc from behind—but he was detected, so he immediately backed away.

Meanwhile, Yume had been nocking an arrow. She let it loose. Three shots; Rapid Fire.

The golden-haired orc easily avoided the first two, and deflected the third one with his katana.

After that, for a moment, he lost sight of Haruhiro.

When he noticed Haruhiro had used Stealth to get into striking distance, even as impressive as the golden-haired orc was, he had to be shocked. From his perspective, Haruhiro seemed to be saying, *Now's the time*—but Haruhiro didn't attack.

He fell back, putting distance between them again.

The golden-haired orc looked surprised and disappointed, but also on guard. It might have already seen through Haruhiro's intentions. Even if it had seen through him, there shouldn't have been anything it could do. At the very least, it couldn't realistically dispatch Haruhiro and Yume in a hurry.

That was because they were buying time. Of course, if it seemed like they could take the orc down, they would. But there was no way they would do anything too risky.

The golden-haired orc had to choose between taking them on in a battle of endurance and letting the difference in strength win it for him, or else quickly crushing Haruhiro or Yume and turning it into a one-on-one battle. Of course, if he could have done the latter, he already would have. He was stronger than either Haruhiro or Yume, but he didn't have that great of a strength advantage. The orc himself knew it, too.

As a result, if they became impatient, it would be easy for him; but that wasn't going to happen. The golden-haired orc settled in for the long course. He likely figured he just had to win in the end. He probably guessed that, even if it took some time, he'd be able to win, so he would attack them slowly and carefully. His confidence was probably unshakable.

The fact of the matter was, if the fight dragged on like this, Haruhiro and Yume might lose without ever finding any chance of victory. That was why the golden-haired orc was doing the right thing. Haruhiro and Yume had also chosen the optimal course of action for their situation, so as long as neither party made a mistake, the one who deserved to win would.

As the golden-haired orc stood there, not showing any sign of overconfidence, an arrow stabbed into the left side of his chest.

"Whuh...?" Yume tilted her head to the side.

Yume's bow still had an arrow nocked. The shooter wasn't Yume.

The golden-haired orc let out a low groan, but braced himself and turned to face in the direction the arrow had flown from. When he did, another arrow pounded into his right arm. Without missing a beat, a third arrow struck the center of his chest. They easily penetrated his armor. What a powerful bow... The golden-haired orc dropped to one knee.

"To think you'd use me." Kuro emerged from the fog. His bow

was slung over his back, and he had a single-edged sword in his hand. It was similar to the katanas the orcs wielded. "You're a cheeky one."

The golden-haired orc stood up, switching his katana to his left hand. Even though it was his off hand, his slashing blows were still sharp. Still, Kuro deflected them easily, then decapitated him.

"Use you?" Haruhiro let out a small sigh. "You make it sound like a bad thing."

"Don't go counting on me. I'm the kind of guy who wants to look the other way when people start having expectations of him."

Kuro collected his arrows from the golden-haired orc's corpse, waving casually to them as he vanished into the fog once more.

"Haru-kun, were you thinkin' that Kuroron would come?" Yume asked.

"I figured, at worst, we could hold out until Kajita finished off the other two orcs and came to help. That was the idea, at least."

Haruhiro looked over in Kajita's direction. The man had just cut down one of the orcs with his massive mushroom sword, so there was just one left to go.

No, it looked like there were reinforcements. It was misty, so Haruhiro could only make out silhouettes at this point, but there were one orc and one undead. He gestured to Yume, and they were about to go intercept the incoming reinforcements when the orc collapsed, and the undead came to a halt. Had Kuro done that?

"Drahhhhhhhhh!" Kajita roared, pressuring the orc he was up against.

He pushed and pushed.

Not only was he not losing to the orc in a contest of strength, he was totally winning. The undead that temporarily came to a halt rushed forward, probably intending to support the orc, but didn't make it in time.

Kajita's massive mushroom sword smashed the katana the orc was desperately flailing around in half. In that moment, the battle was decided.

Kajita stepped in boldly, kicking the orc to the ground, then whaled on him with his massive mushroom sword, splattering the orc's head.

Without stopping to take a breath, Kajita went to attack the undead. He didn't need any help. Haruhiro and Yume nodded to one another, and decided to move forward.

They felt something pulling them further and further forward. The leader of the Typhoon Rocks, Rock, was up ahead.

Kuro, Moyugi, Kajita, Sakanami, and Tsuga. Just what was Rock, the man who led this group of uncommonly intense personalities, like? Would he be as much of a weirdo as the rest of them? Or would he have a surprising amount of common sense? Honestly, when it came to famous volunteer soldiers, especially those who led parties or clans, it felt like there were hardly any that were lacking for personality. If any of them were normal—no, if any of them had common sense—it would be Shinohara-san of Orion, and maybe that was about it?

Someone like Haruhiro would never become famous. Still, given that an ordinary party led by a plain, mediocre leader like him was in the Day Breakers, it was possible they had already been standing out in a bad way. On top of that, they'd been stranded in the Dusk Realm, so everyone must have been convinced they were wiped out. They'd probably already started to forget about them.

When people found out they were actually alive, and they'd made it back, might they actually get talked about a lot? Like, no matter where they went, people would make a joke out of it and tease them? Maybe they'd be better off not returning to Alterna?

Of course, he was getting ahead of himself. Way too far ahead. It wasn't even certain they could make it back yet. For now, he had to focus his energies on making it back in one piece. To do that, they first needed to make it through this battle.

Well, no matter how he psyched himself up, and no matter how he wracked his brains for what little wisdom was to be found in them, there would still be domains he couldn't hope to set foot in.

"They're going at it." Haruhiro came to stop.

Yume came to a stop next to him.

"Hochow..." She let out a weird expression of surprise.

One-on-one.

There was a human man and a double arm fighting in single combat.

That double arm's dangerous. Haruhiro could tell it at a glance. First of all, he was quad wielding. He had a katana in each of his hands, and controlled them freely.

Haruhiro had confidence that if he took it on, he'd get killed before he could do a thing. Though, maybe that wasn't exactly what you'd call confidence.

Also, his movements were clearly very quick. While his speed varied, he never came to a stop, not even for a moment. That double arm was an uninterrupted flow of motion. The strokes of his four katanas had a smooth and natural beauty. They were graceful, even. Yet they still had a fierceness to them. The double arms' attacks were like a clear stream, yet also a raging river, and that man was using just one sword to either deflect or turn them aside.

It was unbelievable.

After all, that man whose hair was standing on end for some reason...he was short.

To look at another famous volunteer soldier, "One-on-One" Max of Iron Knuckle was by no means a big man, but he was still around the same height as Haruhiro.

This man was even shorter than Ranta, who was already shorter than Haruhiro. He may not be much over 160 centimeters tall.

There were times when flexibility beat brute strength. Just because someone was big, that didn't necessarily mean they were strong. Even so, body size was a major weapon. In close combat, the smaller a person's body, the greater the disadvantage they were at. Even Haruhiro, with his 172 centimeters, had to admit he wished he was taller. Even if he couldn't be as tall as Kuzaku, he'd have liked to be 180 centimeters.

The double arm was probably over 185 centimeters tall. He was over twenty centimeters taller than the man, and had twice as many arms, too. When it came to weapons, he had four times as many.

On top of that, the man's sword wasn't long. It wasn't a short sword, but it was on the short side.

He can't win like that, thought Haruhiro.

No matter how he looked at it, the man didn't stand a chance.

In fact, as the man jumped left and right, backed away, ducked, and rolled, he seemed to be having a hard enough time just blocking and dodging the double arm's four katanas. It wouldn't have been surprising to see him get hit at any moment. It was only a matter of time. That man was on the edge, but managing to hold out somehow.

Haruhiro couldn't even gulp.

That's scary, he thought. *The double arm's gonna get him. It'll get him for sure. I want to close my eyes. Wait...*

That man, just now, did he do something? Did he draw another sword, maybe? But he's only holding the one. Does that mean he drew a different sword, then exchanged it with the one he was using before? Looks like he returned the sword he was using before to its sheathe. What for?

Haruhiro didn't know, but the man went on the attack at the same time he switched swords.

"Hahahaha!" the man laughed, launching a fierce assault. The quad wielding double arm was immediately forced on the defensive.

Haruhiro couldn't keep up with the man's swordwork. It wasn't because of the distance, or the fog, he was just that fast. The man swung his sword faster than the eye could see, advancing in almost a straight line. He rushed forward with tremendous force.

Just when Haruhiro thought he understood, the man changed his grip on the sword, this time moving around to the double arm's right-hand side, or maybe to his left-hand side, and launching slashing attacks.

The double arm was amazing, too, for being able to respond to this sudden change-up. On top of that, the double arm began to counterattack. When he did, the man changed his grip on the sword, and went into charging mode.

The double arm didn't back away. He caught the man's sword, using two of his katanas like a pair of scissors, then counterattacked with the remaining two. The man discarded his sword without hesitation, drawing the other one. The two changed roles as attacker and defender at a dizzying speed.

Haruhiro had goosebumps. His breath was short. This was no time to be staring intently, but he couldn't tear his eyes away.

"Yahhhhhhhhhhhhhhhhhhhhhhhhh!" A shrieking battle cry tore through the foggy sky.

He hadn't anticipated the appearance of an intrusion, so Haruhiro was dumbstruck. Could anyone intervene in a serious battle between that man and the double arm?

But she stepped in boldly. Long black hair. That was a human woman. She sprang forward, katana at the ready, launching herself toward the double arm the man was facing.

"Arara?!" the man turned and shouted. The double arm wasn't about to let that opening slip by.

Its four katanas closed in on the man. With no other choice, he leapt backward.

When the double arm tried to immediately follow up with another attack, the woman with disheveled hair took a slash at him.

"This is for Tatsuru-sama! Prepare yourself! Yahhhhhhh!"

This was a surprise. The woman wasn't half bad, either. Holding her katana in two hands, she thrust once, then twice, with a combo attack that was like a line of spears, and made the double arm back away. That said, she couldn't keep thrusting forever. Eventually the woman's hands stopped in order to lure the double arm into a counterattack, at which point she made a return thrust and a return slash targeting his legs. Then, when he dodged that, she thrust, and thrust, and thrust like crazy to push him back.

"Arara!" said the man as he picked up the sword he had discarded earlier, then attacked the double arm once more. "I told you I'd take Arnold!"

Two against one. The double arm was on the ropes. That was how it looked to Haruhiro.

"Do you mean to say I cannot best him with my level of skill?!"

Even as the woman shouted back at him, her katana didn't rest.

"Even if I lack the power," she said, "I must slay this one by myself!"

Haruhiro felt like he was starting to grasp their situation. This woman was Arara, and Arnold was apparently the double arm's name. Arara had said something like *This is for Tatsuru-sama!* when she'd attacked Arnold. He didn't know if this Tatsuru-sama was a relative of hers or what, but it was clear he was someone important to her, and Arnold had killed him. Arara was seeking vengeance.

The short man with his hair standing on end was probably Rock. Rock seemed to be helping her for some reason.

"So it's gonna be a joint project between me and Arara, huh?" Rock called. "Haha! Well, that'll be fun for me!"

"Don't talk nonsense!"

"I'm not kidding, I'm serious here!"

"Then that's even more reason!"

Though they were arguing, Rock and Arara were in sync as they unleashed a fierce attack. They rained blows on Arnold from both sides in rapid succession, so the double arm didn't have much leeway to work with. He was stuck on the defensive, and his moves were clearly becoming more chaotic.

"Hahahaha!" Rock cackled as he got behind Arnold. "This is after I went to all that trouble to fight you one-on-one!"

At the last possible moment, Arnold managed to knock back Rock's sword with one of his katanas.

Instantly, Arara cried, "Yahhhhhhhhhh!" and thrust from directly in front of him.

While Arnold twisted his head to avoid it, he also used two katanas to deflect it at the same time. If he had only dodged, Arara would surely have used a second thrust to inflict a severe wound on him. Having her blow knocked aside by two parries threw her off balance, but Rock was there.

When Arnold began turning, Rock launched a combo attack on him.

"Rah, rah, rah, rah, rah, rah, rah, rah, rah, rah, rah, rah, rahhhh!"

It hit Arnold when he wasn't in a very good stance. He

managed to block with his four katanas up until around the sixth or seventh blow. He missed the one after that, leaving him with a shallow wound on one of his arms. Maybe that made him panic, because he rolled forward as if he had tripped on something.

Now, thought Haruhiro. *You can do this. Right there. Get him.*

No matter how he looked at it, this was the perfect chance. Rock was about to spring on Arnold, too, but for some reason he stopped himself. Not only that, he leapt backward. "Arara!"

Arara inhaled sharply. Maybe she had sensed something. Instead of falling straight back, she tried to move diagonally as she distanced herself from Arnold. It was hard to think she'd been too slow; Arara had reacted quickly. But, still, she didn't make it in time.

In an instant, Arnold transformed into a whirlwind.

That wasn't even a metaphor. When Arnold suddenly leapt spinning into the air, he did, in fact, seem like a little whirlwind, and he tore into Arara's back with the force of one. Having taken a wound deep enough to at least draw blood, Arara collapsed to the ground. If Rock hadn't scooped her up as he fled, who knew what might have happened. Arara might have been chopped up by Arnold's four blades.

"Retreat!" Rock bellowed as he ran. "Arara's down! Retreat!"

"KYYYYYYYYYYYYYYYYYYYYYYYYYYYYYYYYYYYYYYYYY YYY."

It was a noise like miasma violently gushing forth from the bowels of the earth to make all things rot away. Was that a voice?

Arnold had his head thrown back and his arms spread wide. Was he coming? Or wasn't he? Of course he was coming.

Haruhiro grabbed Yume's arm and took off running. Even if he hadn't taken her arm, all it would have taken was one word. That was all, but, for some reason, his voice wouldn't come out. He felt like it would be best if it didn't.

For now, he had to shut up and run. Just run for it. He had to put as much distance as he could between them and this place, and that guy, Arnold, and he needed to do it as fast as possible.

Don't look back, he warned himself. *If you've got time to do that, work your legs harder.*

Yume seemed to agree with Haruhiro. They were almost racing to see who could flee the fastest.

Soon, Kajita's back came into view. Kajita was running for it, too.

For now, let's follow Kajita, Haruhiro decided. *We'll run as far as we can. To the ends of the earth, if we have to.*

It was run or die.

He'd kill them for sure.

Arnold. That undead. That double arm was dangerous.

Haruhiro prayed Arnold hadn't noticed Yume and him. If Arnold wasn't looking for them, they might make it somehow. But, if he was, running might not do them any good. They could struggle all they wanted, but he'd still catch them and cut them down.

Haruhiro was already winded. His throat, chest, and sides were all screaming out in pain. Even so, he didn't slow down. Stopping for a break was out of the question.

"Fwah..."

Yume collapsed.

Haruhiro immediately dragged her to her feet.

When he glanced around, he saw Kajita had stopped and was looking to the rear. He turned to them and gave them the thumbs-up.

It's safe now. Was that what it meant? Could they trust that?

Haruhiro wasn't sure, but he must have run out of steam, because his body felt like it had lost all its bones. He was completely limp. It may not have been completely impossible, but he didn't think he could run any more.

He'd made Yume stand up for a moment, but she'd slumped down again right there.

"Th-th-that sure was scary," Yume said.

As the leader, Haruhiro wanted to put up a false front of bravado. He couldn't.

"I-It sure was..."

7 | Master Choice

*I*T'D BE EASIER *to just die.*

This wasn't the first time Merry had felt this way.

After she'd lost three of her original comrades at once, for a while—quite a long while—day in and day out, she wanted to die. To be more precise, she was at the mercy of regret, self-blame, and loss, and she hadn't been able to think of anything except that death might free her from them.

She contemplated ending her life, but felt it would be wrong. Her comrades basically sacrificed themselves to let her survive. It was thanks to them that she was alive, so how could she die? Unless she suffered far, far more, it would all be a lie. This was a punishment she deserved.

That was how she'd felt, so even when things got so hard that it felt like it would be easier to die, she never died. She couldn't allow herself to.

But this time, it was different. She might actually be better off dead. In fact, she questioned why she had to live.

After all, from here on, they were going to do horrible, repulsive things to her that she didn't even want to imagine. She didn't want to imagine them, but they still crossed her mind. What were the orcs going to do to her? Was that goblin going to humiliate her, too?

No.

I'm not kidding.

I'm going to die.

That's right. I'll bite through my tongue and die.

Oh, but dying might not stop them from defiling her lifeless body. What did she care what happened once she was dead? But still, the thought was hard to take.

No. No. No. No.

"Merry."

"Huh?"

Merry raised her face and looked next to her.

Ranta looked enervated, and he was sweating profusely, like the shadow of death was hanging over him.

Even so, she thought, *You don't have it so bad. They're only going to kill you.*

She was in for more than that. They'd torment her all they liked, torturing her body and soul, then kill her in some brutal way when they were done with her. That was the fate awaiting Merry.

She wanted to scream as loud as she could, *You think you can understand how I feel right now?!*

Of course, that would be taking it out on the wrong person.

Merry desperately tried to steady her breathing.

"What?" she said.

"No... It's just, I called your name a bunch of times, but you didn't answer."

"A bunch of times?"

"You didn't hear me?"

"That's..." Merry shook her head, and blinked. Yes, a bunch of times. "...not true. I could hear you. But even if I responded, it wasn't like anything was going to change."

"You don't have to say it like that," Ranta complained. "I was worried about you."

"You don't have to be."

"Don't try to act tough. It's just awkward if you tell me not to worry when you're looking like that."

"I'm perfectly—"

Her vision blurred, catching her off guard.

Tears. She was about ready to cry.

"I'm fine," Merry said. She shut her eyes tight. "I'm okay."

"Oh, yeah?"

"Yeah."

"You're so not cute."

"You've got that right."

"Seriously, your face is the only thing you've got going for you. Your personality is terrible."

"You're the last person I want to hear that from."

"No, no, no. Even the great Ranta-sama is nothing compared

to you," Ranta told her. "I couldn't possibly compare to your level of spitefulness. That stubbornness could end a love that lasted a hundred years. You've perfected the art of repelling others."

"Be as repelled as you want. It'd be convenient for me."

Ranta clicked his tongue. He didn't stop there, though; he did it a second and third time. There was nothing more annoying.

But, thanks to that, she was feeling a little less afraid. The fear would bubble back up in no time, and she'd be right back where she started, but now she could think more clearly than before. This was how weak fear could make people. If, right now, she was offered conditions that were less terrible than her worst imaginings, she'd easily submit. Merry had no confidence she'd be able to cling to her pride.

That was why she was hoping to die before they made her fall into true despair. It would be easier.

Or perhaps, even if she fell as far as she could possibly fall, she should still cling to her life?

Whichever she chose, she would probably never see any of her comrades other than Ranta again.

Yume. Shihoru. We had finally managed to become friends.

Kuzaku, I'm sorry for what I did to you.

Haruhiro. Haru...

Save me.

That was the one thing she couldn't say. She couldn't think it, either. She was already feeling weak, and it would only make her more fragile.

She didn't want Ranta to see that. When they did whatever

it was they were going to do, she didn't want Ranta—didn't want one of her comrades to see it. However, that wasn't Merry's choice to make. To make her taste the most bitter humiliation, they might defile her right in front of Ranta. She had to be prepared for that.

She would have to bear it without crying and screaming. She'd just have to endure. She'd have to make them think tormenting her any more would be boring. That was the one way Merry could resist. If that was all there was, that was what she would do.

Don't tremble. Don't look down. Keep your chin up.

There was a goblin petting a big black wolf by the mouth of the cave. She couldn't see that middle-aged man. There were several orcs milling about; undead, too. There was a pack of black wolves. Lots of catlike creatures.

Fog. White fog.

She burned all of it into her retinas.

Merry would die here. Probably in the worst way imaginable. But she wouldn't curse the fact she had ever lived, and she wouldn't reject it. No matter what happened, that was the one thing she wouldn't do.

"Ranta."

"Huh?"

"Thanks," she said. "For your concern."

"You id... D-don't be like that, girl. I'm not..."

"'Girl'?" she asked archly.

"S-sorry, Merry-san."

It was so silly, she smiled, even if only a little.

Honestly, she wished she could thank the rest of their comrades, too. She wanted to thank them all properly, in her own words. To tell them they were all important to her, and she loved them. But that wish wasn't going to come true. So, at the very least, she'd thank Ranta.

Honestly, Ranta had done more to offend her than anything else. She could never like him as a person, but he wasn't all bad. She understood he had some strengths, too. Even if she didn't like him, he was an irreplaceable comrade.

Merry spoke. "I have a favor to ask."

"Oh? Sure. Wh-what...?"

"No matter what happens, don't pity me. I want to stay strong, but I may lose. If that happens, you can mock me, but whatever you do, don't pity me."

"Got it," Ranta replied instantly. "I swear to Lord Skullhell. I won't pity my comrades. No matter what happens, okay? Merry..."

"What?"

"Don't give up. Because I won't give up. As long as we're still alive, we haven't lost."

"Sure."

Merry couldn't bring herself to think like Ranta. However, she felt it was important to respect his resolve. She wanted to respect it.

She hoped Ranta would survive somehow. Knowing Ranta, he wouldn't care about appearances, and he'd probably plead for his life or do whatever it took to keep on living.

She sat up straight; puffed out her chest. The ropes bit into her skin, painfully. That was no big deal. This didn't even take perseverance to endure. She put the horrific things she'd imagined out of her mind. When she tried to think happy thoughts, it made her want to cry.

No, she thought. *I want to be with everyone a little longer. This can't be the end. I don't want this.*

But when she remembered someone like her was allowed to meet such wonderful comrades, and spend good times and bad times with them, she reconsidered. She realized she should be grateful for what she'd had.

Her life hadn't been in vain. She'd been blessed. Even if it ended in a horrific way, that didn't make the time she had spent with her comrades worthless.

The moment all the wolves and catlike creatures turned to look in the same direction at once, Merry sensed the time had finally come.

What happened? What was about to happen? Merry didn't know, but it was nothing ordinary. That was the one thing she did know.

The goblin stood up. The big black wolf, on the other hand, lay prone. The rest of the black wolves emulated the big one. The catlike creatures opened their eyes wide, breathing shallowly through their noses. They looked tense. The orcs and undead spread their legs, putting their hands on their hips, and bent at the waist to bow their heads a little.

That middle-aged man appeared from beyond the fog, and he was bringing someone with him. Two people, actually.

It was hard to see them, but one was rather large. That figure had a massive body. Was it an orc? Even if it was, it was way too big. Was it a giant or something?

The other was human, or perhaps an undead. That figure wasn't much taller or shorter than the middle-aged man, so it probably wasn't an orc.

In the time they were approaching, up until she could make out what they looked like, Merry never would have imagined they both were orcs. One was easily two-and-a-half meters tall, while the other was maybe only 180 centimeters tall. Because one of the two was so massive, it made the other look almost delicate in comparison.

It seemed orcs had a custom of dyeing their body hair in vibrant colors. However, these two were different. They both had wavy hair that was black to the point of being glossy.

The small orc was probably the older of the two. It wasn't that the orc looked old; he just exuded an aura of calmness.

It's that orc, Merry thought.

The one the black wolves, orcs, and undead respected wasn't the big one. She'd never seen an orc like that small one before. His skin had a gray undertone and his eyes were a piercing orange, both of which were distinctive; but the most noticeable thing was that outfit.

It was a deep blue fabric with a pattern of silver flowers scattered around. What would it be called? Was it a kimono? Whatever it was, it was beautifully tailored. It was a sleeved outfit that opened in the front, which went down to just below his knees and was tied shut with a thin belt. Instead of shoes, he wore something like sandals. The long object he wore at his belt seemed to be a weapon, but you wouldn't notice it if you weren't looking closely. The beasts and the orcs both clearly feared and respected him. Despite that, he didn't have a particularly imposing or oppressive air about him. He was calm and quiet, and yet, at the same time, though he was short for an orc, he was big. His presence had a sense of grandeur about it. No, of broadness, perhaps. Or depth. That felt like another appropriate way to describe it.

Looking at them again, the massive orc seemed to be trying to imitate the little one. It was clear he admired the smaller orc and couldn't help but emulate his dress and manner.

That little orc, he was the boss. In this group composed of orcs, undead, goblins, beasts, and even humans, that orc was the central figure, the one who had brought them all together.

The next thing Merry knew, the middle-aged man and the two orcs had come up right next to her and Ranta.

Then there was the sudden sound of flapping wings, surprising Merry. Something flew down out of the fogbound skies.

A bird. Not a little one; a bird of prey. An eagle, perhaps?

One black feather fell from those powerful, flapping wings and fell to the ground in front of Merry's knees.

The great black eagle landed on the little orc's shoulder. Though he was little for an orc, he still had broad enough shoulders that such a large bird could use them as a perch. His chest was thick, and his arms and neck were fat. Even so, he gave off the impression of being lithe rather than strong.

"Jumbo," said the middle-aged man. He gestured toward Merry and Ranta with his chin, then said something incomprehensible. It was probably in the orcish language.

The small orc nodded. His orange eyes were fixed on Merry. His pupils seemed to shine. It may not have been the time or place for such thoughts, but Merry found them beautiful. The whites of his eyes were as pale as a baby's.

In her head, she understood orcs were an intelligent race, in no way lesser than humans. But she had to acknowledge she'd been prejudiced against them, viewing them as savage and frightening. That was why Merry was so taken aback.

She couldn't find an appropriate expression for it, but if she was to use the closest word she could think of, that orc seemed noble. He had a grace about him, a refinement. That said, it was still too early to start hoping he wouldn't do anything rough. That would be nothing more than baseless optimism.

"My name is—" Even though the orc's mouth was moving, it was hard for her to believe it was his voice. Of course it was. He was speaking human words, and he was entirely too fluent in the language. Besides, it was a low and smooth, if somewhat throaty, voice, and very pleasant to listen to. "—Jumbo. First, let me ask you: What are your names?"

"Huh...?" Ranta looked to Merry, then back to Jumbo, twisted his head to the side in confusion, and looked to the middle-aged man. When the middle-aged man shrugged, Ranta finally accepted reality.

"R-R-Ranta," he said. "No, I mean, my name is Ranta. No, th-the name's...Ranta...you got that?"

"And you?" Jumbo asked, looking to Merry.

Merry took a single breath. Her entire body was numb. She needed to pull herself together.

"I'm Merry."

"Ranta. Merry. It would seem that you two are not of the village."

"What is the village, anyway?" Merry asked.

"Heyyyyyy, Merry, don't say more than you have to," Ranta said. He shook his head, cursing. "Yeah, that's right! We don't know what village you're talking about. We have no clue what it is, so you can be damn sure we're not from it! So what?!"

"Arabakian volunteer soldiers, then?" Jumbo asked. "Or citizens of Vele?"

Vele was most likely the free city of Vele. There was trade between Alterna and Vele, but despite Vele being a human city-state, they also engaged in trade with orcs and the undead. They were neutral, you could say.

If they claimed to be citizens of Vele, Jumbo might release Merry and Ranta. If he believed them, that was. If he didn't see through the lie.

"We're volunteer soldiers," Merry said. She glared at Jumbo. "What of it?"

Ranta had already told the middle-aged man they were volunteer soldiers. It was hard to imagine that detail hadn't been passed on to Jumbo; he must have known. If he was asking a question he knew the answer to, it was like a trap. If he used such boring tricks, he might be shallower than she'd thought.

Or maybe not.

"Takasagi," Jumbo looked at Merry again as he asked. "Is this true?"

"Yeah," the middle-aged man whose name was Takasagi replied. "Onsa found their Volunteer Soldier Corps badges. I can't see why they'd be carrying around fake ones. There's no doubt about it. No telling what ties they have to the village, though. The guys attacking us are volunteer soldiers, too, so they're still suspicious."

"Suspicious, huh? You wound me," Ranta snorted derisively. If his hands hadn't been bound behind his back, he'd probably have crossed his arms haughtily. "Whaaaat? You're thinking we're spies, or something? Let me tell you, I wouldn't do anything that lame. If I wanted to take you down, I'd do it in a straight-up fight!"

"A straight-up fight, huh," Takasagi said, grinning as the pipe he held between his lips shook. "You're not good enough. Not only would you not be able to take out our boss, I doubt you could even beat me."

"Hey, don't underestimate me, old man!" Ranta's veins were pulsing, his eyebrows raised, and his entire face distorted. Did he think he was being intimidating? Was he stupid?

He was breathing way too heavily from his nose. What was this idiot thinking, getting so worked up? Was he not thinking at all? Normally, that would be impossible, but with this guy, maybe it was. He was just that stupid.

"I'm a volunteer soldier superstar!" Ranta hollered. "I'm the supernova of talent they call the Ultra Idaten! Idaten...?! Well, whatever. Anyway, when they talk about the special swordsman known as the Otherdimensional God of Destruction, they're talking about me, Ranta-sama! Like I'd lose to some old man! Try gauging your opponents a little better before you talk, pal!"

"Cut it out," Merry said urgently. "You're—"

"Shut up! You don't talk now!" Ranta shouted at Merry, raising his voice even louder. "You think you're so hot because you managed to capture us with a big gang! You cowards couldn't handle a fight one-on-one! Who do you think you're fooling with your, 'I doubt you could even beat me!' Say that once we've actually fought! If you're just running your mouth when we haven't even fought, anyone can do that! If you're that confident, then face me!"

"He has a point," said Jumbo, nodding without changing his expression. "Takasagi. You were the one who said you could win. Face him."

"Good grief, that'll teach me to open my big mouth, huh..." said Takasagi. He turned back and looked toward the cave. "Onsa, could you have the nyaas undo his ropes?"

When Onsa the goblin pursed his lips and whistled, the catlike creatures swarmed over Ranta and undid his ropes in short order.

Those creatures, they were called nyaas? It wasn't a very inventive name, but it was cute. They looked like they were trying so hard when they moved their little hands, and that—no, no. This was no time to be admiring the adorable nyaas.

"All right!" Ranta jumped up, twisted his head from side to side, and stretched his arms and legs. "Don't let my hyper-awesome skills blow you away. By the way, you wouldn't fight with weapons while I'm unarmed, right? If you want to settle this with our fists, I don't mind, though. I'd be down for that, too. I'm a master of everything, after all."

A short time later, three nyaas brought Ranta's RIPer from the cave. The nyaas straining themselves as they rushed over carrying the sword were adorable, of course, but it went without saying that Merry didn't have the presence of mind to properly savor their cuteness. In fact, her jaw had dropped.

Rather than choosing to watch things play out, the flow of events had left Merry behind. She blamed Ranta. Ranta was an idiot. Everything was stupid Ranta's fault.

The black wolves and nyaas, the orcs, the undead, and Jumbo and the big orc all moved, making space for the duel. Merry could only sit there in silence.

Perhaps this was Ranta's plan. Whatever the case, Ranta was free now. He'd even gotten his weapon back. Which meant maybe it wasn't impossible to escape?

When Ranta glanced over in Merry's direction, it made her want to think, *I knew it*—but it was just that, a single glance, and then Ranta turned to face Takasagi, drawing RIPer from its sheathe. He dropped the sheathe right there. She was embarrassed that, even for that one moment, she had started to think, *I knew it.*

"Okay!" Ranta slapped his own face with his left hand. "I'm good to go! Come at me any way you like, old man Takasagi!"

"I can't tell if you're serious, or just desperate." Takasagi chewed on his pipe, slowly drawing the katana on his back with his right hand. "If you like, I'll let you move first."

"You sure?" Ranta asked. "I don't want you regretting it later."

"Don't hesitate to take me up on it. I've probably lived twice as long as you. If you want, I'll give you an even bigger handicap."

"The wisdom of age, is that it?" Ranta lowered his hips a little, readying his sword. "Well, I'll gladly take the right to strike first. Don't go down on the first blow. I don't get to do this often, so make it fun for me."

"You talk a good game."

"I'll show you I'm more than just talk soon enough."

Could it be? This seemed like the only possibility, but could it be that Ranta thought he could beat Takasagi? That he could win the duel, and, in winning it, drag some sort of compromise out of them?

Takasagi had taken a wound to his left eye, or had something else wrong with it, and was seemingly blind on that side. On top of that, he probably wasn't hiding his right arm. He had one eye, and one arm. He was middle-aged, too, so Ranta could probably handle him. If Ranta was thinking that—and knowing Ranta, he probably was, which worried her—it was frivolous of him.

Takasagi slowly raised his katana, pointing the tip toward Ranta. The moment he did, Ranta stopped moving entirely. He probably couldn't move. The damp air suddenly began to feel chilly.

Merry's eyes were drawn to Takasagi's sword, unable to focus on anything else. If Ranta was in the same state as Merry, it was over; the battle was decided. He couldn't possibly win.

"I won't be hypnotized," Ranta muttered to himself.

In the next moment, he burst forward with Leap Out. With the force of an eruption, he shot to the left of Takasagi. From there, he used Hatred. Takasagi swayed to avoid it.

Ranta used Leap Out again to go to Takasagi's right side, and swinging his sword in a figure-eight motion, he used Slice. Takasagi easily dodged that one, too.

Ranta fought in a very un-Ranta-like manner, barely using his voice as he pressed the attack. His feet never stopped, and he kept on moving and attacking.

Merry didn't want to praise Ranta, but the way he moved around with such bewildering speed as he fought had to be rather troublesome for his opponent. When fighting that way, Ranta seemed to gain an abnormal strength. On top of that, he wasn't just moving around randomly; he was always trying to attack from an angle that would make it hard to block. It was like he was an entirely different person from the one who had been in the party when Merry first joined. Ranta had gotten so much stronger now that he was almost unrecognizable. However, there was always someone better.

Even for Merry, a priest, it was clear to see. For now, at least, no matter how earnestly Ranta stretched out his hand, he could never reach Takasagi.

Ranta could jump to the right and swing, or spring to the

left and thrust, and Takasagi would always be facing him, ready to evade it with one or two steps. Takasagi could see it. He had completely seen through Ranta's unorthodox fighting style.

It was no exaggeration to say that Ranta was no match for him. Ranta, more than anyone, must have been aware of the gap in their power. Despite that, Ranta kept attacking. Incorrigibly, he repeated his meaningless attacks.

Just stop it, Merry wanted to say. But what would happen if he did?

Don't give up, Ranta had said to Merry. *Because I won't give up,* he'd said.

This was very much a battle where, if he gave up, it was all over. Though he definitely couldn't win, he had to keep fighting so it didn't end. That was why Ranta was fighting so desperately. Until his last bit of energy was spent, or until Takasagi cut him down, Ranta wouldn't give up.

"Go for it..." Merry said, forcing the words out. "Go, Ranta! Go!"

"Ohhhhhhhhhhhhhhhhhhhhhhhhhhh!" Ranta yelled.

Ranta wasn't responding to Merry. He was focused on the battle, and probably couldn't hear her voice. But the sharpness of Ranta's moves, along with his speed, went up a notch. It might have been an illusion, but that was how it looked to Merry.

If he stepped into his strikes by a few more centimeters, his sword reached that much farther. Takasagi's evasive maneuvers were getting larger, too. Up until a moment ago, he had been lazily evading, but now it was a little different. Occasionally his feet moved a little faster, becoming hurried. He had less room for error than before.

"That's not the best you've got, is it?!" Merry called. "You can give it more! There's no way you can't!"

This wasn't true at all. Ranta was giving it all, going past his limits. Even though she knew that, all she could do was cheer him on like this. It made her hate how nasty she was. Her comrade was burning out the very fire of his life, so why couldn't she offer him some kinder words?

"This time...!" Suddenly, as if he'd been blown away, Ranta moved back several meters. It was Exhaust. He'd put distance between them, but what was he planning to do with it?

Takasagi stayed put, as if waiting to see what he could do.

"Secret technique..."

Ranta held RIPer in both hands, his entire body swaying.

"Hachioji Beta Cleansing... No, forget that, it needs a cooler name. Thousand Arms Kannon Boddhisatva... No, wait, that's no good either. Fragrance Bitter... Huh? That's off, too. It's not special attack-y. Uhh... Ultimate Skyboy?"

Merry was appalled. What did the name matter? It didn't even need one. In the end, Ranta was Ranta. An idiot. No matter where he went, a true idiot was always an idiot.

Takasagi was gaping, too.

Wait, was that what Ranta had been aiming for?

"Gotcha!" Ranta used Leap Out to charge at Takasagi. He leapt in from outside his swinging range, thrusting with all his might and all his anger. "Take that!"

Takasagi's legs were frozen stiff. He couldn't dodge.

This might be it.

For the first time, Takasagi used his katana, and—

"Ungh!" He simply swept Ranta's sword aside.

"Gwuh?!" Just from having his sword deflected, Ranta lost his balance.

Takasagi finally went on the attack. Or rather, he settled it with one swing, if it could even be called that.

Takasagi used his katana like it was his own arm, wrapping it around Ranta's sword. RIPer spun around as it flew about five meters before falling to the ground.

"You've got spunk," Takasagi said as he pressed the tip of his sword against Ranta's forehead. "But that's all you've got. Well, ten years from now, I'll have weakened with age, so maybe you would've won then. Right now, it's just not gonna happen."

It was over.

It was all over.

So easily.

Merry smiled wryly, all her strength having left her. How very like Ranta. But, well, for Ranta, he'd done the best he probably could.

That was right. He'd done well. Merry hadn't done anything; she hadn't been able to, so she was in no position to gripe.

"You think this is over?" Ranta said in his trembling voice, and she was moved a little.

Not yet. Even now, Ranta hadn't given up. He was an idiot.

An idiot, but incredible. He was great. As his comrade, she

GRIMGAR OF FANTASY AND ASH

felt proud, though only a little. The corners of her eyes started getting hot.

If Ranta hadn't kowtowed at light speed, she might have teared up.

Merry thought her eyes were going to fall out of her skull. She'd never felt such confusion and shock before.

"Huh?" Takasagi asked.

"You got me! Please, make me your disciple! I'll carry your sandals, wash your sandals, polish your sandals, whatever you want, so please! Do you like strong men?! I loooove them! Me, I wanna be strong! Seriously, seriously, I do! I've been looking for a way to, you could say, always searching, and, at last, I've finally found what I need! You, Takasagi-sensei! I've found you! I mean, you're way too strong, and I was so much more powerless before you than I thought I would be, I fell in love! Please, please take me on as your disciple! I'll start out as your gofer if I have to! I'm begging you! Pleeeeaaaase!"

"Listen, I'm not taking disciples..." said Takasagi. He frowned, resting the flat side of his katana on his left shoulder with a sigh. "Besides, don't you get it? We don't serve any king. But, nonetheless, people from Arabakia are still our enemy. There's no way we can get along. Don't you know what that means? Let's assume for a moment that I do make you my disciple. It'll never happen, but if I did, you'd be betraying Arabakia."

"That's A-OK!"

"Huh?"

"Nah, Sensei, Master, I think you may be misunderstanding

here, so I'll tell you, okay? I just became a volunteer soldier because things turned out that way. It's not like I've sworn my body and soul to the Kingdom of Arabakia. I've never once felt like doing so. I just happened to find myself here in Grimgar, flat broke, and they said they'd cover my personal expenses for the time being if I became a volunteer soldier trainee. And I didn't seem to have any other options at the time, so I did. Well, in a way, you could say they tricked me into it, yeah? That's how I got made into a volunteer soldier!"

"I was a volunteer soldier myself, so I can see where you're coming from," said Takasagi.

"Wow! You're a former volunteer soldier, Sensei? Master?"

"I'm not your sensei or master, though..."

"How'd you end up working for Commander Jumbo, then?" Ranta asked eagerly. "I'd love to hear about that, too."

"It's a long story..." said Takasagi. He clicked his tongue lightly. "You're a smooth operator, you know that? I almost went along with you there, just now."

"Darn straight! Me, I've got a silver tongue! I've got the gift of the gab! I talk all the time, so people always say I'm annoying! But, you know what?! My heart is hot! My soul is full! I wanna be your disciple to the max, Takasagi-sensei! I seriously wanna get stronger, for real! The way I am now—a volunteer soldier, doing the same things as anyone else—I can't expect to grow! It just hit me!"

"What just hit you...?"

"That, there, that's the point! Or rather, this place is!" Ranta spun around, looking to Jumbo, the big orc, the goblins, the black wolves, and more. "You, a human, are working under Commander Jumbo! You've gotta have a damn good reason! But, more than that, I feel something here! To be frank, that's what attracts me! If I become one of you, maybe I can find something?! Maybe the path that I, in my quest to become the greatest and most invincible fighter to ever live, need to follow has been here all along?!"

"Okay, tell me if I've got this right," Takasagi said. "Setting the bit about becoming my disciple aside, you want to quit being a volunteer soldier, and join Forgan, even if it's as a petty underling."

"Uhh, Forgan?"

"Forgo," Jumbo said, looking at the giant black eagle on his shoulder. "That's the name of my respected friend. In human language, it means 'black eagle.' I suppose that would make Forgan the Black Eagle Band."

"There!" Ranta nodded, as if Jumbo had said exactly the right thing. "That's it! Please, let me into Forgan, I'm begging you! I'll do the cleaning, laundry, cooking, chores, anything! Pile all the work you want on me, because I'll keep pushing upward! I'm confident I've got the talent, the potential, the guts, the nerve, the cojones, the Jones! Makes you wonder who this Jones guy is, but, seriously, I'm seriously super serious about all this!"

As Ranta rubbed his head against the ground repeatedly and begged, Merry couldn't decide if he really was super serious about this, or if this was a way of begging for his life, or if he was just spouting nonsense. Any of them seemed possible, and she didn't think any of them was okay.

Maybe Merry had misjudged him. Ranta might have been a bigger piece of trash than she had ever thought.

She wanted to cry now, but for a different reason than before.

As his comrade, she felt ashamed of Ranta. She was hopelessly ashamed that anything he'd done had moved her heart even the slightest.

"Well, regardless, if that's the case," Takasagi said as he returned his katana to its sheath, "I'm not the one who makes that decision. It's Jumbo. Jumbo makes the decisions. The rest of us follow them. That's the rule in Forgan, after all."

Forgo the great black eagle let out a shrill cry, then took off from Jumbo's shoulder.

Jumbo walked over. It was like there was a light breeze around him. He was quiet, coolly approaching, stopping in front of Ranta, then of all things, crouching down.

"Ranta," said Jumbo.

"Ye—" Ranta said. He straightened his back, kneeling formally. "Yes, sir!"

"I am not fond of needless killing."

"Yes, sir! Huh? Sir?!"

"Of course, we sometimes kill those who oppose us," said Jumbo. "We steal sometimes, too. We hurt people. Because some among our companions are of a special nature, you see. There are also those who will slander Forgan, claiming we are cruel and merciless. I won't deny it. However, I, personally, do not take lives needlessly."

"Y-yes, sir."

"If you wish to become my companion, I will welcome you."

"Yes, sir. ...Huh?! Welcome me?! You mean...you'll make me your comrade?!"

"If that is what you wish," said Jumbo. "At present, Takasagi is the only human among my companions, but it will only mean taking on a second. That, too, could prove entertaining."

"I...I did it?!"

"However," Jumbo added.

"H-howev...?!"

"What will that woman do?" Jumbo gestured to Merry—or rather, he turned his orange eyes toward her. "Will that woman become my companion along with you? Is that what she wishes?"

8 | Pride

IN THE VILLAGE, there were four samurai houses. The foremost was the House of Nigi, followed by the House of Shigano, House of Ganata, and House of Mishio, in that order. These, with the addition of the House of Katsurai, who managed the onmitsu spies, and the House of Shuro, who carried on the tradition of necromancy, made up the Six Houses.

There was a young man; he was of the House of Mishio, but in the village, women were the ones to inherit the house, and it was the matrilineal line which mattered most. Boys did not carry on a family name, no matter who they were born to. Only by marrying a girl with a family name could a boy finally be recognized as a man, and he would take the name of his wife.

This young man was unmarried. Furthermore, his mother was not the head of the Mishio, and he seemed to have no aptitude for the sword—something which decided the value of those born to a samurai family. He was an attractive man, but his beautiful countenance actually made him an object of scorn. His inborn kindness, which he showed to all equally, only encouraged further mockery, and it showed no sign of letting up.

His name was Tatsuru.

Nigi Arara, born the eldest daughter of the head of the House of Nigi, had, for as far back as she could remember, always watched Tatsuru, who was a year older than her, with a sense of irritation.

Those of the four samurai houses were put through training from a young age that, even by the standards of samurai houses, was especially strict. Being roughly the same age, it was normal for them to shed sweat and sometimes blood together, but Tatsuru was, to put it kindly, seen as unfit, and, to be blunter about the situation, the subject of bullying.

The treatment he received would have made anyone gloomy. It wouldn't have been surprising if he turned cynical. But Tatsuru wasn't like that. Even when they jeered at him, insulted him to his face, and left him out of things, it never warped him. He would work even harder at his training, trying somehow to make them acknowledge him. He was ever polite, bowing his head to ask for guidance even at a young age, and he never complained that he was dissatisfied or that things were unfair.

It is of special note that, when he spoke to others, he always looked the other person straight in the eye. Though humble, he was not servile. His face was also not all that beautiful. But he was a youth whose actions, and whose very heart, were beautiful.

That made it all the more irritating for Arara. Tatsuru was of mediocre skill, to be sure, but by training more than others, he was well on his way to becoming a viable samurai. To Arara's eyes, the contempt she saw directed at Tatsuru was clearly unfair, and Tatsuru accepted it gracefully.

Arara had her position as the heir to the House of Nigi to consider, so she was hesitant to criticize everyone loudly for what she saw. However, when she was fourteen, she could bear it no longer, and consulted her uncle about it.

"Uncle, you know of Tatsuru of the House of Mishio," said Arara. "He is one year older than me. Why is he the way he is? It frustrates me to no end."

"It frustrates you, does it?" her uncle asked. "Even so, he is not one so significant that you, who will one day be head of the House of Nigi, need concern yourself with."

"I am not concerned for him. It simply angers me."

"Why would the treatment of one such as he anger you? Ah—"

Arara's father was of the House of Ganata, and her uncle, who was eight years younger than him, was an eccentric who had stayed single even past the age of thirty. He had wandered freely since he was young, did not have property, and wore a strange pair of glasses that he had obtained from somewhere.

Arara had a great fondness for this vagrant uncle. He was a man of meager talent—unlike his brother, who, despite being a man, came to be called a war god and married the head of the House of Nigi. Honestly, if she were asked to think of a relative, this uncle's face would come to mind before her own parents. Her uncle, in turn, adored Arara.

"I see, I see," her uncle said. "Arara, you find this young boy not entirely disagreeable, do you?"

"What are you saying, Uncle?! I am merely saying that I find it unbearable to watch that man act so weak, not objecting in the face of everyone's unfair treatment of him!"

"We could say that you are righteously indignant, then. In that case, could you not simply speak to everyone about it, and admonish that boy?"

"As daughter of the family head, I can do no such thing."

"Hmm. I suppose, as daughter of the family head, you cannot always say what you wish to say. What an uncomfortable position to be in. You have it hard, too, being born into the House of Nigi."

"I take pride in being my mother and father's child!" she retorted.

"I see, I see. Good girl."

"How dare you pat a girl's head!"

"Sorry, sorry. I'll not do it again, so please forgive your inconsiderate uncle. If you came to hate me, I couldn't go on living."

"I could never hate you, Uncle!" Arara said. "Besides, I never said to stop. No…"

Before they were Arara's parents, her mother and father were the heads of the foremost of the four samurai houses. Their relationship was not that of parent and child; it was that of master and disciple. Furthermore, the heads of the House of Nigi were the strictest of masters, and Arara needed to be a loyal and earnest disciple.

Her uncle could be irresponsible, but he was a warm person.

He had hugged her often when she was young, and even now would pat her on the back and head. It embarrassed her when he did it, but she felt a kinship with him, and it made her happy.

Her uncle was the one person Arara could tell anything to. There were many subjects upon which she could only share with her true feelings.

That was why, at seventeen, while walking with her uncle, who had returned once more from his travels, Arara secretly confessed to him.

"Uncle, it seems...I'm in love with Tatsuru."

"I see." Her uncle smiled. "That's splendid. My niece has finally discovered love. Yes, splendid indeed."

"Do you think that we can be wed?" Arara asked.

"That was sudden!"

Arara was aware it would be difficult.

First of all, she had to consider Tatsuru's feelings. Though they had trained together as fellow children of the four samurai houses, Arara had never spoken to Tatsuru on a personal level. Marriages weren't always the idea of those who were to be wed, so that in and of itself might not be an obstacle. If Tatsuru refused, however, that would be the end of it. Even if Arara proposed a marriage, and Tatsuru accepted, there was still the issue of whether the heads of the House of Nigi would allow it. In fact, that was perhaps the biggest problem.

It was a harsh way to put it, but Tatsuru was a hanger-on of the House of Mishio. Being the eldest daughter of the House of Nigi, Arara had considerable influence. It would be a simple matter to force Tatsuru to her will, but if the heads of the house, her parents, were not in favor, she couldn't move ahead with it.

There had been offers of marriage for her going back years. If the heads of the house agreed to one, no matter how Arara might feel, or what she might say, she would be wedded off on the spot.

The current candidates were the second and third sons of the House of Shigano, the eldest son of the House of Ganata, and the eldest son of the House of Mishio. Rather than being hard to decide which of these four was the best prospect, in Arara's eyes they were all more or less the same. Their ages and physique varied a little, but in a fight with Arara, they may or may not win. None of them were extraordinarily talented.

The heads of the house had pondered the matter, but they'd been having trouble deciding on a marriage partner for their daughter.

Until she realized her yearning for Tatsuru, Arara had no interest in marriage. She would have been fine with any of them. She had figured she would marry who she was told, bear children, then raise and train them. That was fine. She would merely do her duty; that was a given to her.

If she had not fallen in love, she never would have agonized over it. Once she began to, though, she couldn't stay put.

Not long after telling her uncle about her love, Arara dragged Tatsuru into a secluded place where no one could see them and revealed her emotions to him like she might deliver a letter of challenge.

"Tatsuru-sama, I am in love with you. Please, marry me!"

"Whuh...?" Tatsuru stared at her vacantly, his mouth agape for some time, but then responded that he wanted to think over the matter properly, and politely asked her to wait seven days for his reply.

Arara waited.

She slept well at night, but it occupied her mind and kept her from focusing on her training during the days, so she was scolded by the heads of the house. Even when she tried to pull herself back together, thoughts about what she would do if he gave her a less-than-favorable response, or what to do if he didn't respond after seven days, kept filling her mind, and there was nothing she could do about it.

After precisely seven days had passed, Tatsuru came to the House of Nigi. Arara thought he was there to see her, but that wasn't the case. It turned out that Tatsuru had requested a meeting with her parents, the heads of the house. Her parents, unaware of the situation, had happened to be free at the time, and so agreed to meet with him.

When Tatsuru had walked up in front of the heads, he suddenly prostrated himself before them. "I humbly, humbly beseech you to allow me to marry Arara-sama."

In an instant, not just the House of Nigi, but the entire village became as noisy as a nest of wasps that had just been poked. At first, they thought Tatsuru had fallen for Arara, and was getting ahead of himself, but that wasn't the truth of the matter.

If she left things to run their course, Tatsuru might find his head on the end of a spear, so Arara hurriedly explained to the heads of the house that it was her who had fallen for Tatsuru and proposed they marry. Tatsuru had, after seven days of deep thought, consented to this, and had felt it was only polite he go to request it himself.

After all, marriages were an important issue between families. Arara was the eldest daughter of the House of Nigi, foremost among the four samurai houses, so it was only appropriate he address the matter with the heads first. This was all so very like Tatsuru. He'd followed the proper protocol. He was right in what he was doing, but he could have said a word to Arara about doing it first.

But that was good. This part of him was one of the things that Arara found so agreeable about Tatsuru. At this point, she could think of marrying no one else. She would have no other man. To begin with, she had never, not even once, thought of anyone but Tatsuru as a man. Tatsuru was the only one. Tatsuru was her one and only.

The heads seemed unwilling to even consider it, but Arara went on bended knee and tried to persuade them. She bowed her head, too. She pleaded with them to let her marry Tatsuru.

Naturally, part of it was that she wanted to save Tatsuru, who was not only harshly criticized by the people of the village, who now threw stones at him openly rather than just speaking ill of him behind his back, but reprimanded by his parents and siblings. Tatsuru wasn't just isolated; he was persecuted. Many samurai were bloodthirsty. If she left him be, there could very well be an incident of bloodshed.

"My lady! No, Mother! I beg of you! I beg of you, let this happen! I, Arara, ask you this one selfish favor, hoping you will allow me to be wed to Tatsuru-sama!"

"It cannot be," her mother said.

"That is why I am here, asking you to bend on that!"

"I will not bend."

"You're so hardheaded!"

"How dare you call the head of this house hardheaded!"

"What's wrong with calling a hardheaded person hardheaded?!" she shouted.

"If you cannot understand what I am saying, then you are the one who is being hardheaded! You will stay in a cave until you've cooled your head!"

It was the first time in all her life that Arara had argued with the head of the house. She was sealed in a cave and expected to repent. She spent five days in the lightless cave, without eating or drinking, and was finally released. Arara was completely exhausted, so she hoped that maybe the head of the house would relent and indulge her daughter's wishes.

Arara's hope of that was shattered to pieces.

"Mother, please…I beg you, let me marry Tatsuru-sama…"

"It is not possible," her mother said. "It seems you've not reflected on your actions enough. Back to the cave with you."

She must be joking, thought Arara. If she were returned to the cave like this, she'd die.

But it was no joke. By the orders of the head of the house, Arara was thrown into the cave once more.

The second time she was released, after three days, she had only survived because of the training her body and spirit had been put through, and because she had swallowed her pride to lap up what little moisture there was on the cave walls.

She had to consider that the head of the house might be serious. If she wouldn't do as she was told, whether she was her daughter or not, the head might not mind seeing her die. Or perhaps she was confident that, if she was ready to kill her, she could make her daughter obey her.

Arara had no intention of doing as she was told. She couldn't let the head of the house kill her, though. She couldn't be with Tatsuru-sama if she was dead, after all.

If Arara stayed stubborn and lost her life for it, Tatsuru would grieve. He might take his own life. That wasn't what Arara wanted.

So Arara gave up on appealing directly to the heads of the house. On the surface, she returned to training in the sword as before, but she and Tatsuru had many secret trysts. Trysts though they may have been, neither of the two were particularly skilled with words. They would just talk a little, and exchange letters.

On the orders of the head of the house, the onmitsu's nyaas were monitoring them, so even managing that much took a great deal of effort. They had to dispose of the letters immediately after reading them. If the two kept the letters hidden somewhere, and the skillful and clever nyaas went looking, the nyass might find them.

The head of the house would eventually move forward with another marriage for her. What would she do then? If push came to shove, the head of the house would do what it took to make her comply. Even if she refused, would she be able to reject it? Wouldn't the head of the house get her way in the end?

Even as Tatsuru was isolated and without support, suffering incredible harassment, unending slander, and straight-up abuse, nothing ever clouded his eyes. What was more, he saw it as inevitable, so he didn't resent anyone for it, and repeatedly told Arara she mustn't resent anyone, either.

It seemed to Arara that he spoke from the heart when he said these things. Her respect for him deepened, as did her love. When it got to be too much for her, she let slip to her uncle that she wanted to just elope with him.

"If that is what you want to do, I won't stop you, but I would feel a wee bit uneasy sending you two out into the unfamiliar outside world alone," he said. "Let me guide you wherever you would like to go."

"Uncle, I am serious about this."

"As am I. Well, if the truth came to light, I am sure your parents would kill me, but if it was for your sake, I would gladly give my life."

"I'll believe you."

"Sure, go ahead, go ahead."

Half because her uncle had instigated her to do so, Arara brought up the idea of eloping during one of her secret meetings with Tatsuru. Surely, Tatsuru wouldn't refuse her.

Arara was wrong.

"We mustn't, Arara-sama," he said. "Eloping is out of the

question. I can't abide it. Even if we escaped successfully, it would bring ill fortune to all involved."

"But Tatsuru-sama. Is there any way but eloping that we can be together in this life? The head of the house will find a man for me soon. Even if I fight against it, I'll have no say in the matter."

"The truth is, I do have a plan."

As she listened to him, she learned Tatsuru had been formulating a plan, and training day and night so he might execute it. In fact, compared to the time when Arara was sealed in the cave, Tatsuru's body had grown much larger, and manlier.

According to Tatsuru, this was all a result of his lack of skill, and if he had attained a level of prowess that even the heads of her house were forced to recognize, they wouldn't have opposed their marriage.

Indeed, a samurai had to be strong. Strength was not a thing to be flaunted, but if it was never demonstrated, others wouldn't know about it. Tatsuru explained he had taken the wrong path, and gotten the order of things incorrect. To gain the head of the house's approval, he first needed to become a samurai worthy of her. It had been a mistake to ask for her hand before that.

"But how will you make everyone acknowledge you?" Arara asked.

"By striking down a powerful foe, of course."

"You don't mean..."

"Indeed I do, Arara-sama. Recently, there is only one foe who has made the people of the village tremble in fear."

"You would slay Arnold the Bloody Whirlwind?"

The village didn't stay in one location. Ever since they'd lost their homeland, it had been their custom to perform an augury, and move the village on the day it was determined it would be auspicious to do so. In addition, everyone was accomplished at using the labyrinthine terrain of Thousand Valley to their advantage, so it wasn't often that external enemies threatened the village.

Neither the undead who infested the domain of the former Kingdom of Ishmal nor the orcs who built their Kingdom of Vangish in the domain of the former Kingdom of Nananka went out of their way to strike the village. Of course, that was because the villagers were always on alert, and they spent their days tirelessly working to improve themselves. It was better to be prepared than to regret it later.

The village was always prepared, and the undead and orcs who had destroyed their homeland knew this, too, so they didn't attack.

It wasn't that the village had let their guard down. Around half a year earlier, in the dead of night, that double-armed undead, Arnold, had broken though the defenses with brute force and entered the village.

Seven died; twenty-three were injured.

The undead who swung his four katanas around, cutting down the samurai one after another, and chopping the flesh golems that served the necromancers to ribbons, clearly enjoyed the slaughter from the center of the bloody whirlwind he formed around himself. Shockingly, that undead came alone. Just one person had entered the village, taken many lives and injured so many more, then shook off the samurai of the four houses and the onmitsu that pursued him.

It went without saying that this had been a painful incident for the village. It had been an incredible tragedy, and a great humiliation.

They had soon identified the undead responsible. He was a member of the Black Eagle Band, Forgan, led by Jumbo the Orc, and his name was Arnold. It was said he was among the strongest members of Forgan.

Forgan operated across a fairly wide area, including the former domains of the kingdoms of Ishmal, Nananka, and Arabakia. Their true nature remained unknown, but they were seen as a drifting group of refugees that came into conflict with factions everywhere.

That said, they were no mere refugees. They had been involved in a large number of bloody incidents, including some battles that were on a large enough scale it would be fair to call them wars.

They had taken their fair share of casualties, too, but their renown had only grown with time. It was said the king of the new Kingdom of Vangish once asked Jumbo to serve under him but was summarily rejected. It was a harsh blow to his prestige. Out of resentment, the king sent his army in an attempt to subdue them. However, though the force from Vangish had put up a valiant fight, and outnumbered Forgan many times over, they'd been wiped out. Instead of restoring his authority, the king had fallen from power.

The strange thing was that Arnold had come into the village alone. The onmitsu had been able to determine that Forgan had made camp at a location only around ten kilometers from the village. Yet Arnold hadn't continued to attack the village. In fact, he hadn't seemed interested in the village at all.

Would they take revenge, or watch and wait?

The heads of the Six Houses held a joint council and came to an answer.

They would strengthen their security, then take revenge with ambushes and surprise attacks, and see what Forgan did.

They immediately formed and dispatched a retribution force of samurai, onmitsu, and necromancers, but Forgan split up as if they had anticipated this, making them hard to capture.

If the enemy was aware the houses had set out to attack them, the village might be attacked instead. Though the houses had beefed up their defenses, with the retribution force outside, the village's combat potential was reduced by that much. The retribution force had to consider the possibility of being caught in an ambush, too.

The path the village had walked was by no means flat, and they had faced several crises in the past. It wasn't as if the current heads of the six houses had never faced an emergency that threatened their survival before. However, the people of the village, including the heads of the six houses, had never known war.

Long ago, their homelands struggled against the great army of the No-Life King, fought valiantly, and were struck down and miserably destroyed. That was why they now so thoroughly avoided war. Because of that, they set themselves up in a way that no one would attack them. That was the major policy of the village.

The heads of the six houses made the decision to call back the retribution force, thicken their patrols, and remain in a state of readiness for battle. There were those who criticized this as weakness, but everyone obeyed.

Forgan didn't seem to do anything particularly special. They were definitely in Thousand Valley, but they were quiet, as if they were avoiding contact with the people of the village.

A month passed like that, then two, then three...

Soon, it had been half a year.

It got to the point where the majority view was maybe Forgan had no intention of fighting. Still, they couldn't let their guard down. Arnold's rampage through the village had taken place shortly after the second time Arara had been sealed in the cave. The whole village was on edge, so perhaps Tatsuru was serving as an outlet for some of that.

If Tatsuru could slay Arnold, no one could ignore that accomplishment. However, it might also be the trigger that started a war.

Even if she didn't always want to be, Arara was the eldest daughter of the House of Nigi. That concern immediately crossed her mind, but she was hesitant to use it as a reason to persuade Tatsuru to stop. It was hard to tell him the enemy was too great for him, too. She didn't want to wound Tatsuru's pride.

"I think we should elope after all, Tatsuru," Arara said. "If you are with me, I have no need of anything else. Even if it means throwing everything else away, I would have no regrets."

"I don't want to throw anything away, Arara-sama," said Tatsuru. "The heads of your house are especially concerned for

your well-being. If we tread on the hearts of your parents by eloping, we will surely come to regret it later."

"Those two only care about the house and the village!"

"No. You're wrong, Arara-sama. The heads of your house are
people, too. However, as the ones charged with leading the greatest of the four samurai houses, they must bite back their tears and
kill their own selfish desires. Do you not understand that?!"

When he scolded her, she was overcome. Tatsuru's consideration and brave resolve touched her heart.

Even so, she shouldn't let him go. No matter how he trained,
Tatsuru couldn't become a master swordsman. He might make for
an experienced instructor someday, but he could aspire to no more.
Having been born with potential befitting the eldest child of the
House of Nigi, Arara had an almost perfect grasp of Tatsuru's talent, and his limits. Short of being blessed with incredibly good
fortune, Tatsuru couldn't defeat Arnold the Bloody Whirlwind.

Though she knew this, Arara didn't stop him. No, she couldn't
stop him. He was a samurai warrior, risking his life to accomplish
something. Even if it was rash, or reckless, she couldn't ask a samurai to bend his will.

Because she loved him, that was the one thing she could not do.

Because that was the way of the samurai warrior, there were
times when the heads of the house would issue high-handed orders for them to stop. But as long as those above them didn't hold
them back, allowing no room for disagreement, a samurai never
stopped.

The following day, Tatsuru left the village, never to return.

Grimgar
of
Fantasy and Ash

9 | Lighting a Fire in Someone's Heart

"**S**O YEAH, that's Arara's grudge against Arnold," Rock said. As he spoke, Rock would stand up, sit down, walk around, and generally act restless. Also, his hair was standing up. How was he making it stand up? Was he using gel or something to make it stiff? Whatever it was, he gave off the impression of having more energy than he knew what to do with.

There was a broad-mouthed creature with tiger-like fur riding on Rock's shoulders, wrapped around his neck, but it was impressive that it didn't fall off. The creature was called a mirumi, and they were relatively common in Grimgar. It turned out this one was Rock's pet, and its name was Gettsu.

"Basically, she's out for revenge," said Rock. "Well, can you blame her? I would be, too. The love of her life got done in by the guy. You guys have gotta understand that. Right? Haruhiro? Yume?"

Haruhiro hung his head and furrowed his brow, sighing. "Well, yeah."

"Hrm..." Yume puffed up one of her cheeks, tilting her head hard to one side.

The fog thinned out a fair bit, but now it was gloomy instead; it was quickly darkening. However, for a little while now, little green lights had begun to dance around here and there. These insects, which were apparently called rurakas, supposedly produced light from early evening until late at night. It was a scene that had a sort of illusionary beauty.

The fact that seeing it only made Haruhiro feel like, *Yeah, but so what?* made him feel a little sad.

Sad? Actually, to be honest, Haruhiro was feeling pretty irritated.

With Rock carrying the wounded Arara, everyone had run away as hard as they could on their own, and then they regrouped here. Haruhiro had no clue where "here" was, but they had apparently decided in advance that this was the spot to meet back up if anything happened.

The big bald guy, Kajita, had his massive mushroom sword thrust into the ground and was sitting cross-legged. He hadn't so much as budged for a while now. Had he fallen asleep while sitting? It was hard to tell with him wearing sunglasses.

The strongest dread knight in active service, Moyugi, was sitting on a bump in the ground with one leg crossed over the other, drinking something from a cup. Not that it mattered, but wasn't he a little too relaxed? He was even giving off the sense he was having an elegant time.

Moira the demon wasn't around. There was a "Noooooo..."

every once in a while, though, so she was apparently hiding somewhere.

Why was Sakanami the thief lying face-down? Was he all right? Haruhiro was a little concerned, but everyone else was ignoring him, so it was probably fine. Besides, that guy was probably not quite right to begin with. Since he had never been right, it was all right if he wasn't all right.

When Tsuga, the priest with the buzz cut, finished treating Arara, he began meditating in the lotus position. Since then, his eyes had stayed shut, and he hadn't moved.

Incidentally, Kuro, the former hunter, wasn't here. He had a little business to attend to, so he left on his own.

"We failed to avenge Tatsuru-sama." Arara was sitting on a tree stump and hanging her head in shame. "It was my fault. It's because I was injured!"

"Don't let it get you down, Arara," Rock said, crouching down right in front of her. "There'll be other chances. We'll make them for you. Okay?"

Gettsu the mirumi squeaked loudly. It was like both pet and owner alike were trying to cheer Arara up.

"Thank you," Arara said. She sighed and looked up. "I am in your debt, Rock. How can I ever repay you for this?"

"Silly Arara, you don't need to think about that. We're doing this because we want to."

"But..."

"Seriously, it's all cool! Let's just focus on beating down that Arnold guy for now. Moyugi'll come up with a way. We'll follow his plan. If we fail, we'll just try again until we succeed. Simple, right?"

"When you are the one saying it, for some reason, it really does start to feel that way."

"There's nothing hard about it," Rock said confidently. "You just leave it to us. The Rocks."

"However." Arara looked down again, gripping her left arm tightly with her right hand. "You people are under no obligation to help me seek vengeance."

Haruhiro and Yume looked at one another.

Yeah, that, Haruhiro thought. *That's it. That's the issue.*

Arara's beloved Tatsuru tried to kill Arnold, the enemy of the village, but was defeated. Arara wants to avenge the man she loved. I get that. But where do Rock and the Rocks come into this? They're volunteer soldiers. Obviously, they're not from the village. This isn't really their business, is it?

"Arara. Arara. Hey, Arara!" Rock suddenly stood up, spreading his arms wide. Gettsu nearly fell off his shoulders, but managed to hold on somehow. "What're you acting like a stranger for? Of course we're obliged to help! We totally are!"

"You say that, but we only met recently..." Arara began.

"Who cares?! Time has nothing to do with it!"

"If I hadn't told you my circumstances back then, you wouldn't have been dragged into this."

"We don't feel like we're being dragged into anything! Right, Moyugi?!"

"No. I very much feel like I am."

"Whaaaat?!" Rock shouted.

"Not that it's anything new," Moyugi added. "For as long as I keep working with you people, I'll keep getting dragged into trouble like this."

"Ha! And you're in the Rocks because you can't get enough of it, right?"

"You've got that right," said Moyugi. "Life's too short to waste time on boring stuff."

Kajita gave them a thumbs-up. "Indeed."

"Urgh," Sakanami groaned and writhed around on the ground. He looked like he was in pain.

Tsuga was meditating with a smile. Was he on the verge of enlightenment or something?

There was...an awful lot Haruhiro could have turned into a punchline here. In fact, it felt like maybe there wasn't a single thing he could accept at face value. If he were to sum up the reason the Rocks fought simply, they were doing it on a whim. That was what Moyugi had said.

Ohh, thought Haruhiro. *I see, I see.*

These people are all weird.

They're a band of weirdos.

He'd had the feeling they were. They weren't ordinary people like Haruhiro and his group, so there was no way they were normal. Besides, it probably didn't matter in the least to them whether a mediocre guy like Haruhiro thought they were normal or not.

People who weren't plain and ordinary were always a little

extreme in some way. Were they extreme to begin with, and that was what let them go beyond mediocrity? Or when they went beyond the realm of mediocrity, did it make them a little extreme? Or, perhaps, was it impossible to escape from mediocrity without becoming extreme? Haruhiro didn't really know.

Still, even if he didn't understand it, that wasn't going to cause him any trouble. The dispositions and motivations of a band of weirdos like this weren't his problem. Or they wouldn't be, except he was currently in a situation where he was forced to work with them.

"Murrrgh..." Yume nodded, as if trying to forcefully convince herself she'd figured it out. "Basically, here's how it is, yeah? Rockun and all them only met Araran a li'l while ago, but they're dead set on helpin' her, 'cause they're good guys, right?"

"Hm? Us? Good guys?" Rock looked at Yume and scowled.

Uh, that's a serious bad guy look you've got going on there.

"Huh? What's that supposed to mean?" Rock demanded. "You making fun of us?"

"How's sayin' you're good guys makin' fun of you?" Yume wanted to know.

"Listen, Yume, being called a good guy isn't a compliment, or anything. Basically, it means they're someone you don't have to care about, right?"

"Yume wasn't meanin' it that way when she said it!"

"Oh, yeah? Well, we're not good guys. We don't look like we are, now do we?"

"Yeah," Yume agreed. "You don't."

"Hahaha! I know, right? We aren't motivated by justice, fairness, morals, or any of that stuff."

"Well, what're you all motivated by, then?" Yume asked.

"All sorts of things, really. But this time..." Rock brought his hands to his chest with a look of pride. "It's love."

Haruhiro stared blankly.

"*Love?*" he asked in disbelief.

"No, not *love*. It's love, man. Love."

Where's the difference? It's all the same word. Geez. Haruhiro felt a little dizzy. *He's making no sense.*

"Huh? Wait, love...for whom?" Haruhiro asked.

"Well, for Arara, of course."

"No... B-but...?" Haruhiro looked back and forth from Rock to Arara. Rock was speaking proudly, but Arara must have been embarrassed, or not sure what to say, because she was still looking down. "But, erm, Arara-san had a lover, didn't she? And it's because of what happened to him that she's doing this, so..."

"Does that have anything to do with it?"

"Doesn't it...have something to do with it? I mean, I don't really have any experience with this sort of stuff, so I wouldn't know, but—"

"When we first met, Arara was carrying a katana. She suddenly jumped out of the fog and came swinging at us."

"Th-that was—!" Arara pouted like a child. "I-I was in a state of confusion. Avenging Tatsuru-sama was the only thing on my mind, and I left the village despite Uncle's attempts to stop me, so I was convinced everything that moved was my enemy."

"She was beautiful," Rock said with a broad grin. "Her hair was disheveled, her face was a mask of rage, and she was crying a little. She got me good. It was love at first sight. 'Why is she crying? What happened? Is there anything I can do for her?' I couldn't help but wonder."

"She lit a fire in his heart," Kajita said in a husky voice.

"That's it." Rock turned his fist toward Kajita. "With my heart and body burning with the fires of love, there ain't no man who can stop me. I'll keep running till I burn out."

"He's easily infatuated," Moyugi said dismissively. "And it's never with someone he can have. What's the allure of a woman you'll never sleep with? I can't understand it."

"That's what's boring about you, Moyugi," said Rock. "If you give love to get something in return, that isn't love. It's just lust, right? Well, that's not what my love is like. My love is given freely. I fell for Arara. I love her. That's why I want to make her wish come true. For that, I'd do anything. It gets you fired up, doesn't it? It's fun, right? Right, Haruhiro? You get it?"

"No, I don't get it."

"You don't?!"

"I, uh, don't have much in the way of experience with romance, so..."

"Oh, so you're a virgin!"

"Is that such a surprise?"

"A virgin..." Yume said. She was nodding along with a knowing look, but did she really understand what that meant? Knowing Yume, wasn't she misunderstanding it somehow?

"Of all things, he had to be a virgin." Rock clicked his tongue. "A virgin, huh. I dunno if a virgin can get it."

"Could you stop repeating that word?" Haruhiro asked.

"Haruhiro." Kajita looked at him and gave him a thumbs-up. "Beginner's luck."

"I don't understand."

"Gyahahaha!" Sakanami suddenly began laughing as he writhed in agony. "Hilarious! Virgin, virgin, rose! If they put you on the throne, you'd be the Rose Emperor! A title fit for a premature ejaculator! Gyahahaha!"

"I understand you even less."

"Well, yeah," Rock agreed, stroking Gettsu's throat. "I didn't really understand it, either. Sakanami's nuts. You should try not to get him mad, Haruhiro, Yume. Even I have no idea what he might do."

"I'm amazed you can work with a guy like that," Haruhiro said.

"Isn't it interesting?"

"It's a lot of trouble for me." Moyugi passed the cup over to his left hand so he could use the middle finger of his right hand to press on the bridge of his glasses. "I have to include the guy in my calculations when putting together a strategy."

"Isn't that what makes it interesting?" Rock asked.

"I won't deny it."

To sum things up, this was the situation:

The group had been motivated by Rock's falling in love at first sight. Other than that, the Rocks were helping Arara with her vengeance because it seemed like it might be interesting. They really were doing it on a whim.

"So, when you joined the Day Breakers, was that because it seemed interesting, too?" Haruhiro asked.

"That's part of it." Rock's eyes narrowed, and both corners of his mouth curled upward. "We have another reason, too, though. I won't tell you what it is, Haruhiro."

"Huh? Why not?"

"Isn't it more interesting if I keep quiet about it? Oh—" Rock stopped, and even before Rock did, Gettsu turned his head to the right. "Is that Kuro?"

Looking in that direction, there was a humanoid figure walking through the evening gloom where the lights of the rurakas danced about. The figure was approaching it waved. It was Kuro.

"They weren't there." When Kuro came over and sat down next to Haruhiro, looking exasperated, that was the first thing he said. "Went to that cave you mentioned. No sign of your friends."

"No way..." Haruhiro was at a loss for words. "B-but, hey, maybe you had the wrong place?"

"Not a chance. That, what was it? That cave leading to another world, I already had some idea where it was. And there were traces that someone had been there."

"Hrm..." Yume made a difficult face and pressed her index fingers into her temples. "That means... What does it mean? Yume wonders..."

"Since you weren't coming back, they probably went looking," Kuro said. "Then they got into trouble. Seems likely."

"You say that so easily," Haruhiro murmured.

"You people don't even know the damn way there, and it's

easier and safer for me to go alone anyway, so I went out of my way to go there for you. For nothing, I might add."

"Sorry. I...guess you're right. Thank you, Kuro-san."

"Yeah. You owe me one. Pay me back with interest, got it?"

Even setting aside the debt he had just incurred, their comrades not being near the cave exit was a huge shock for Haruhiro.

Whoa—I can't think about anything right now, he thought. *No, even if I can't think, I have to think. Should I go there myself after all? Go, and search for the other four? But it's already dark. Also, enemies. There could be enemies.*

Haruhiro didn't really care about Forgan, but they probably didn't feel the same way about him.

Well, I did kill them with my own hands. If they attack me on sight, I have no right to complain.

"Hey, hey!" someone called out to him. Startled, Haruhiro turned to see Sakanami was right beside him and wriggling around. "How's it feel? How's it feel? Hey, tell me, how's it feel right now? Sad? Or painful? Heart wrenching? Like you want to cry? Like you're going to puke? How do you feel right now? Well? Well?"

"For a start, that you're kind of annoying."

"Gyahoh! Gyahahahaha! Hilarious! My sides..."

"What's with this guy?" Haruhiro muttered.

"Oh, him?" Kuro said, sounding pleased. "Just a guy with a defective personality."

"That was harsh!" Sakanami turned on Kuro. "Kuro, I don't want to hear that from an inhuman monster like you! You prey on other people! Well, not me! I won't prey on people, but I will eat gods! I am the God Eater! So cool! Gyahahahahaha!"

I should ignore him. Yeah. Ignore him. I need to ignore this guy and think. Think.

"Now, then." Moyugi stood up. "In my diagnosis, it wouldn't be surprising for Forgan's people to start reaching this general area any time now. We're moving."

"Okay." Rock looked around to the rest of the group. "Let's go, Arara. You people, too."

It was apparent Haruhiro and Yume were included in that "you people." Well, Haruhiro didn't want to be left behind, so he'd have to go. He'd have to think on the move.

"Haru-kun..." Yume said, tugging on Haruhiro's cloak. She looked worried, as may be expected. "Where do you think everyone's gone off to?"

"They're fine. I'm sure of it." Even as he said it, he wasn't sure if it was to console her, or because he wanted to believe it himself. "I mean, they've got Ranta with them. He's a tenacious one."

"Guess so..." Yume let go of Haruhiro's cloak. Then she immediately grabbed Haruhiro's sleeve.

He understood what it was she wanted from him, so he had to give it to her.

Haruhiro held Yume's hand.

Yume squeezed his hand back tightly.

10 **For What Reason?**

IT WAS DIZZYING. The countless lights flashing in the darkness swayed about like crazy, and it felt awful. Whenever Shihoru tripped over something, or stepped in a hole and almost fell over, Kuzaku caught her. She'd stopped apologizing every time. She didn't have it together enough to form the words.

I can't do this anymore. I can't run any further. She'd been thinking that for a long time now. *I wish they'd just leave me here.*

Even if she said it, Kuzaku wouldn't abandon Shihoru, and Katsuharu probably wouldn't, either. Because she knew that, she couldn't say it.

"Katsuharu-san!" Kuzaku called out to the man ahead of them. "How do you think it looks?! Can we get away?!"

"Who can say?" Katsuharu was winded. "It's still some way to the village, so that may depend on the two of you."

"Damn it! Because I was so noisy, the nyaa found us, and...!"

"It does little good to dwell on it. I was the one to invite you along, after all. It was careless to get so close to them. The fault lies with me."

"Wait, why are you sounding so relaxed about this?!"

"Were I to panic, no good would come of it," Katsuharu said.

Nyaas. There were nyaas behind them, of course, but also to the right and left. Even with the shining bugs that were called ru-rakas flying around, it was dark. Though they couldn't see the nyaas, they could still hear their voices. *Nyaa... Nyaa... Nyaa... Nyaa... Nyaa... Nyaa... Nyaa... Nyaa...* Meowing from all directions.

Were the nyaas close? Were they far? How many were there? Shihoru had no clue. From what Katsuharu had told them, tamed nyaas would sometimes take their time, slowly pushing their targets into a corner like this. It was true; they were beginning to feel cornered. At least, Shihoru and Kuzaku were.

"Well," Katsuharu said in a voice that was far too relaxed for a man who was running, "for now, it would seem we only have the nyaas pursuing us. The way things look now, we may yet make it to the village somehow. Give it your all."

Give it your all, he said. That was what Shihoru thought she was doing. She was trying as hard as she could. But, try as she might, there were limits to what she could do. Once she was exhausted and couldn't go another step, she was going to be a burden on Kuzaku and Katsuharu.

Hold on.

Suddenly, she lost all the strength in her knees, and she could no longer keep her feet moving forward. Shihoru quickly supported herself with her staff. That managed to keep her from falling over, but she couldn't run anymore. She didn't think she could walk, either. This was it. This was her limit.

"Shihoru-san?!" Kuzaku stopped. "What's up? Why'd you stop?"

"Good grief." Katsuharu turned back, crouching down in front of Shihoru with his back turned to her. "Here. I'll carry you on my back. Grab on."

"N-no, I can't ask you to..."

"Shihoru-san, let him carry you!" Kuzaku cried. "If it comes to it, I'll tank for you two!"

"Hurry it up, would you?" Katsuharu asked. "This position is painful on my lower back, you see."

"S-sorry. Then, e-excuse me...!"

Katsuharu's back was broader than Shihoru expected, and it gave her a sense of relief. The ability to carry Shihoru, who was pretty heavy, and to not have it do much to throw off his running form, this man must have been more reliable than he looked.

"Sorry, but could I ask you to cling just a little tighter?" Katsuharu asked.

"R-right!"

"Yes, I am a lucky man indeed."

"Huh...?"

"No, just talking to myself. Think nothing of it. However, I should have done this from the beginning. Heh... I jest, of course. Trying to lighten the mood, you see?"

He may have been reliable, but he also seemed just a little dangerous.

Speaking of danger, what about the nyaas? Shihoru had done a great job of slowing everyone down, so it was hard to imagine the situation had improved. Thinking about it normally, it should have gotten worse.

A wolf howled in the distance.

"Just now, was that...?!" Kuzaku looked back without stopping.

"Not good," Katsuharu said in a low voice, quickly looking left then right. The left side was flat, but the right side sloped upward. The paths ahead and behind them were narrow. "This is a bad place. Guess I'll do it once we reach somewhere a little better. I'm going to carve a bloody path for you, so you two run away."

"No, Katsuharu-san, there's no reason you should have to do that for us!" Kuzaku cried.

"Were you two older than me, I would sacrifice you to save myself, but watching those younger than me die always turns my stomach. Oh, don't you worry, I won't go down easily. I have experience on my side, if nothing else."

"I wouldn't be able to run far, anyway..." Shihoru said, clenching her teeth. Even though he'd helped by carrying her, she was still winded. "I'll fight with you. I have to. I'll support you with magic."

"I wanted to show off, but I suppose this is how it has to be."

Not long after that, when they entered a flat area with many trees, Katsuharu let Shihoru down and drew his katana. Kuzaku readied his black blade and his shield, moving up in front of Shihoru.

There weren't many rurakas here. *Nyaa... nyaa... nyaa... nyaa...* Based on the meowing, the nyaas must have been pretty close. The wolves were howling, too.

"Dark…" When Shihoru focused her mind and called his name, the elemental appeared as if coming out of a door that had opened up from an unseen world. Shadowy strings twisted into a spiral and took on a human-like form. Dark floated through the air to sit on Shihoru's shoulder.

Katsuharu took one look at Dark, then said "Oh," in admiration. "Now there's an unfamiliar spell."

"It's an original, Shihoru-san's own." While paying attention to the area around them, Kuzaku took a deep breath. "Will the nyaas attack us directly, you think?"

"They don't often fight, no. When one of their kind gets roughed up, they have a tendency to all become uncooperative as a group. That is why nyaa handlers don't like to make them fight."

"So, the ones that'll be coming—" Kuzaku started to say, but then shut his mouth.

There was a noise. Footsteps? It's charging in. From the left. A wolf. A black wolf, huh?

Shihoru was going to send Dark to intercept it, but she thought better of it. He wouldn't make it in time.

Katsuharu headed to the left using a unique method of walking where neither his head nor his waist moved up or down. Before the black wolf could jump up at him, Katsuharu was already swinging down at it with his katana. He smashed the black wolf's head open, and it collapsed. Katsuharu then used the same walking technique to return to his original position. "The next one is coming."

"Uragh!" Kuzaku knocked something back with his shield. Had another black wolf tackled him?

"If you try to follow them with your eyes, you'll act too late." Katsuharu swung his katana. It looked like he'd hit it. "Don't look. Feel."

There was no way Shihoru could do that. She was a mage. No, saying she couldn't do it because she was a mage was just acting weak.

One was coming from behind. As she turned toward it, she gave the order. "Go!"

Unlike the magic Shihoru had learned in her time at the guild, Dark didn't just fly in a straight line. He was guided, to a degree.

There was a black wolf. It wasn't that she was actually able to see it lunging at her from the darkness. What Katsuharu had told her immediately came in handy. *Don't look, feel.*

Something came rushing at Shihoru, and she willed Dark to collide with it. That was all. Dark protected Shihoru.

The black wolf yelped, then turned and ran.

Shihoru immediately summoned Dark again. "Come, Dark!"

"Sorry, Shihoru-san!" Kuzaku was using his sword and shield to knock back the black wolves, and somehow managing to cover Shihoru. "Aren't there an awful lot of them?!"

"At times like this, you should assume there are more than you can actually see." Katsuharu moved with that particular walking style, the same as always, swinging his katana to land a precise blow on a black wolf's head. It wasn't flashy, but even a mage like Shihoru could tell he was skilled. "There'll be a short break."

It went just like Katsuharu said. The black wolves suddenly

stopped charging in, growling at them from a little way away instead. Shihoru nearly breathed a sigh of relief despite herself.

"Now!" Katsuharu said. He took off running. "Follow me!"

"Shihoru-san!" Kuzaku called.

"R-right!" she called back.

She'd been lost in thought. Was this the right thing to do, or wasn't it? She didn't even have time to think. Shihoru chased after Katsuharu.

Katsuharu cut down one of the black wolves to break a hole in their encirclement, then kept on running. The black wolves tried to swarm Katsuharu, as if they were being sucked in by him. He made sharp swings to the left and to the right with his katana, opening a path.

Kuzaku and Shihoru ran down that path. Kuzaku helped, too, driving off two or three of the black wolves with his sword and shield. Shihoru wasn't trying to conserve Dark's power, as she had bigger concerns. She was quickly winded. Her heart pounded, ready to burst. It may already be too much for her.

Then Katsuharu came to a stop.

Kuzaku and Shihoru shot past Katsuharu on inertia. Having performed an about-face that almost caused him to trip, Katsuharu was holding his blade a little below the middle level and staring down the black wolves. The wolves spread out to the left and right, while remaining cautious of him. Were they trying to encircle the group again?

"Are we just going to keep repeating this?" Kuzaku said with a groan. "It feels so overwhelming. But I guess we've gotta do it."

Shihoru wanted to say something, but her voice failed her.

Katsuharu began pulling back, so Kuzaku and Shihoru backed away along with him. This really was overwhelming. Just how many times would they have to repeat this before they reached the village?

Nyaa...nyaa...nyaa... The nyaas were meowing. *We're here. We're right here. There are so many of us. We'll follow you wherever you go,* those meows threatened them.

If Shihoru had been the way she used to be, her heart may have broken. Now, though, even if she was on the brink of that, she could tough it out just a bit longer. Even if, at the very worst, she had to let Katsuharu and Kuzaku go on ahead and stay here by herself, she wouldn't just accept death with resignation. She didn't think she had become strong, but she wanted to be.

"It's going to be fine." Shihoru nodded. "I have to see everyone again...because I want to see them."

"Yeah." Kuzaku smiled just a little. "Can't let ourselves get killed by a little thing like this, can we?"

"That's the spirit." Katsuharu turned and began running again. "Onward!"

Shihoru and Kuzaku tried to follow, but Katsuharu came to a sudden stop. He had no choice but to.

There was something big standing in his way. It hadn't been there originally. If it had, there was no way Katsuharu would have gone that way, after all.

For a moment, Shihoru thought it was a tiger, lion, or other big cat. But she was wrong.

Judging from its outline, that thing was—or rather, that thing was *also*—a wolf. It was much too big to merely be a wolf. What was more, on its back, there was something...riding it?!

"Ow..." Katsuharu slapped his forehead with his left hand. "The beast master's here, huh? Sorry to say it, but we can't get away from this."

"It's not *just* the beast master," echoed a man's voice. It came from behind them; in other words, the area where the black wolves first surrounded them.

When Shihoru turned back, the wolves bared their fangs; there was a humanoid figure standing behind them. Not just one; there were several.

But a human...?

"I'm here, too, trespassers. I'll punish you to kill some time."

There was no doubt about it. It was a human voice, male. That alone would have been a shock, but there was something far, far, far more shocking.

The figures were approaching them. The leader was a human, like Shihoru had thought. The human man had five or six orcs in tow. However, one of them was awfully small.

"No...way..." Kuzaku shuddered. "What's that supposed to mean?"

Shihoru blinked, shaking her head. "Why...?"

"Hey, Ranta." The man from earlier gestured to him with his chin. "Go crazy for us right now. I won't ask you to prove your loyalty, but if you're our comrade, you can at least join our fights."

"That's a given." The small man lowered the visor on his

205

helmet, and drew RIPer. "I don't mind fighting myself. Just watch, old man Takasagi. Soon enough, I'll have you begging me to become your disciple, I guarantee it."

"Ranta-kun," Shihoru whispered.

The ground felt like it was shaking violently. This had to be some kind of mistake. That, or a bad dream.

Oh. Knowing Ranta, this had to be another of his bad jokes. He wanted to surprise them and make fun of them.

But if that wasn't it...

"You know him?" Katsuharu asked Shihoru and Kuzaku, and at practically the same time, this old man Takasagi, or whoever he was, asked Ranta, "Do you know them?"

"We don't just *know* him," Kuzaku said through grit teeth.

Shihoru could only nod.

"Well, yeah." Ranta gave a nasal laugh. "Not that it matters. I'm part of Forgan now. No matter who they are, I'll crush anyone who lays a hand on our guys. We can't let them mess with us."

"I hope that's not just tough talk." Takasagi stuffed his hand down his collar. His right arm was... He apparently didn't have one.

"You'll see soon enough." Ranta twisted his neck back and forth. "Prepare yourselves. It's massacre time, guys."

Shihoru still couldn't believe it.

He sprang toward them. Leap Out.

This was Ranta.

Katsuharu questioned whether he should intercept him or not, but he retreated. Kuzaku was standing there, standing practically stock still, when Ranta came swinging at him violently.

Kuzaku quickly brought his shield up to defend himself. "Wah?!"

"Take that!" Ranta gave him no time to stop and breathe, launching into a slashing attack. "You beanpole!"

"Urgh! Ah! Wha...?!" It was all Kuzaku could do just to block the attacks with his shield. No, he'd already taken a number of hits. Kuzaku was wearing tough armor, which was the only reason he hadn't gone down yet. "R-Ranta-kun?! Whoa, wait!"

"What kind of idiot would wait when you ask them to wait?!" Ranta used Leap Out to suddenly get around to Kuzaku's right side, then took a big swing, holding RIPer in both his hands. "Ooorahhhh!"

Kuzaku was holding his shield in his left hand. If he was attacked from the right side, he wouldn't be able to block with the shield. Even if he was going to deflect it with his sword, Kuzaku's response was too slow. He stopped it with his right arm instead. "Guh...?!"

His arm was covered by his armor, too, so it didn't get cut off. Kuzaku nearly dropped his sword, however, and it hurt him pretty badly.

Katsuharu immediately stepped in, so Ranta used Exhaust to leap back and get some distance.

Thank goodness, thought Shihoru. If Katsuharu hadn't backed him up, Kuzaku might have gone down with the next attack.

The next attack from Ranta, who was supposed to be their ally.

"Dark." Shihoru went to order Dark, who was sitting on her shoulder, to do something. But what, exactly, should she order him to do?

"Let's see." Takasagi drew the katana that he carried on his back. "Maybe I'll play a bit, too. Even if it's just the three of you, I see one of you is capable, at least. At least try to resist, okay?"

The orcs each readied their weapons, as well.

"You don't get a turn, old man." Ranta bent his entire body to lower himself. "I'll take these guys. Kuzaku. Shihoru. You two are mine. Think of it as the little mercy I can offer. I'll put you to rest."

"If that's your idea of mercy..." Kuzaku said, digging his heels in and lifting his sword overhead. It looked like his right arm still hurt, but he could tough it out and make it move somehow. "You can keep it! Ranta-kun, what happened to you, man?!"

Shihoru had a sudden realization.

"Where's Merry?"

There was a shudder that shook through Ranta's head and shoulders. That was when it happened. Suddenly, the nyaas began meowing like crazy, and the humanoid creature on the giant wolf's back shouted something.

Takasagi said, "Huh?" and looked around the area. "Enemy reinforcements, you say?"

The nyaas scattered in a hurry. Though they were out of sight, you could tell it from their meows. The black wolves seemed uneasy, too, but when the giant wolf let out its horrifying howl, they all fell into line. Takasagi was shouting in some unknown language. The orcs seemed to be trying to harden their defenses.

"Hey," Katsuharu said without looking to Shihoru. "Now's our time to get out of here."

"But...!" Kuzaku kicked the ground. "Damn it! This makes no sense!"

He was so right. Ranta becoming their enemy... It was so incomprehensible, she wanted to cry.

"Ranta-kun!" Shihoru burst out with a sob. Before she cried, she had to find out this much, at least. "What about Merry?! What happened to Merry?!"

Kuzaku turned back in shock. Ranta said nothing. Could he not answer? Could he not afford to do that?

"Aaaaarnooooold! Where are you?!"

An awfully loud voice echoed through the area. It wasn't far from here; it was close.

The giant wolf jumped and changed direction. Something—someone—had attacked it. The black wolves all began to move at the same time. Were they trying to help the giant wolf?

"Oh?" Takasagi knocked something out of the air with his katana. An arrow, huh. "We've got ourselves a sniper, I see. I'm not interested in getting hurt. The end!"

Was "the end" the signal to retreat? They pulled back. They retreated, without any regard for Shihoru and the others. The giant wolf, the black wolves, the orcs, Takasagi, and even Ranta.

"Wait, Ranta-kun!" Shihoru almost chased after him despite herself, but Katsuharu stopped her.

"Stop it!" he ordered. "I don't know the situation, but not now!"

"B-but, Merry...!"

"Hey! Ranta-kun!" Kuzaku took off running, but quickly

came to a stop. "Ugh! It's no good, not against that guy! Damn it, Ranta! He's more than just fast when he's running away!"

Shihoru couldn't stand any longer. She sat down where she was, Dark disappearing from her shoulder, looking disappointed.

This... This is just too much. It's awful. Too awful.

"Ah!" Kuzaku shouted.

When he looked, Ranta was at the tail of the enemy group and something jumped him from the side. There was a struggle, one of them got on top of the other, then they switched, flipping over and over. When he noticed, Takasagi swung his katana, but it looked more like he was trying to split them in two than to split them up. Neither of them wanted to get killed, so they both leapt apart at the same time.

Ranta immediately took off running. Takasagi left, too. That left only the other one behind.

"Haruhiro-kun," Shihoru whispered.

Even if it was dark, there was no mistaking him. That was Haruhiro.

Haruhiro was on one knee, watching the enemy leave.

What was even going on here? Shihoru couldn't think straight. Even if she could think, it wasn't likely she'd understand it.

I don't want to think about anything right now.

11 | Deep in the Night

*S*ORT IT OUT. *I need to sort all of this out, thought Haruhiro.* Moyugi indicated it was time for them to move.

Rock headed in the direction Moyugi pointed with Gettsu the mirumi on his shoulder and the rest of his party in tow. That included Nigi Arara, the eldest daughter of the House of Nigi, Haruhiro, and Yume.

Not long after heading in that direction, they detected something out of the ordinary. It seemed Forgan was in combat with someone. The enemy of their enemy wasn't necessarily their friend, but Arara and the Rocks's goal was vengeance, and their target was Arnold of Forgan. If Arnold was one of the enemies there, they might be able to catch him by surprise.

When it came to Haruhiro and Yume, they had a different motive. What if Ranta and the others were the ones Forgan were attacking? It felt like a distinct possibility. If that was what was happening, they had to help them.

Haruhiro went ahead of the group with his fellow thief Sakanami, as well as Kuro the former hunter.

Sakanami was the one who got spotted by the nyaas. Or rather, for some unexplained reason, Sakanami found a nyaa and tried to grab it, resulting in the nyaas finding them and raising the alarm.

Still, while Sakanami continued with his bizarre antics, Kuro and Haruhiro were able to get closer to the enemy.

It looked like three humans were surrounded by wolves and orcs. One of them was unfamiliar, but Haruhiro knew the other two. They were Shihoru and Kuzaku. They were all right. Thank goodness.

But why was it just the two of them? Where were the other two?

Half of that question was resolved a moment later. No, maybe resolved wasn't the word for it.

There were humans with the enemy. Two of them, even, and one of those two was Ranta.

As for what happened from that point on, honestly, it was a blur. Haruhiro couldn't put the events in order.

He recalled Rock and the others attacking Forgan, and he recalled being relieved that, for now at least, Shihoru and Kuzaku were all right.

Shihoru and Kuzaku were shouting at Ranta about something. Haruhiro chased after Ranta. He leapt on him and put him in a hold. He said something like, *What are you doing, man,* or, *What are you thinking,* or, *We're going home.*

That and, Merry, what happened to Merry?

The one-armed man came at him with a katana. If Haruhiro didn't get out of the way, he sensed both he and Ranta would be cut in two. The man was probably serious. He had to get away.

He remembered what Ranta said as he left, word for word.

"That woman belongs to me! If you want her back, just try and steal her from me!"

Seriously, what was that about? What did it mean?

"That woman" had to be Merry. No question about it.

She belongs to me? Just try and steal her? What was that guy saying? Was he an idiot? He was. Haruhiro already knew that much. But he never thought he was that kind of idiot. He never thought that idiot would treat Merry like his property or turn traitor.

Haruhiro wasn't sure it was appropriate to call what Ranta had done turning traitor in this situation, but he'd stabbed them in the back. That was how it felt. Ranta had stabbed Haruhiro and the rest in the back.

Thanks to Ranta, even though they'd managed to meet back up with Shihoru and Kuzaku, Haruhiro couldn't be happy about it, no matter how he tried. Even when he learned that the man with them was Arara's uncle, "Oh" was about the only reaction that escaped him.

Moyugi seemed to have some sort of plan, so the Rocks, Arara, and her uncle said they would be heading to the hidden village. The idea of parting ways with them didn't even come to Haruhiro's mind, so they tagged along.

After passing a number of traps, fortifications, moats, and more, they gave a password to the guard to let them in. When they arrived in the village, around ten men and women armed with katanas appeared and took Arara away somewhere. Rock seemed to want to raise a fuss over it, but Arara stopped him.

According to Arara and her uncle Katsuharu, she was probably going to meet with her parents. Well, not so much meet them as be dragged in front of them, but, well, she was the heir to an important house. They probably had a lot going on.

The Rocks, Haruhiro, and the rest were led to Katsuharu's retreat on the edge of the village. It was kind of him to show them the way there and all, but Katsuharu's "retreat" was just a hovel with no floor. It was only large enough for five, maybe six, people at most. That being the case, it seemed appropriate to let their seniors have priority. Besides, Haruhiro didn't really want to go in there anyway, so he and the other three decided to wait outside. They were used to roughing it from their time in Darunggar.

It didn't feel like any time to be taking it easy and sleeping, but they couldn't go anywhere until dawn broke. Besides, even if they could go somewhere, he had no idea where that somewhere ought to be.

Katsuharu told them they were free to make use of his firewood, so Haruhiro had Yume start a fire. Fires were nice. When the four of them sat around a fire like this, it felt like he might somehow manage to retain his sanity.

On Haruhiro's right, Yume and Shihoru were sitting shoulder-to-shoulder. They both looked completely spent. Kuzaku, on his left, was kneeling formally for some reason, pressing down on his knees with both hands.

"Kuzaku," Haruhiro began.

"Yesh."

"What's 'yesh'?"

"Sowwy."

"Are you crying...?"

"I'm not crying," Kuzaku said defensively. "Like I'd cry. Crying's not gonna do us any good."

"Well, no, it's not."

"What is it?" Kuzaku asked.

"Oh, I was just wondering why you're kneeling."

"I just sorta felt like it?"

"Okay, then."

Yeah, this was no good.

It's just no good, Haruhiro thought. *If I relax, my mind goes blank. I need to think, but nothing comes to mind. Besides, think? About what? Ranta stabbed us in the back. We don't know if Merry is safe or not. No, Ranta was saying she belongs to him. That means she's still alive. I'd like to think that. It's safe to assume she's alive, I guess?*

Setting aside the question of whether she was fine or not, Merry hadn't been killed. That being the case, whether Ranta told them to or not, their party had to take her back. They had to save her.

Ranta seemed to have joined Forgan. Merry must have been taken prisoner by them. Hopefully she wasn't being treated too badly.

Or was she? It was hard to be optimistic. There was that human, Takasagi, with them for some reason, but their boss was an orc named Jumbo.

They were an independent, multi-racial group mainly consisting of orcs and undead. It went without saying that orcs and undead were the enemies of humanity. Despite that, Takasagi and Ranta were working with them.

Haruhiro couldn't figure them out, but it was hard to imagine they were treating Merry with the proper respect. If anything, it seemed like it wouldn't take much for them to get rough with her. Was this just Haruhiro's prejudice? Really, he hoped it was. They might be a surprisingly gentlemanly and unexpectedly good gang, one that wouldn't hurt Merry or do anything untoward to her. If they weren't, that was a problem.

"Y'think she's gonna be all right?" Yume said all of a sudden. "Merry-chan."

"Yeah..." Shihoru rubbed Yume's back and shoulders, probably trying to reassure her, but she was crying herself. "I believe she will be..."

"Arghhhhhhhhh!" Kuzaku punched the ground. "Rantaaaa! That bastard, he's screwing with us, damn him! I never thought he was the type!"

Yeah, that, Haruhiro thought. *That's really what it comes down to, huh.*

It wasn't like Haruhiro was firmly convinced Ranta hadn't, and he didn't have enough evidence to claim otherwise, but he wasn't ready to decide for sure that Ranta had betrayed them yet. Even if Ranta had stabbed them in the back, he might have been put in a position where he had no other choice.

Merry, Haruhiro thought. *I'm concerned about Merry. I'm*

worried for her, of course, and there's something that bugs me about the way Ranta talked about her.

First, the way he'd said, "That woman belongs to me." Taken at face value, it was a declaration that Merry was his. It was hard to imagine the feeling was mutual. Ranta was one-sidedly declaring Merry was his woman.

Why would Ranta say that about Merry? Sure, Merry was beautiful, and could be tender, so it wouldn't be all that strange if Ranta secretly harbored feelings for her. But he'd never shown any sign of it. If anything, the way Haruhiro saw it, Merry wasn't Ranta's type. To go a bit further, he was probably more into Yume. As a matter of fact, Haruhiro suspected that Ranta really liked Yume.

Ranta was all bluster. He'd go on about how he wanted a woman, or he wanted to do this or that, but he'd never take direct action.

A line like "That woman belongs to me" just didn't suit Ranta. On top of that, he said, "If you want her back, just try and steal her from me!" There was something strange about that, too. Why did Ranta go out of his way to say that? To provoke Haruhiro? Well, it wouldn't be that uncommon for him to do so, but something was strange about it.

What was strange, and how? Think. He had to think.

"Ranta said Merry was his," Haruhiro said slowly. "He also said that if we want her back, 'just try and steal her.' Before that, I asked him, 'What happened to Merry?' That was his response." Haruhiro bit his lip lightly. "First, we can draw one conclusion:

Merry is alive. If she wasn't, he couldn't make her his. I couldn't steal her from him, either."

"Ranta-kun..." Shihoru forced herself to speak. "...was trying to tell us that?"

"I dunno." Haruhiro shook his head. "I couldn't tell you that much. But maybe. In terms of possibilities, I think, broadly speaking, we have two of them. Either Ranta stabbed us in the back, or, for some reason, he's pretending to have done so. Either way, in that situation, he couldn't just tell us Merry was fine, and not to worry. Ranta was on the other side, after all. But still. The 'If you want her back, just try and steal her' bit is a little weird. I mean, did he need to go out of his way to say that? If it was 'She's mine now, give up,' or something like that, I'd understand. But 'just try and steal her'... Maybe he's telling us to come take her. Maybe it meant that Merry is where he is, and he wants us to come save her. That's only one possibility, but..."

"Listen." Yume leaned against Shihoru. "Yume, she's always thought Ranta's a hopeless idiot, and she's still thinkin' that, but him betrayin' Yume and everyone else, doin' somethin' like that, that's just not Ranta, now is it?"

"Nah, I dunno about that." Kuzaku was pressing down on his knees. "At the very least, he was serious there. He came at me ready to kill. If Haruhiro and the others hadn't shown up, I think it would've gotten real bad for us. They were nearby, so we got rescued, and it was all fine. But if they hadn't been, Ranta, that bastard, I think he'd have killed both me and Shihoru."

"Well..." Haruhiro scratched the back of his neck. "He can get strangely into things, you know."

"I don't want to get killed because he got too into his role," Kuzaku said. "You know?"

"Well, yeah...."

"Um." Shihoru raised her hand.

Haruhiro didn't feel like there was any need for her to raise her hand and ask for permission before speaking, but he said, "Go ahead."

Shihoru nodded, then cleared her throat a little.

"If thinking about it isn't giving us any answers," she said, "I think we should come back to it later. In the end, Ranta-kun is the only one who knows what his true intentions are. Before that, what should we do from here on? What should our priority be? I think those are the more important questions."

"In that case, it's gotta be Merry-chan, don'tcha think?" Yume put in.

"I've gotta agree," Kuzaku said.

"Yeah," Haruhiro said. He sighed, then looked to Shihoru.

When she smiled just a little, Shihoru seemed awfully reliable. Talentless and immature as he was, Haruhiro needed to think, and think, and think until they got through this, but there was no need for him to be the only one wracking his brains. It was okay to lean on his comrades' wisdom at times.

Besides, if he was aware he was talentless and immature, he should rely on his comrades where he was able to. If he could do everything by himself, he wouldn't be so talentless or immature.

So what meaning was there in cornering himself, thinking, *I have to do it myself, I have to do it myself,* when he couldn't do it at all? That only served to satisfy himself.

Shihoru was shy, but that also made her cautious, and it meant she watched her surroundings carefully, thinking deeply about them. Her powers of observation and analysis were beyond Haruhiro's. Haruhiro needed to rely on Shihoru more.

"Saving Merry," Haruhiro agreed. "That's our top priority. For now, Ranta comes second. Merry's probably been taken captive by Forgan. It's not realistic for us to do anything about them by ourselves. If we're going to get the Rocks to help us, since they're going after Arnold of Forgan, we'll need to lend them a hand, too."

Shihoru's brow creased with worry, and she looked down, but when she noticed Haruhiro's eyes on her, she nodded slightly.

"I think that's our only choice. If we could have the Rocks attack Forgan...then rescue Merry while they do..."

"Use the Rocks as a decoy, you mean?" Kuzaku asked.

"Kuzaku." Haruhiro lowered his voice. "You're being too blatant."

"Oh. Right." Kuzaku glanced quickly at the retreat. "But that's basically what it'd be, right?"

"Nah, I mean, we can't do that," said Haruhiro. "The Rocks are fellow Day Breakers. If we're going to get their help, we'll be open about it, bow our heads to them properly, and ask. Naturally, we'll thank them, too."

"What do you think's happenin' with Araran?" Yume looked in the direction Arara was taken.

"They looked intimidating." Shihoru touched her lips.

That was right. If Arara was punished for picking a selfish fight with Forgan, and she got locked up, what would happen to them taking vengeance? If that plot got put on hold, it was going to be a problem.

Still, there was nothing Haruhiro and his group could do about that. For now, they would have to think things over while watching how events developed.

And then, someone's stomach rumbled loudly.

"Whoa!" Yume's eyes went wide, and she held her belly. "There's a surprise. Never knew it could rumble that loud. Y'think some sorta creature's livin' in there?"

"Ahhh..." Kuzaku hung his head. "Man, I'm hungry. And tired."

"It shows you're still alive," Shihoru murmured. She looked like she was having a tough time, too.

Haruhiro looked up to the sky and sighed. *Ranta. Is it okay for me to trust you, man? Your contemptible face is the only thing coming to mind. Maybe I shouldn't trust you after all?*

Whichever the case, he had to do something about the food situation.

When Haruhiro went to stand up, Katsuharu came out of his retreat. He was carrying something like a sieve that was full.

"You all must be hungry. I've not much to offer, living in a thatched hut like I do, but eat some of this."

Kuzaku put his hands together and looked at the man. "Thanks!"

Haruhiro and Shihoru looked at one another. Was this okay? It would have to be. It was said you couldn't fight on an empty stomach, after all.

The food Katsuharu brought them included some sort of sticky cake made with potatoes or some other vegetable, some sort of dried meat, and some sort of bittersweet dumpling. They were all unfamiliar, but none of them were bad. No one was going to be calling any of them a delicacy, but they seemed nourishing enough. Katsuharu even went and drew a bucket of water for the group. He was an awfully caring man. What was more, he crouched down nearby, smiling and seemingly enjoying watching Haruhiro and the others eat.

"Um, thank you," Haruhiro said awkwardly.

"It's fine, it's fine."

"Erm... What about Arara-san? What do you think's actually going to happen with her?"

"Well, that's not for me to decide."

"But if you're her uncle—" Haruhiro began.

"When it comes to a mere wanderer like me, it's all the same to the village whether I'm here or not. I wanted to stop my niece before she took action, but I was too late. Now that she has, it's out of my hands."

"That's awful..."

"Well, my older brother, one of the heads of the House of Nigi, is not the heartless sort who would make his own daughter commit seppuku because he can't manage her. So long as she is still alive, she can do anything. Right?"

"You figure?" Haruhiro asked.

"Luckily, as a wanderer, I can abandon this village at any time," Katsuharu added.

Oh, so that was it.

This guy's probably already made up his mind, thought Haruhiro. *No matter what happens, he'll save his niece, and support her. That's why he can act so relaxed.*

"Those people." Katsuharu gestured to the retreat with his chin. He must have meant the Rocks. "They say they'll go on the move first thing in the morning. If you people intend to follow them, get some sleep."

"Right."

"Darn, my lower back hurts." Katsuharu stood up and rubbed the small of his back. "Having to worry about the house and all that must be such a pain. Even though all of us are born, meet people, part ways, laugh, cry, and die just the same, I can't help but feel sorry for my brother and his wife. Not that they'd want to hear that from a lowly man like me."

Yume was already snoring softly, having fallen asleep while still sitting, using Shihoru's shoulder as a pillow. Shihoru looked pretty tired, too. When Haruhiro laid Yume down on her side, Shihoru lay down next to her.

"Thanks, Haruhiro-kun," Shihoru said sleepily.

"No, I should thank you," Haruhiro said.

"I'm sure...she's definitely going to be okay."

"Yeah."

Kuzaku curled his big body into a ball, shutting his eyes tight, and trying his hardest to fall asleep. No doubt he was worried sick for Merry, and that was keeping him awake.

In his heart, Haruhiro whispered, *I know that feeling. Because I feel the same way.*

Grimgar
of
Fantasy and Ash

12 | A New Feeling

THE WORD "CAMPFIRE" suddenly came to mind. Vaguely, he felt like he'd seen this scene once before. He'd probably been part of it himself.

There wasn't just one fire. There were a number of them spread out. It was loud and boisterous.

The orcs were talking about something as they drank, laughing occasionally, their arms around one another's shoulders. Little fights would break out, but all in good fun. They only looked rough because they were so big. The things they were doing were no different from what humans would do.

It was surprising to see, but the undead ate and drank, too. Though there were some groups of orcs or undead who stuck only with their own kind, they weren't the majority. Most of the orcs and undead didn't make distinctions as they told stories, drank booze, and ate fried meat and fish.

Though Onsa the goblin kept his distance, surrounded by his

wolves and nyaas, he didn't reject the orcs or undead who occasionally came over with drinks. He'd talk with them for a bit, and smile, too.

There weren't many, but there were races other than orcs and undead represented here, too. One was a half-man, half-horse centaur. That thin, pointy-eared guy with the ashen skin had to be an elf. There were a number of dwarves, too. There were guys who looked like humans shrunk down to less than half the size, and even guys who looked so inhuman they wouldn't have been out of place in Darunggar. It didn't look like they all got along, but they were partying without any trouble.

Ranta turned his eyes away from his jolly new comrades, sipping at a cup of spiced mead as he walked. Two or three nyaas were watching him from a distance; Ranta was being monitored.

Was Onsa the beastmaster using the nyaas to watch him on his own initiative? Or was someone like Takasagi the one behind it? He didn't know, but they didn't trust Ranta yet. Of course not.

"Hey." Ranta came to a stop, looking down at the woman who was hanging her head. "I said, 'Hey.' You could respond, at least."

Not far from his jolly comrades around the campfire, there was a woman sitting still, not moving. Though she was handcuffed, her hands were no longer bound behind her back. She was chained to a stake, so she couldn't move around, but she could at least stand up. Despite that, the woman was sitting with her legs to one side of her, practically motionless.

There was a canteen filled with water and a plate with food sitting at her knees. She hadn't so much as touched either of them.

"Drink some water at least, Merry. You're gonna die."

Merry just shook her head a little.

Ranta sighed. "You're so stubborn. Give up already. If you'll just be my woman, I can get you untied."

"I'd sooner die," she said weakly.

"You would, huh? Well, go ahead and die right there, then."

"Traitor..."

"Call me what you want, but it doesn't hurt, or even make me itch."

Ranta turned around. How would he get along with that jolly bunch? What did he have to do to meld into the group? Most of them didn't speak the human language. That was the first problem.

Well, back in Darunggar, he'd managed to get reasonably close to the people in Well Village. If he just got fired up, threw himself into it, and partied like a fool, he could make most things work out.

"I'm not getting fired up, though," Ranta muttered.

Guess I'll go find Takasagi, he thought.

But Takasagi was having a grand old time drinking with some orcs and undead. The centaur, dwarves, elves, and midgets were with him, too. For a human, they showed him a lot of respect. He wasn't necessarily a father figure, but maybe he was like a big brother to them.

For some reason, Ranta just couldn't convince himself to join the ring that had formed around Takasagi. He was being uncharacteristically passive. The way he was acting just wasn't like him.

When Ranta happened to glance over, a number of undead

229

had surrounded Merry. Merry was looking down. What were they planning to do? He wanted to rush over there right away, but he held back.

This was her fault. Wasn't it, though? If she wanted to survive, and wanted to avoid bad things happening to her, she should have just joined Jumbo.

She would've been the lone woman in an otherwise all-male group. Sure, it'd be a bizarre situation to be in. Still, Jumbo probably would have said, *That, too, could prove entertaining,* or something like that, and accepted her. If Jumbo agreed to something, all of these guys would go along with it.

She had come right out and said clearly that she'd never join Forgan. She had to be an idiot. Letting an opportunity like that slip by—she was too damn stupid. Ranta had snapped.

Fine, let her have it her way, he thought. *Let them screw her, beat her senseless, kill her, and throw away the body. It's no skin off my back.* That was what he thought, but then he had to go and open his mouth. "I've been meaning to make this woman mine for a while now. So, please, don't let anyone else touch her for a while. If she keeps insisting she won't be mine, then you can do whatever you want with her. I won't have any regrets."

She was technically his comrade. If he abandoned her without at least trying to do something, he'd have trouble sleeping at night. He knew they'd probably reject his request anyway, but he figured he had to try.

He'd been in for a surprise.

"Very well," Jumbo had responded all too easily. "You may

keep the woman tied up until you are satisfied. Leave the human woman alone," he'd ordered the others.

It was Jumbo's order. Those undead probably weren't going to eat her or anything. Well, they might mess with her a bit.

—*Mess with her?* Ranta wondered. *How? Do a little of this, a little of that?*

"This'll be something to see." Ranta forced himself to laugh. "She's got it coming to her. I went out of my way to try and save her. Screw that ungrateful harpy…"

As he watched with bated breath, the undead walked away from Merry. Ranta felt a sense of relief, but also irritation at himself for feeling relieved. Why should he have to worry about that bitch? This was stupid.

Suddenly, there was an outburst of laughter. The giant orc had put Takasagi up on his shoulders, and the guy was shouting, "Hey, stop it! Let me down!" in a panic.

If Ranta remembered correctly, that orc who was big even for an orc was called Godo Agaja. Looking at his clothes, his weapons, and the way he acted, he was clearly trying to imitate Jumbo, but at times like this, he was completely different. The way he fooled around more than anyone didn't quite put a smile on Ranta's face; but it was so innocent. Even with the way he looked, he might be surprisingly young.

It looked like they were having a lot of fun. He wanted to join them. No, it wasn't that he wanted to fool around with them—it was that he thought it would be best to join the group. But he couldn't quite bring himself to.

Jumbo was sitting atop a little hill, drinking. It might have been a coincidence, but he was alone.

"Okay..." Ranta said, quietly trying to motivate himself. He approached Jumbo.

He thought the man was alone, but he wasn't. Ranta was shocked. There was someone sitting there, near the foot of the hill, cowering before him.

The other person had his four arms out of the sleeves of his robe, leaving him unclothed from the waist up, but, because his whole body was wrapped in blackish bandages, his skin wasn't exposed. The mouth that peeked through those bandages was nothing more than a gash. There was no life in his eyes; they were like the eyes of a dead fish. He was an undead, so that was to be expected—or was it? Still, from the looks of it, the other undead weren't like that, so it seemed fair to say his eyes were especially dead.

"H-hey there, Arnold-san," Ranta said nervously.

It seemed like Arnold was a pretty big deal, so Ranta figured he should at least greet the guy, but he got no response.

What, you're ignoring me? he thought.

When he somewhat timidly tried to walk past Arnold, he felt a cold, damp wind blow past him.

It went, "Ohhh..."

Was that a voice? Maybe? Did Arnold-san respond?

Ranta laughed, saying, "N-nice to meet you," then climbed up the hill to sit next to Jumbo.

That was scary just now.

No, maybe not?

Yeah. There was nothing to be scared of. That was just the un-dead Arnold's way of reacting. It was an Arnoldian answer. That was all. Ranta had just been a little startled by it, was all.

He cleared his throat, then it was time to decide how to address Jumbo. While he was thinking, Jumbo interjected.

"Have you been drinking?" he asked quietly.

"W-well, yeah." Ranta hurriedly took a sip of mead. "Um, er... So, you aren't gonna go hang out with the rest of them?"

"I'm too much of a snob for that, you see."

"Huh?"

"I'm not good at letting loose."

Jumbo wasn't the type to get out there and mingle. Was that it? But if he really was a snob, he wouldn't go calling himself one, would he? Besides, Jumbo was smiling. Occasionally, he would let out a low laugh. He enjoyed watching his comrades drink, talk, and play around from the bottom of his heart. That was what it looked like.

"Arnold and I are alike," said Jumbo.

"Ohhh. Y-you are?"

You're not like Arnold, Ranta couldn't help but think.

He got the feeling that, left to his own devices, Arnold would always be alone. That was why Jumbo was going out of his way to be like, *I get you, I get you, I'm the same way,* and sticking with him.

Ranta would never do something like that himself, but he knew some guys who cared too much about others that would. He hated their type. If someone was alone, let them be isolated.

If they found themselves tormented by the feeling of loneliness as a result, it was their own fault.

Was Jumbo a surprisingly sensitive man?

That was kind of a letdown. Despite his appearance, he was way too normal.

There was a saying, "If you want to shoot a general, start by shooting his horse," but really, if you just shot the general to begin with, the rest would more or less fall into place. Forget the small fry, if he was going to curry favor with someone, it was going to be Jumbo.

"Erm, how about trying to join them, maybe?" Ranta asked. "Everyone would like that, wouldn't they? I think so, at least."

"I don't want to ruin their fun," said Jumbo.

"Nah, I don't think you would be. No way. I think just having you there, it'd get them excited—like, everyone would get all fired up, you know?"

"This works best for Arnold and me," said Jumbo. "My companions understand that, too."

"Ah..." Ranta felt himself grimacing. "Was I out of line there, maybe?"

"You needn't be so guarded." Jumbo's tone was gentle. "You, too, are one of my companions."

"Yeah, but I'm a total newcomer..."

"A companion is a companion."

"Well, yeah...sure, but..."

Ranta rubbed his face with his left hand. This was weird.

If Arnold was a big deal, Jumbo was obviously an even bigger

deal. He could do more to act the part. If he had been more ar-
rogant, Ranta would be able to tolerate that, and it might even be
easier for Ranta to accept.

But what had he done instead? The way Jumbo spoke was
always frank, never keeping him at a distance. There was even a
warmth to it.

"So, like, why are you so darn fluent in the human language?"
Ranta asked.

"I was raised by a man."

"Oh. I see, you were raised by a man, huh." Ranta's eyes nearly
shot out of his skull. "Whaaa?! By a man?!"

"Yeah."

"By a man, you mean, like, a human...right?"

"Of course. In my earliest memories, I was already with that
man. I don't know his name. To the day he died, he never gave
me his name. I, myself, had no sense that I was an orc. I thought
myself the same as that man, and never questioned it."

The man never even told Jumbo his name, so, of course, the
man never said anything about where he came from, his history,
or anything else about himself.

Anyway, the man walked all over Grimgar with the young
Jumbo. According to Jumbo's recollection, the two of them spent
a little over ten years traveling together, from the frozen lands of
the north to the Tenryu Mountains in the south; from the blue
seas of the east to the rusty seas of the west.

The man may not have spoken at all about himself, but that
didn't mean he was the silent type. Whenever there was time, he

told Jumbo the legends, traditions, narratives, stories, and histories of each place. The man could speak many languages. He was fine no matter where he went, from steep mountains to deserts, wastelands, major cities; yet he never got careless. The man was well versed in the ways of avoiding danger and getting out of a crisis when he found himself in one. Naturally, Jumbo learned from the man, and mastered such skills himself. If he hadn't, he wouldn't have been able to stay with the man. He'd have been left all alone.

For Jumbo, traveling with the man had been his entire life. He'd believed, if he just followed the man, the journey would go on forever.

Then, one day, the man lay down complaining of a headache, and he never rose again. The next thing Jumbo knew, the man's heart stopped.

Jumbo knew the proper way to bury the dead, so he did it. Then he was left with only himself.

"I see," Ranta said slowly. "So you learned the human language from him."

"I've probably inherited nearly everything he had."

"You have to wonder, though, who was that guy?" Ranta asked. He noticed that at some point he'd started talking to Jumbo like an equal. But he didn't feel like correcting himself, and he didn't think he ought to. "There're all sorts out there, huh. So many people, living lives I couldn't even imagine."

"And your path, too, is one no other can walk."

"Well, yeah, if you put it that way."

"Each of us lives and dies in a myriad of different ways."

"You lost a number of comrades today, huh."

"I mourn the loss of my companions. I was just offering a drink to them earlier."

"Everyone else, they don't seem that sad," Ranta commented.

"We are all equal in death. Even the undead, who are without life, will lose their forms and be destroyed. What is there to be sad about?"

"But still." Ranta hung his head.

What is this? he wondered. *He's making me want to say how I really feel. Or rather, I can't say anything else.*

No, that's not it.

I don't want to tell him anything but how I really feel.

"But if you can't see your friends, your comrades anymore, doesn't that make you feel lonely?" Ranta asked.

"We all must part eventually," Jumbo answered.

"Even so, if I don't want to part just yet... Is that selfish?"

"Many orcs think like this," said Jumbo. "We are each born fated to die. When death inevitably comes, our bodies rot away to become the soil, and we go through the cycle to be born once more."

"Do you think that, too?" Ranta asked.

"I don't know how this world works."

"Ohhh. So there's stuff even you don't know, huh. It's just, somehow, it feels like you know everything."

"I don't know what I don't know," said Jumbo. "We can only learn a small portion of all there is to know in our short lives. That is true for all of us."

"Jumbo."

"What is it?"

"Sorry for asking you for that favor, about the woman," Ranta said hesitantly. "I..."

"Drink." Jumbo lifted his glass and smiled at Ranta.

There was something weird happening here, if Ranta did say so himself. When he saw Jumbo smile, he felt his chest squeeze tight, and he teared up, without understanding why.

This was—love?

No, no, no. That wasn't it. Obviously. As if he'd fall in love. But he felt his emotions being shaken intensely. That was a fact.

Ranta knocked back his wooden cup, downing the rest of his mead.

"Damn, this stuff's sweet."

"Is it not to your taste?" asked Jumbo.

"It's not like I hate it or anything. I figure, soon enough, I'll get used to it, and I'll be able to think it tastes good."

"You will?" asked Jumbo.

"Hey..." The voice that spoke was like a damp wind blown up from below.

When Ranta glanced over, Arnold was looking up at him, about to throw something. It was a container with a cork in it.

When Ranta stuck out his hand without meaning to, Arnold tossed it up to him. He managed to catch it without dropping it somehow. He gave it a little shake, and there was a splashing sound.

"Juin," Arnold said, making a drinking gesture.

"Huh? For me? Drink it?"

"Ahhh... Yah..."

"Well, just a little, then."

Ranta uncorked the container, pouring its contents into the wooden cup. His mead had been an amber color, but this was whitish. When he took a sip, it was a bit sour, but not too harsh. It was a fairly dry taste, and he downed it in no time.

"Yeah," Ranta said. "This is good stuff."

Arnold let out an unnerving "Heee..." sound. It might have been a laugh.

Ranta naturally laughed back.

"Thanks, Arnold."

"...elcome..."

"Heh..." Ranta looked down, whispering to himself. "If that doesn't beat all. Damn."

Grimgar
of
Fantasy and Ash

13 | Don't Decide to Do Something, Resolve Yourself To

WHEN DAWN CAME, the village was enveloped in morning mist. The thickness of this mist was just seriously not normal. It was bad enough that you couldn't see your own outstretched hand.

Haruhiro had thought maybe when the morning came, he'd get a view of the whole village. Not a chance. He couldn't even make out Katsuharu's retreat, which was right next to him, and he didn't notice Rock until the guy kicked him in the back.

"We're going, Haruhiro. Tag along."

"Huh? Where to?"

"You guys want to save your comrade from Forgan, don't you? We want to crush Arnold. I can't say our interests are perfectly aligned, but it'd be impossible for you guys to rescue her on your own. We want all the help we can get. So, cooperate with us. You do that, and we'll help you, too."

Haruhiro had no objection. It was just what he wanted to

hear; but Arara hadn't come back, and he hadn't heard anything about them having decided what to do with her, so what were they going to do?

They said Haruhiro was the only one who needed to come along for now, so along with Rock, who had Gettsu on his shoulder, Moyugi, the strongest dread knight in active service, Tsuga, the priest with a buzz-cut, and Katsuharu, the group of five people and one animal pushed through fog so dense you couldn't see more than an inch ahead.

There were many elevation differences inside the village. The ground was well-trod like a game trail, but they could hardly see the buildings through the fog, and there were no signs of any people.

However, Haruhiro soon began to sense some sort of presence. Probably nyaas. Those catlike, monkey-like creatures were surveilling them from beyond the fog. It wasn't just one or two of them, either. There were far more.

The reason for that became clear very shortly. Haruhiro's instincts had been on the mark. The building was twice as tall as Katsuharu's retreat, with probably more than three times the frontage and depth.

There were furs plastered to the walls and roof. Also, nyaas. Nyaas at the windows, outside, and on the roof, too. Nyaas everywhere. An incredible number of them. All the nyaas were scrutinizing them closely. It was pretty scary.

"I-Is this the nyaas' house...or something like that?" Haruhiro stuttered.

"This is the abode of one called Setora, of the House of Shuro," Katsuharu answered. "You people wait here. If you intrude any further without permission, there's no telling what might happen. Let me go explain your business here."

"We'll have to wait and see how it goes, huh?" Rock was grinning.

Moyugi pressed the middle finger of his right hand against the bridge of his glasses without a word. Actually, he'd hardly spoken all morning. He seemed to be in a bad mood somehow and was being pretty blatant about it.

"He's always like this when he gets up," Tsuga whispered in Haruhiro's ear. "For all the self-important things he says, he's pretty childish, huh."

"Tsuga," Moyugi said in a frightening voice. "I can hear you perfectly."

"I'll bet," Tsuga said, as if it was nothing. "I said it so you could hear. If I hadn't, that'd be talking behind your back."

Moyugi clicked his tongue, and Rock guffawed.

Katsuharu approached Shuro Setora's house, which wasn't actually the nyaas' house. Immediately, the nyaas' eyes all focused on Katsuharu.

If Haruhiro ended up at the center of attention like that, he'd probably stop moving despite himself. Katsuharu kept going like it didn't matter. But he didn't make it to the door. Before he could, the door opened from inside, and someone came out.

It's...a human? Haruhiro realized. That's Shuro Setora?

None of the man's skin was exposed, face included. His face

was all covered with scarlet-and-indigo-colored fabric, or leather, or some other material.

He was about the same height as Haruhiro, maybe. But he looked big. The fact of the matter was, he *was* big. As for what was big about him, it was his arms. His arms weren't just long; they were thick. Then, on top of that, they were wrapped in what looked like metal armor.

Just what was Shuro Setora?

"Oh," Katsuharu said, taking a step back. "Enba, huh."

Apparently this wasn't Shuro Setora. Enba remained silent, turning his head right twice, then left three times.

That's kind of scary, you know? thought Haruhiro.

"Enba." Katsuharu took another half-step backward. "The truth is, I have something important to discuss with Setora."

"Something to discuss with me, you say?" said another person, sticking their head out of a window on the second floor.

This person also had their skin covered with scarlet and indigo cloth and other materials. But in their clothing, there was a large gap for their eyes, from behind which two eyeballs peered out.

"What is it, wanderer?" Setora asked. Judging by the voice, they were a woman. "Nothing useful, I'm sure."

"That's some way to greet me, Setora," Katsuharu shot back. "This, after I spent all that time playing with you when you were just a little girl."

"That just means you were a good-for-nothing with too much time on your hands even back then. No respectable person wastes their time playing with little brats."

"Indeed. There's nothing I can say to that."

"Setora," Rock called out to her. What, he was dropping the honorific already? "I've got a favor to ask you."

"I refuse." Setora pulled her head back inside.

"You're always so rude, Rock," Moyugi said spitefully with a sigh, brushing his bangs back with his fingers as he looked up to the window. "You, the lovely young lady up there. Might I ask you to grace us once more with a glimpse of your beauteous form? Even for just a moment. Please, allow me to offer a poem extolling your greatness."

Whoa, what was that? He's being kind of creepy, thought Haruhiro. But, in the surprise to end all surprises, after a short while, Setora stuck her head back out the window.

"What is with that outsider?" she demanded. "Is his brain full of maggots?"

Moyugi said, "See, I've got her now," under his breath, then turned to Setora with a smile. "Shuro Setora, I am Moyugi, the strongest dread knight in active service, here just to see you."

"What a bizarre fellow," she murmured.

"Do you prefer the ordinary?" Moyugi asked. "You don't look like it."

"Enba, dispose of him."

Before Haruhiro even had time to be surprised, Enba attacked Moyugi. If those arms hit him, there was no way he wouldn't die instantly. However, Moyugi seemed to have anticipated this, evading Enba's right arm in one smooth motion.

As Enba followed up with a swing of his left arm, Rock closed in. He slipped past Enba's left arm, getting in close, and just as Haruhiro was wondering what he was going to do—incredibly, Rock wrapped his arms around Enba's torso. Then he braced himself and lifted Enba up.

"Hoooorah!" Rock shouted.

He threw him. Enba may not have been that massive, but he was still much taller than the diminutive Rock. Based on his overall thickness, he had to weigh more than twice what Rock did. Yet Rock was easily able to throw Enba. What sheer idiot strength he had.

Enba braced himself for the landing and got back up again quickly.

When he went to lunge at Rock again, Setora called out, "Stop! Enba, the way you are now, he'll just break you. Forgive me for lacking the ability to have made you stronger."

"Nah, I had no intention of breaking him, anyway." As Rock flashed her a grin, Gettsu climbed up onto his shoulder. "This is one of those golems, huh? Just like Pingo's Zenmai."

"Pingo..." Setora said. "You're acquaintances of Soma's, are you?"

"We're in his clan. You know what a clan is?"

"I don't. But I can guess. Enba, catch me."

As soon as Setora said that, Enba ran over underneath the window. She made a nimble jump down from the window, landing on Enba's left shoulder.

"I'll deign to hear whatever it is you have to say. But first, let me check one thing. Does it have something to do with Arara?"

It turned out, Setora and Arara were around the same age, and they had been childhood friends. Because she was the third daughter of one of the six houses—the House of Shuro, which carried on a tradition of necromancy—she'd associated with Arara, the eldest daughter of the House of Nigi, foremost of the four samurai houses.

Despite that, while Arara was the heir of her house, Setora had two elder sisters and was not the heir. On top of that, despite being born into a house that practiced necromancy, she'd come to devote herself to the skills of the onmitsu. As was apparent from looking around here, it was the nyaas. She had gotten completely hooked on the creatures, which were primarily raised by the village's onmitsu spies.

Though she still made flesh golems as a necromancer, most of her passion went into raising and breeding nyaas, so Setora was seen as a nuisance, and a stain on the good name of the House of Shuro.

Haruhiro might have thought, *Well, what's the big deal?* but they probably had their own traditions, their common sense, their standards, and all sorts of other things to consider.

One was the heir to the House of Nigi, the other was an embarrassment to the House of Shuro. That had made Arara and Setora a contrasting pair, once upon a time. Still, that didn't necessarily mean the two of them had grown distant.

"What a fool Arara was, falling for a weakling like Tatsuru," commented Setora. "Still, I always had a feeling she'd go astray somewhere. If she were the sort of woman who could keep quiet and inherit the House of Nigi, she'd never have paid me any mind."

"I was wrong, too." Katsuharu slumped his shoulders. "I should have stayed a wanderer, and not gotten involved with Arara. I may have been a bad influence on her."

"You can say that again, Wanderer," Setora said scornfully. "You're the root of every kind of evil."

"That's awfully harsh. I've been trying to reflect on my actions, you know."

"It's too late. If she picks a personal fight with Forgan, and that leads to sparks reaching the village, they won't let her off with being sealed in a cave. They may well cut her hair and expel her."

"Cut her hair..." Rock's eyes went wide. "Wait, how short are we talking here?! They wouldn't shave her bald, would they?!"

"This short, I'd say." Katsuharu pointed to his shoulders. "When the women of the village turn six, they grow their hair long. That means a short-haired woman is no member of the village."

"Like a bob cut, huh?" Rock nodded. "That'd look pretty good on her. Well, anything looks good on Arara."

That aside, what were they doing visiting Setora the nyaa-wrangling necromancer during a situation where that might happen to Arara? Haruhiro more or less had it figured out. It was just like he'd thought.

"I didn't expect the hair cutting thing, though," Rock said. "Her being disowned and expelled was more or less assumed. Either way, we're still going to avenge Tatsuru. I want your help with that, Setora. Forgan has this goblin beastmaster called Onsa, and he's keeping a lot of nyaas, you see. You've got to fight nyaas with nyaas. I can't turn anywhere else for help with that."

It was true, these nyaa critters were trouble. It still wasn't clear how effective they were in combat, but they seemed excessively nimble, and could hide themselves and move around silently. They'd no doubt been trained to alert their trainer if they detected enemies. That meant they could be laid out in a network. If their opponent was operating a nyaa security network, they had no choice but to try to break through with force.

That meant even if they could find where Forgan was, searching for Arnold's specific whereabouts would still be difficult. The same went for finding where Merry was being held captive. Obviously, it would be practically impossible to rescue Merry quietly.

"How many nyaas does Forgan have?" Setora's expression was completely unreadable, and her brusque tone hardly changed at all.

"Maybe ten, maybe twenty..." Rock held up both hands, tilting his head to the side. "No clue."

"I keep a total of one hundred and twenty-four nyaas. Of those, eighty-two are usable."

"I'd say the enemy has maybe thirty, at most," Katsuharu said, stroking his chin. "That's only my intuition, though, so it may not be reliable."

"Indeed, I can't rely on it." Setora snorted. "Still, I doubt they'll have more than double that. If that's all, my nyaas can keep them under control."

"You'd do that for us?!" Rock said, his glee showing clearly.

"I refuse."

"Seriously? It sounded like things were leading up to you agreeing to do it, just now."

"That was your imagination. For a start, would there be some merit for me in doing so? I could ask the same of you people. The wanderer aside, what do you outsiders have to gain from helping Arara with her worthless revenge?"

"I fell for her, so there's that," said Rock.

"Say what?"

"I fell for Arara. If the woman I fell for is putting her life on the line to accomplish something, I've gotta be willing to take a risk or two for her."

"Do you think if you do all that for her, the woman in question will fall for you, too? You're wasting your time."

"Huh? Why would that make Arara fall for me? Hardly any time's passed since Tatsuru died. It'd never happen."

"This is making less and less sense," Setora fumed. "What are you doing it for, then?"

"I already told you, it's because I fell for her. I'll make the woman I love's wish come true. What happens after that doesn't matter."

"I understand," Setora snapped. "You're a complete fool. No, you all must be fools."

"I'd appreciate it if you wouldn't lump me in with him," Moyugi said, pointing at Rock. "This man might be a fool, but by no means am I one."

"That's right." Rock stretched a bit, then threw his arm around Moyugi's shoulder. "I might be a fool, but my comrades are just having fun tagging along. Right, Moyugi?"

"Would you let go of me? I hate being touched by other men."

"In a way, we may be even worse than Rock." Tsuga's smile was so peaceful it was kind of scary.

"Regardless," Setora said. She sighed a little. "Even if you people have a reason, I have none. If Arara is expelled from the village, she can live freely. Revenge is pointless. Tell that fool she should forget Tatsuru already, and—"

"A-a deal!" Haruhiro burst out.

Uh oh...

He couldn't help but go and open his mouth.

Haruhiro glanced to Rock, Moyugi, Tsuga, and Katsuharu. None of them were going to try and stop him. Well, it looked like he was stuck. He'd have to finish what he'd started saying.

"Can we make a deal?" Haruhiro asked. "We could give you something in exchange for your help. If we do that, there's something in it for you."

"Do you believe you're able to offer me what I want?" Setora demanded.

"That...I'm not sure of. It would depend what it is."

"If I had to choose a word for it, it would be material."

"Material... Wait. For what?"

"Golems," Setora began, patting Enba on the head, "are made by stitching together parts from corpses. The more freshly dead, the better, they say. But, the truth is, they apparently don't even have to come from the dead. I've yet to try it myself, but I hear there are methods for using parts from the living."

"So, basically, what you're saying is, 'Give me a part of your body'?" Haruhiro asked.

"One arm." Setora looked Haruhiro's body up and down with awfully cold eyes. Those were the eyes of someone evaluating a product. "No. It's only an experiment, so I can let you off with just one eyeball. Why, yes. I think an eyeball will do quite nicely. It will be something to toy with."

"Just so you're aware," Tsuga explained calmly, "if she takes your arm, or your eyeball, light magic can't bring it back. Even a shaman shouldn't be able to do that."

"Isn't that common sense?" Moyugi pressed on the bridge of his glasses with the middle finger of his right hand while letting out a gentle sigh. "It seems we have no choice. Let's give up on the nyaas. Our optional objective will be more difficult, but the main one is still doable."

"Oh, yeah?" Rock frowned. "Too bad, huh."

The optional objective. Was that what he thought it was? Haruhiro and his party's objective, rescuing Merry.

Well, Moyugi may have been right. If they could confuse the nyaas, it would make having Haruhiro use Stealth to sneak into enemy territory, then rescuing Merry and running, a viable option. If they were going to do something about the enemy's nyaa security network, they absolutely needed Setora and her nyaas.

Haruhiro pulled out his dagger with the hand guard. He tried to bring it up to his own eye, but he had no confidence he could do it right. Setora was sitting on Enba's shoulder.

"Um, sorry." Haruhiro approached Enba, offering the dagger

hilt first. "Could you use this to do it? If I try to do it myself, and screw it up, it'd be a waste. I'll sit still the best that I can. If possible, I'd prefer you take the left eye. Because I'm right-handed, you see. If you could do it real quick, I'd be much obliged."

Setora's eyes narrowed slightly. "You're saying you'll make the deal?"

"Yes," Haruhiro said. "Oh, right. Also, Tsuga-san, when she's done, heal up the wound, please."

"I can do that." Tsuga was still smiling. The guy had clearly reached enlightenment.

"You're okay with this?" Katsuharu seemed a little flustered.

"I'm not *okay* with it, but it's just one eye, not both, so fine, whatever," Haruhiro said. "My comrade's life is at stake. I want to raise our odds, even if only a little. If I don't do everything I can, and then end up regretting it later, I wouldn't like that, you know?"

Rock and Moyugi looked at one another. *This guy's an idiot,* they must have been thinking.

Was he an idiot? It was hard to say. Whatever the case, he'd said everything he had to say. There was something he could do to accomplish their goal, so he was going to do it. Haruhiro didn't exactly have a level head right now. He wasn't thinking deeply about it. He felt like he'd get scared if he did, so he was deliberately not thinking.

"Put that thing away." Setora nimbly hopped down from Enba's shoulder, drawing the thin short sword at her waist. "I'm more used to using my own blade. You're absolutely sure about this?"

"Go ahead." Haruhiro returned his dagger to its sheath, clearing his throat. "So, should I bend over? To get to the right height. Or should I crouch down?"

"Sit."

"Right. Okay then."

Haruhiro sat with his knees in front of him. He wasn't feeling that tense. Or afraid. That only lasted until Setora crouched down and opened his left eye with her left hand.

Ohhhhhh, crap. Seriously? She's seriously doing this? Will it hurt? I bet it will.

The dagger closed in.

Hurry up. Get it over with already.

Haruhiro held his breath. Right after he did, she inserted the knife between his eyeball and eye socket. What he felt was not so much pain as an intense feeling that there was a foreign body that didn't belong there. The pain was sure to come. He winced without meaning to. That must have caused the blade to nick something. He heard something like a small puncturing sound, and then came the pain.

Hurry, hurry, do it, do it, do it, he screamed internally. *Huh? Why?*

Setora pulled back her blade. "It can wait..."

"Huh...?" Haruhiro blinked. There was a pain in his left eye. The tears started to run.

"You have things to do, don't you? I can take the material from you once you're done." Setora turned her back to him. "I'll handle Forgan's nyaas. Rest assured. My nyaas would never lose."

DON'T DECIDE TO DO SOMETHING, RESOLVE YOURSELF TO

"Ah..." Haruhiro shut his left eye tight, pressing down on it from above his eyelid. Damn, it hurt. "Thank you..."

"I'll be taking my payment. There's no need for thanks." With that, Setora went inside the building along with Enba.

Tsuga tapped Haruhiro on the shoulder. "You want me to heal that?"

"Please..."

"Why, everything went exactly as I expected," Moyugi whispered, gloating, but Haruhiro thought that absolutely had to be a lie.

"Well, whatever the case, it's all good, huh?" Rock winked to Haruhiro.

Maybe Haruhiro was supposed to wink back, but his left eye still wasn't healed, so he wasn't quite sure he could do it, and he didn't want to, either.

Katsuharu raised his goggles up on top of his head, crossing his arms.

"Now, that just leaves Arara."

Grimgar of Fantasy and Ash

14 | With These Hands

IN THE END, their reading of the situation may have been too optimistic.

In the midst of the fog, four men moved forward carrying a palanquin.

Though it was called a palanquin, it was a simple one: just a rectangular board with two long poles beneath it. A woman dressed in a crude, unbleached cloth robe sat on top of the board. Or rather, she was being forced to sit there. Her hands were bound behind her back, and the ropes around her neck, chest, hips, and thighs were tied tightly to the poles. The way she was tied, she couldn't move. If she moved carelessly, she'd likely strangle herself.

The woman was sitting with her back straight, but her face was looking downward. Her hair was short. They hadn't just cut it to shoulder length; they had gone all the way to just below her ears.

Haruhiro, who was hiding on a hill in the shadows of the trees to watch events unfold, assumed all of this had to be hitting her pretty hard. He didn't know how much, but he assumed it had to be shocking. After all, even for Haruhiro, who didn't know the situation that well, his first impression upon seeing her had been, *They took off a lot more than I thought they would.*

And even if that was fine because her hair would grow back, she was still being banished and expelled from her village.

The palanquin headed westward, further westward.

According to the information Setora had gathered using her nyaas, that was where Forgan had made camp. The men carrying the palanquin surely knew that.

Incidentally, at the point when the palanquin left the village without so much as a sendoff, the village readied themselves for battle. They weren't setting out to attack; they were hardening their defenses. It was a stance that said, *If you're going to come, come.* While cautious of an attack by Forgan, they were also trying to communicate, *We have no intention of starting anything ourselves.*

The other day, a group attacked Forgan, and it included people from this village, but that was by no means a representation of the will of the village, and it in fact had nothing to do with us. That was what the village was trying to say.

Arara was no longer Nigi Arara. Now that she had been disowned by the House of Nigi, she was simply Arara. The present head of the house's younger sister had two daughters, and it seemed the eldest of those two had now become heir to the House of Nigi.

When he heard that, Haruhiro had been taken aback. *Is it just that simple?* he thought.

Being the eldest daughter of the House of Nigi, foremost of the four samurai houses, he'd been sure they wouldn't just say she was no good and switch her for someone else. Besides, Arara was the daughter of the head of the house by blood. Haruhiro had expected, somewhat arbitrarily, that her mother would cover for her, and she would get off with a slap on the wrist.

He had been very wrong.

The village was throwing Arara out on her own, with none of her possessions. That was almost a death sentence.

Haruhiro and the others had planned to regroup once Arara was released, then try to take out Arnold and rescue Merry. However, now that this was happening to Arara, their plans were disrupted.

How far was the palanquin carrying Arara going to go? They wouldn't turn her over to Forgan, would they?

The people of the village seemed prideful, so they wouldn't try to appease Forgan like that. Or so Haruhiro hoped, but he couldn't say anything for certain.

Whatever the case, when someone was in a position of leadership in the village like the head of the House of Nigi, they would cut even their own daughter loose if she was deemed a detriment to the village. It was easy to condemn that as cruel, cold blooded, and inhumane. But if the head of the house showed mercy out of affection for her daughter, and that in turn put the village in danger, she would face more than just condemnation. Whatever her true feelings, her position as head of the house may have forced her to do this.

"This is bad." Haruhiro couldn't see the palanquin from his position. "They're getting pretty close to Forgan."

There were two broad directions he could see things going from here.

The first was that the men would lay down the palanquin before they came into contact with Forgan. In that case, it would just be a matter of collecting Arara right away.

However, in the second possibility—the one where they made contact with Forgan, essentially—that was going to become difficult. It seemed unlikely, but if the village contacted Forgan somehow, and there was an agreement to turn Arara over, that would be worse.

Haruhiro walked quickly along the top of the hill, going further and further to the west.

This hill was to the north of the course the palanquin had taken. Forgan was camped west-northwest of here at a spot where the ground was comparatively level, and the palanquin really did seem to be heading that way. The palanquin was going fairly slowly, so he could circle around ahead of them without too much rush.

Despite himself, he ended up thinking about Merry. Ranta, too.

Damn you, Ranta! he thought.

Not now. He banished the thoughts from his head.

The fog had gotten deeper. He didn't actually see it, but he thought he noticed something moving to his left. A nyaa, maybe? Was he imagining it?

Haruhiro nearly came to a stop, but he thought better of it and sped up instead.

Faintly, he could hear wolves howling. He had an incredibly bad feeling about this.

Why does nothing ever work out? he thought. It made him want to gripe a little. Not that he had anyone to listen to him, or anyone he would actually say that to.

He was done with this hill. The palanquin was still out of sight. Haruhiro descended the slope.

He really did sense some sort of presence. Had he been found by a nyaa that was tailing him? Should he verify that? No, he had to hurry on ahead right now. Westward. It was okay if his footsteps made some noise. Westward.

The ground of Thousand Valley had patches of damp soil and slippery rocks here and there, and almost none of it was flat. In some places, there were moss-covered fallen trees lying atop one another, and there were deep, gash-like holes everywhere. It was strangely difficult to walk here, but he'd gotten used to it.

Westward.

He saw it; the palanquin.

It seemed, at some point, he'd passed it. The palanquin was now heading toward Haruhiro.

The fog still showed no sign of clearing. He could probably see fewer than a hundred meters around him, but the sky was slightly blue. He could tell where the sun was, too. It was maybe ten o'clock in the morning.

According to the rough map that he had memorized in advance, there was a land formation that was like a little ravine about a kilometer past here. If they passed through that valley, they'd come to Forgan's camp. Was the palanquin going to stop before the ravine or not?

Hoping it would, Haruhiro continued westward while remaining careful not to be spotted by the palanquin bearers.

Oh, but—no, this wasn't his imagination. He was probably being monitored by nyaas.

When he suddenly heard the small, sharp cry of some animal, his heart jumped in shock. What? Was it a nyaa?

Moving forward with nervous steps, he found a black nyaa holding a striped nyaa down and biting at its throat. The striped nyaa was thrashing and resisting, but it was weak. The black nyaa glanced at him. The two were roughly the same size, but the black nyaa had the clear advantage.

It wasn't long before the striped nyaa went limp, at which point the black nyaa wagged its tail while opening its mouth as if to meow, but no sound came forth. This was called a silent meow, and it was apparently a way of signaling, *I'm a friend.*

Was it one of Setora's nyaas? He'd heard some nyaas might use a silent meow to trick humans, so he couldn't be sure. He also heard that a nyaa handler could see through an insincere silent meow, but that was beyond Haruhiro.

The black nyaa disappeared into the fog. For now, Haruhiro would have to assume it was on his side.

The palanquin was still moving forward. Weren't they going to stop? No. They showed no sign of it.

"Haruhiro," a voice called out from behind him.

He wished people wouldn't surprise him like that.

WITH THESE HANDS

Looking back, it was Kuro. He was crouched down and beckoning.

When Haruhiro approached, Kuro whispered in his ear. "Good news, or bad news. Which do you want to hear first?"

"Okay... Start with the good news."

"There is..." Kuro smiled maliciously. "...no good news."

"Then don't act like there is. What's the bad news?"

"Forgan seems to have noticed their delivery from the village. They're on the move."

"Yeah, I had a feeling that'd be the case," Haruhiro said grimly.

"The plan's to lay in waiting at the entrance to the ravine," Kuro said. "Once we've snagged the package, you guys can go steal the treasure."

"Sorry for the trouble...and thank you."

Kuro slapped Haruhiro on the shoulder lightly, then gave him the go sign.

Haruhiro nodded.

It was starting.

Because of Arara's harsher-than-expected punishment, they hadn't had the leeway to make adequate preparations. Haruhiro was feeling uncertain, but they'd have to go for it.

He followed Kuro. He was beginning to feel a fluttering in his chest. He had to make sure he didn't get too stiff. Even if there wasn't much time, he couldn't act haphazardly. He had to think as much as he could, then choose the best option.

The flow of time suddenly seemed to quicken. They reached the ravine in no time.

263

The ravine was a valley, maybe around twenty meters wide, between steep slopes to the north and south. The north and south sides were thick with trees, offering plenty of places to hide.

Rock, Moyugi, Kajita, Tsuga, and Sakanami were already on the north side, while Yume, Shihoru, Kuzaku, and Katsuharu were in position on the south side. Setora and Enba were elsewhere, giving orders to the nyaas. Kuro naturally went to join the Rocks, and Haruhiro headed toward where Yume and the others were.

Yume was the first to spot Haruhiro, and she waved to him. Shihoru, Kuzaku, and Katsuharu seemed to have noticed him, too. Haruhiro crouched down next to his comrades.

"I think we'll probably end up rescuing Arara-san around here."

"Meow." Yume nodded, biting her lower lip.

"'Kay." Kuzaku was sitting still, doing his best not to let his armor make noise. He was already wearing his helmet, and his shield was in hand, too.

"For our part," Shihoru said in a whisper, "once we've rescued Arara-san, Merry's next?"

"Yeah," said Haruhiro. "The Rocks and Arara-san will start a fight with Forgan. We support them while looking for Merry."

"It will depend on the situation, but...it may be better for the rest of us to act as decoys while you to go in alone, Haruhiro-kun," Shihoru said timidly.

"True. If that's what we do, Shihoru, I'll be counting on you."

Shihoru nodded, without even asking him what for. "Got it."

Of course, if she asked for an explanation, he'd give her one. But it was highly reassuring that she didn't need it. He didn't want to rely on Shihoru too much, and he had no intention of relying on her completely, but it would make a lot of difference to have a second pillar that could support the party.

The wolves howled. They weren't far from here.

He could just barely make out the palanquin.

It stopped.

There were still nearly another hundred meters to the ravine.

"Indeed..." Katsuharu said. He wiped his goggles with a finger.

The palanquin began moving forward again. If the men had just laid down the palanquin there, it would make this a lot easier, but there was no way things would be that convenient.

At this point, both the Rocks and Haruhiro's party were unwelcome guests in the village. They would likely never be able to enter again. Even so, as much as possible, they wanted to avoid any acts of open hostility against the village. If the village sent pursuers after them, the villagers knew Thousand Valley like the backs of their hands, which would make them more than just a pain to deal with. That was why, frustrating as it was, they couldn't assault the palanquin to save Arara. They had to wait.

They had to just wait until the situation changed.

"They're here," Yume whispered.

Beasts. They were racing through the valley in this direction. Wolves? It was a pack of black wolves.

The Rocks still hadn't moved. Katsuharu put his hand on the hilt of his sword.

265

It was hard to breathe. It felt like something was pressing down on his chest.

The black wolves howled, one after another. The leader of the pack was already two, three meters from the palanquin.

The men finally dropped the palanquin. With their weapons at the ready, they began to back away.

"It should be fine now!" Katsuharu raced out.

Though it felt a little too soon, Katsuharu had been holding himself back until now, even though he had to be worried sick about his niece. It was hard to blame him.

Now that one of them moved, the rest had to follow. When Haruhiro waved his hand and gave the signal, Kuzaku jumped out and Yume followed. Haruhiro would stay in the rear, protecting Shihoru for now.

The Rocks acted in response to Haruhiro and the others. Kajita led the charge.

"Ohhhhhhhhhhhhhhhhhhhh!" Kajita let out a great War Cry.

The black wolf pack flinched, coming to a stop, then all looked up to the north slope in unison. By that point, the rest of the Rocks had already split up and were nowhere to be seen.

Katsuharu headed straight for the palanquin, shouting, "You people!" at the men, who still hadn't turned around. "Forgan is coming! Pull back!"

"You vagrant!" one of the men shouted back as he turned. "The next time I see your face, you'll become rust on my blade!"

One after another, the other three also ran away.

"No, I've not fallen so far that I could be cut down by the likes of you!" Katsuharu rushed to the palanquin, cutting the ropes that bound Arara to it with his katana. "Arara, are you all right?"

"Yes, uncle! I'm so sorry you had to do this for me!"

"Indeed! I had to help my darling niece!" Katsuharu got Arara to her feet, then handed a second katana he was carrying to her, sheath and all. "If we were to fail in your goal now, there would be nothing left but regrets. Take your vengeance for Tatsuru, Arara. If that satisfies you, you can find another love or two after that."

"I will not," said Arara as she shook the sheath off of her katana, "find a new love! I will slay Tatsuru's killer with my own hands, and remain loyal to him! That is my only wish!"

Rock had said he didn't want anything in return, so maybe it was fine, but when Haruhiro heard Arara declaring that so clearly, he felt a little sorry for the guy, even if it was none of his concern.

The black wolves were racing up the slope to attack Kajita. Were there more?

There were. Incoming. Orcs, undead. More and more of them, coming from beyond the valley.

"Show yourself, Arnold!" Arara shouted. She readied her katana, but she seemed to have trouble moving.

It had to be the robe. When they first met her, she'd worn a coat and riding pants, much like Katsuharu, but now she was wearing a kimono that went all the way down to her ankles, tied tightly with an obi.

It was apparently as constraining as it looked, because Arara suddenly shouted, "Argh!" and cut a vertical slit in the hem. "This will do!"

True, it was no doubt easier to move in now, but she didn't seem to be wearing pants underneath. Haruhiro didn't know whether to think she was too exposed or what, but it didn't really matter.

Without going all the way down the slope, Haruhiro and his party pressed to the west. The wind blew; the fog suddenly thickened. In no time, visibility was reduced to less than ten meters.

Yume nocked an arrow to her bow.

There was something up ahead. An orc?

"O light, O Lumiaris." Kuzaku held up his black blade, making the sign of the hexagram on the center of the sword's guard. "Bestow the light of protection on my blade."

Instantly, the black blade began shining. It was the paladin's light magic spell, Saber. The light of Lumiaris sharpened the cutting edge of a paladin's sword engraved with the hexagram. That light would dazzle anyone who looked directly at it up close, and it had one other important effect: When the sword was shining like that, it really stood out.

"Wohhhhh!" When Kuzaku held up his sword and charged forward, the enemies gathered. Like moths to the flame.

Don't take on more than you can handle! Haruhiro wanted to shout out to him. But he held it in. That was Kuzaku's role. Kuzaku with his heavy armor was the only one who could handle multiple enemies at the same time. Haruhiro and the rest had other work to do. Obviously, cheering Kuzaku on wasn't it.

Anyway, there were three orcs. Three whole orcs beating on Kuzaku.

Kuzaku deflected an orc's katana with Block.

"Kwah!" He used Bash to drive them back. Swinging his sword around earnestly, he tried to make the orcs back down.

The orcs were as tall or taller than Kuzaku, and far thicker than he was, too. They were trying to gang up on Kuzaku and beat the stuffing out of him. It seemed like he should be crushed in no time, but Kuzaku hung in there. What was more, he was far from being pushed to the edge.

Kuzaku was predicting their attacks' strengths and angles in an instant, nailing the call on whether to block with his shield, dodge, or take the blow. In a three-on-one fight, Kuzaku basically had no chance to counterattack, but looking at that from another angle, it also meant he could focus fully on defending. If all he had to do was protect himself, Kuzaku knew a lot about how to do so. When an opponent was confidently defending himself, breaking him down was hard even for the most experienced of warriors.

"Dark." Shihoru stopped to summon her elemental.

Haruhiro moved up to the left of Kuzaku, while Yume went to his right. He didn't want to leave Shihoru alone, but there was no helping it when they only had four people. It was fine, though. Kuzaku would hold the enemy back, no matter what.

Yume loosed an arrow at close range. The fog meant she couldn't see, let alone hit, distant targets, but if she got up close like that, she wouldn't be able to miss that easily.

It looked like she hit one of the orcs. Where exactly wasn't clear.

Haruhiro, for his part, was using Stealth to get around behind the orcs. Kuzaku was drawing their attention, and Yume was in their line of sight, too. Thanks to that, they hadn't noticed Haruhiro.

Any more enemies? No sign of them yet.

Haruhiro got behind the orcs. The copper armor they were wearing seemed thin and light, but it guarded them securely all the way up to their necks. It was probably good quality. They were wearing protectors like elbow guards, knee guards, shin guards, and gauntlets, too, and though their helmets were the type that left the face exposed, their heads were securely protected. They were more than twenty centimeters taller than Haruhiro, and their bodies were the picture of health. It was easy to see how strong they were.

Think. Think. Think. Think fast, and come to a conclusion.

It didn't look like he could finish them with Backstab. Spider was very likely to end in failure. Which meant...

Haruhiro landed a jumping kick on the back of Orc A, the orc who was on the right-hand side from his perspective, and the left-hand side from Kuzaku's.

When Orc A nearly pitched forward, unable to keep his balance, Kuzaku shouted, "Rah!" and used Bash.

The orc in the middle, Orc B, tried to cover for his comrade. Kuzaku didn't pursue too far. While Orc A regained his balance, he turned to look for Haruhiro.

By that time, Haruhiro had already set his sights on Orc C, the one on the left from his perspective, and the right from Kuzaku's.

Yume's arrow was lodged in Orc C's left arm. Despite that,

he was holding his katana in both hands, and was about to take a swing at Yume.

This didn't need to kill him. Backstab.

Haruhiro's stiletto couldn't penetrate Orc C's armor, but he never intended it to. Unable to ignore Haruhiro, Orc C turned his way.

Using that gap, Yume fired at point blank range. "Meow!"

Contact Shot. No, this wasn't just one shot. She followed up immediately with another. Rapid Fire.

She was using a combination of the skills Rapid Fire and Contact Shot. One arrow missed, and one bounced off his armor. Still, it was enough to intimidate Orc C. Seeing her opponent shrinking back, brave Yume wasn't about to back away.

An arrow. Yume didn't nock it to her bow; she stepped up with the arrow in hand, stabbing it into Orc C's right thigh.

Narrow Spear. This was apparently a skill for use in emergencies, but it was just like Yume to use it when attacking a retreating enemy.

Haruhiro wasn't going to let the groaning Orc run away or strike Yume with his katana. He used Arrest on Orc C's arm. He locked the orc's left elbow joint and swept his leg.

Orc C braced himself, trying not to fall, but because he'd taken an arrow in the thigh, he couldn't quite manage it. When Orc C fell to one knee, bending backward, Haruhiro shifted the stiletto to a backhanded grip and slammed it into the orc's left eye.

Yume drew Wan-chan and knocked the katana from Orc C's right hand.

Haruhiro twisted the stiletto, pulled it out a bit, then screwed it back in. He pulled it out and stabbed it back in, but Orc C was still alive.

"Yume, go support Kuzaku!" Haruhiro shouted as he finished off Orc C.

There were still no enemy reinforcements, but they couldn't afford to let their guards down.

While using Block on Orc B's katana, Kuzaku shouted, "Zwah!" and used Thrust on Orc A. Orc A turned this aside with his katana.

Next, Kuzaku used Punishment on Orc B. At the same time, he used Bash to knock back a thrust from Orc A.

When that made Orc A back away slightly, Yume attacked. It was a somersault followed by a powerful strike: Raging Tiger.

With what was probably a reflexive reaction, Orc A jumped sideways to evade it.

"Go!" Shihoru launched Dark.

Orc A tried to twist out of the way, but Dark turned. He hit and slipped inside Orc A's body, like he was being sucked in.

Convulsions. Orc A frothed at the mouth. His legs gave out.

Haruhiro couldn't be like Moyugi and say, *Just as planned,* or *Just like I thought.* They hadn't signaled each other, and his hope that Shihoru might do it had been only a hope. It had been incredibly close to a haphazard decision.

I've got a long way to go still, he thought, admonishing himself as he grappled Orc A from behind. Spider.

Shihoru's Dark was doing its thing, so Orc A's reactions were dulled. Haruhiro quickly jabbed his stiletto through the orc's right eyeball and into its brain.

That wasn't all. He used all the strength in his body to twist Orc A's neck while falling to the ground with it. No matter how tough an enemy's body was, it became surprisingly fragile when hit in a vital spot by a surprise attack.

Orc A went limp; he nearly expired. Haruhiro leapt away from him.

"Nuwahh!" Kuzaku was continuing to defend himself against Orc B's katana with his shield while occasionally using his sword, but he wasn't going in to finish the orc.

Now that Orcs A and C were down, it wouldn't be too strange for him to want to go on the attack, but Kuzaku continued enduring. Being almost stupidly committed to his role was one of Kuzaku's strengths. It was also a mark of his faith in Haruhiro and his other comrades.

Shihoru was keeping her distance. Any new enemies? No. Haruhiro signaled to Yume with his eyes.

It would have been possible for Kuzaku, Haruhiro, and Yume to attack from three directions, but they'd do something else here instead.

Haruhiro rushed over behind Yume.

Yume closed in from behind Orc B.

Orc B quickly noticed her and jumped backward at an angle, trying to get it so that both Yume and Kuzaku were in front of him.

Haruhiro lowered himself and leapt out from Yume's shadow. Outward. Outward.

Kuzaku and Yume closed in on Orc B. Orc B backed away; he had no choice but to do so. He'd completely lost sight of Haruhiro.

When he got into a position to look straight at Orc B's back, Haruhiro took a short breath. His target hadn't noticed him. Haruhiro was staring right at his back. In an instant, it felt like he understood his opponent. Of course, that was merely an illusion, but Haruhiro theorized that, while people believed the eyes said more than the mouth, they ought to instead believe the back said more than the mouth. At the very least, what he should do next was apparent at a glance.

Orc B put his weight on his right foot which had stepped back, sticking his right elbow out so his katana was to the right side of his face.

When Haruhiro slammed his stiletto into that right arm, Orc B first reacted with shock. *Who're you? What're you doing there?* That was the kind of look it was.

While the fingers of his right hand weren't completely severed, he wasn't going to be getting much use out of anything but his thumb. Orc B gripped the katana's hilt with his left hand. That was all he could do.

"Gaarah!" Kuzaku tackled Orc B with his shield, pushing the orc down. He pressed his shield against the fallen orc's left arm, locking down the orc's katana. Without missing a beat, he used his black blade to cut up Orc B's face, and there was nothing the orc could do to stop it. It looked like Kuzaku could handle the rest, but this was no time to feel relieved.

"Haruhiro-kun!" Shihoru shouted.

They're here, huh, Haruhiro thought. *Reinforcements.*

Was that it?

There was something big charging in from beyond the fog.

"A giant?" Haruhiro was reminded of the white giants from the Dusk Realm. It looked that big.

No, it wasn't that big in actuality. But it felt nothing if not dangerous.

Once we've snagged the package, you guys can go steal the treasure, Kuro had told him.

Haruhiro's party's goal wasn't to fight Forgan. That big guy was coming their way, but, if at all possible, they didn't want to run into him.

"Come on," Haruhiro said in a low voice, walking off to the southwest. His comrades followed in silence.

While climbing the southern slope of the ravine on a diagonal, he watched the big one's movements.

We're good! Haruhiro wanted to cry out in glee, but he obviously refrained. The big guy hadn't changed course. He didn't seem to have a fix on their location. Even so, once he found the orcs' corpses, he may start looking for the culprits. They needed to get away quickly.

The fog made it impossible to know how the battle was going, but there were definitely clashes going on here and there between friend and foe. Were they winning or losing? If the Rocks, Arara, and Katsuharu were killed or retreated, Haruhiro and the others would be left behind. That would be incredibly bad.

There was also the issue of whether they could find Merry. Even if they did find her, could they rescue her? Looking back, having misread how serious Arara's punishment would be had hurt. It had hurt them badly.

The slope was getting steeper. It would be hard to go any higher.

"Can hardly see a thing..." Kuzaku muttered to himself.

Haruhiro was about to say something, then shut his mouth. There was a sound above, and some gravel rolled down the slope.

Haruhiro looked up and immediately shouted, "Above!" But, to be honest, he had no idea what to do.

It wasn't the big guy from before, but this enemy still looked plenty dangerous. It was that one: the giant wolf. It was nimbly loping down the slope. On the giant wolf's back was a goblin: Onsa the goblin beastmaster.

"Get away!" Kuzaku spread his arms wide, pushing Shihoru and Yume away.

No, that's not going to work!

Haruhiro tried to stop him. It was too late.

The giant wolf plowed into Kuzaku with a growl, but Kuzaku wasn't sent flying. Had he grabbed on and clung to it? He'd done more than just that. He tried to brace himself, but when it became apparent that wouldn't work, he twisted his body.

"Rahhhhhh!" Kuzaku screamed.

The giant wolf toppled over sideways with Kuzaku. The two of them slid down the slope together. Onsa grabbed the back of the giant wolf's neck like it was a set of reins; he must have been trying to get the wolf to stand up.

But Kuzaku didn't let him. He rolled.

The giant wolf and Kuzaku wrestled with one another as they rolled down the southern slope.

It wasn't long before Onsa was thrown off. He quickly got up, chasing after the giant wolf and Kuzaku.

"Kuzaaaaku!" Haruhiro chased after Onsa like he was jumping down a flight of stairs two to three steps at a time. "Yume, watch Shihoru!"

Kuzaku! Kuzaku! Kuzaku! Damn it! Haruhiro cried out in his mind.

He hadn't been able to move; hadn't been able to do anything. Kuzaku had saved him.

"Hou, hou, hou, hou, hou, hou, hou, hou, hou!" Onsa was making a strange noise.

What was that supposed to be? Haruhiro had a bad feeling about it. Was he calling something?

Kuzaku and the giant wolf finally came to a stop. The giant wolf shook its head.

What about Kuzaku? Haruhiro couldn't see him. Where was he? Was he underneath? He started crawling out from under the giant wolf.

Kuzaku.

He's moving! He's alive! Haruhiro wanted to shout out.

But not yet. It was too early to celebrate.

The giant wolf got on top of Kuzaku.

Kuzaku shouted, "Screw you!" as he struggled.

Onsa would soon reach the giant wolf and Kuzaku. He'd get to them.

"Funahhh!"

That was Yume; Yume's voice. An arrow; an arrow was flying.

It grazed Onsa's shoulder. He ran into the shadow of a nearby tree without looking back.

All right, thought Haruhiro. *Good! Now's our chance!*

Haruhiro didn't so much run as jump. Every time he kicked off the ground, he went two to three meters, jumping, jumping, jumping. It was dangerous, and super scary, but this was far faster than running. Finally, he passed Onsa. He kept going and leapt onto the giant wolf.

"Get off of Kuzaku!" Haruhiro screamed.

He clung to the giant wolf's back, stabbing his stiletto into its neck. He pulled it out and stabbed it in again repeatedly. The giant wolf writhed in agony, thrashed around, and tried to throw Haruhiro off, but to no avail.

I'm not letting you go!

Maybe the giant wolf had decided that doing something about Haruhiro was its priority, because it stood up and began running.

What? What? What? Huh? Why are you running toward that tree?! Have you gone crazy? We're going to collide!

"Ngah?!" Haruhiro shouted.

Haruhiro released the giant wolf at the last possible moment and ended up rolling around on the ground. The wolf ended up striking the tree, but it seemed fine. By the time Haruhiro leapt to his feet, the wolf was baring its fangs and facing him. It hadn't felt like his stiletto was doing much, either. The wounds probably weren't that deep, thanks to its hard fur and the fat beneath its skin.

Kuzaku had risen to all fours, but he wasn't standing. Was he hurt? He couldn't be completely unharmed.

How bad was it?

Where was Onsa?

No. Now wasn't the time to worry about him.

The giant wolf lunged.

It was impossible to think. The next thing Haruhiro knew, his body was moving on its own.

The giant wolf sailed above him.

Why was Haruhiro lying on his back? He didn't know, but it seemed he'd ended up in that posture by sliding to the ground. Thanks to that, he'd dodged the attack somehow.

However, the giant wolf turned immediately, and was about to come at him again. Haruhiro scrambled to his feet, but—

Isn't this kind of impossible?

He couldn't dodge the next one. It'd get him.

It wasn't that he'd given up, though.

His throat; he'd protect that. If it sunk its fangs into his throat, that'd be the end. Rather than make a poor attempt to run away, he'd be better off standing ready and trying to avoid taking a fatal wound. Not dying was the key. He wouldn't die instantly. No matter what, he could guarantee that.

The giant wolf was coming.

Coming.

Closing in.

When an arrow sank into its right eye he thought, *Yume?*

The giant wolf's head shrank back. It winced, shaking its head and whining.

"It's not like I care about my juniors," Kuro said coldly.

Kuro, huh? thought Haruhiro.

The warrior who was a former hunter was surprisingly close by. He'd appeared from the shadow of a rock not five meters from Haruhiro.

Kuro unleashed two arrows.

"Don't misunderstand that, Junior."

The giant wolf suddenly changed the way its head was facing. Because of that, the arrows struck its shoulder. Haruhiro didn't know how serious the damage was, but the arrow was firmly lodged in there. What a powerful bow.

There was the sound of a whistle, and the giant wolf turned. It was Onsa whistling. Would they run?

"Kuzaku?!" Haruhiro glanced over to him.

"I'm okay." Kuzaku had risen to his knees. He turned his head to look at Haruhiro. "Somehow."

"I want that guy dead." Kuro went to take a shot at Onsa.

Onsa jumped to the side, dodging it, then jumped onto the giant wolf's back. Kuro loosed another arrow, but Onsa lowered his head and avoided it.

"Hou, hou, hou, hou, hou, hou, hou, hou!"

There was that weird vocalization again.

What is that supposed to be? Haruhiro wondered.

Haruhiro rushed over to Kuzaku. Kuzaku rose under his own strength, then looked up the southern slope. Haruhiro turned his gaze in that direction, too. Yume and Shihoru were coming down.

"Damn that uppity little goblin." Kuro nocked an arrow to his bow. He drew back the string. Halfway, he stopped and looked up to the sky. "Huh?"

There was a beating of wings. Was it birds? They were close; getting closer. Large bugs? Birds? Or bats, maybe? There were many of them.

Haruhiro ducked down, screaming, "Whoaaaaa?!" as he swung his arms around.

The birds, or bats, or whatever they were... Those things were running into him. Into his arms, back, chest, head, and face. They hit him hard.

He saw them, though not that clearly. They weren't birds, and they weren't bugs, either. They were close to bats, but different.

Lizards? Like winged lizards.

The size of his two hands put together and spread out. Dragons? They were like little model dragons, but it was clear these were no models. They moved and flew. They were attacking Haruhiro and the others. But if they could fly around so nimbly, they had to be fairly light. Even when they hit him, it only hurt a little, so it wasn't a big deal. They were just a huge nuisance.

"What the hell?!" Haruhiro used his stiletto to lop a wing off of one of the mini wyverns. The mini wyvern let out a screech and fell to the ground. When he saw that, it was time to—well, no, even if he hadn't seen that, it would have been time to run.

The swarm of mini wyverns dispersed as he ran. Haruhiro couldn't see the giant wolf anymore. Had Onsa used that weird vocalization of his to call the mini wyverns as a distraction?

The mini wyvern Haruhiro had sliced a wing off of was waddling away. He thought of giving it a good kick but refrained.

"That surprised me..." Kuzaku raised the visor on his helmet and sighed.

"Lost him, huh." Kuro gave a hearty guffaw and clicked his tongue. "Oh, there's Kajita."

True enough, they could hear a whole lot of manly battle cries in a husky voice. But who did the other voice belong to? It was deep and low, like the rumbling of the earth. It didn't sound human. So it was an enemy, then.

Somewhere nearby, Kajita was going at it with an enemy. A powerful one, most likely.

"Kuzaku-kun!" Shihoru ran over to Kuzaku. She was carrying his shield. Had he dropped it in the middle of the battle?

Yume was beside Shihoru with her bow ready, looking around restlessly.

"Maybe you guys had better stick near us, after all. For now, at least," Kuro said and disappeared into the fog.

Haruhiro wanted time to sort his thoughts out. He knew, though, he'd get no such thing.

Something was coming from the west. Enemies, no doubt. From the east, too.

Here; this place was probably going to see heavy fighting soon.

"Stick together!" Haruhiro raced over to where Kuzaku was. "For now, let's support the Rocks here!"

That figure he could faintly make out in the fog, was that Kajita?

"Zweh!" Kajita swung his massive mushroom sword, and the ridiculously big guy they saw earlier, probably an orc, bellowed, "Fuuuuuungh!" as he blocked it with his katana.

Kajita was pretty tall himself, but that orc was still a good head or two taller—no, even more than that. Three meters tall seemed like a bit too much, but he had to be at least two and a half. And because of that—

"Goahhhh!" The giant katana the giant orc had raised over-head on the diagonal must have had an incredible amount of power behind it. It was clearly a blow to be avoided at all costs, but Kajita tried to catch it with his massive mushroom sword.

"Doehhh!" Kajita shouted.

There was no way he could stop it. Kajita's body soared through the air.

Hey, wait, Haruhiro realized. *He's flying toward me.*

What now? Should I catch him? No, I can't do it. But, that said, I don't know if it's okay to dodge him, either.

For better or worse, Kajita slammed into the ground with a loud thud, right in front of Haruhiro. He was completely spread-eagled. His sunglasses were starting to fall off.

"Ka... Kajita-san?" Haruhiro timidly called out to him.

The giant orc was trudging toward him.

"Ha-Haruhiro-kun, run!" Shihoru shouted.

The giant orc raised his giant katana overhead.

No way! He was already in range? Could he reach from there? He could? It felt like he could, too. Because the giant orc was so big, it might have been throwing off Haruhiro's sense of distance.

No other choice, thought Haruhiro. *I'll have to run.*

"Heh!" Kajita rose with a frightening display of leg, abdominal, and back muscle strength that seemed unnatural. His massive mushroom sword turned sideways; he blocked the giant orc's giant katana. This time, it stopped. Not just that, Kajita pushed back and made the giant orc bend backward. He stepped in, then swung down diagonally.

The giant orc didn't block with his giant katana. With a "Gwah!" sound, he just turned it aside. He was surprisingly dexterous.

Kajita spun his massive mushroom sword around, locking blades with the giant orc.

"Nghhhh! Nuhhhh!"

"Guhhhh! Ohhhhhhhgh!"

"Zwehhh! Humph! Zeahahhh!"

Kajita used brute force to push back the giant orc, then, quickly taking a moment to adjust his sunglasses, held his massive mushroom sword in a low stance.

"Hmph... *What's your name?*" Kajita said in a language that was foreign to Haruhiro.

"Gai, Godo Agaja! Danjinba?"

"My name is Kajita."

"Den, dogaran..."

"Hahaha! *Me, too.*"

What is with these people? Haruhiro wondered. *They both clearly speak different languages, but they're managing a conversation?*

I shouldn't get involved. Leave them to it. Well, it's not like I could get involved, and the two of them seem to be having fun, so let them have at it for as long as they like. Looks like I've got things of my own to do.

More and more orcs and undead were coming in from the west. They were going to the east—was that Arara? Katsuharu was there, too. And Rock.

Gettsu the mirumi was running right behind Rock. They were three people and one critter, pushing westward through the valley. Not far behind was Tsuga with his buzz cut. Then Moyugi. Sakanami the thief was nowhere to be seen.

Tsuga and Moyugi seemed to be being chased by orcs and undead. No, since this was Moyugi, maybe he was deliberately not turning to fight, and pulling the enemy along with him that way.

It looked like enemies were coming for Haruhiro and the others, who still weren't fully down the southern slope yet, either.

Two orcs, and two undead. Four on four, huh. Tough, but they couldn't run away now. They'd have to prepare themselves for the worst. They'd have to fight.

"Kuzaku, you handle the front! Shihoru, Yume!" Haruhiro shouted.

"'Kay!"

"Okay! Dark!"

"Meow!"

Yume loosed an arrow. Dark flew forward. Kuzaku acted as a shield.

Haruhiro looked for openings, going in for a single decisive blow when he could. If he could, that was. It turned into a chaotic melee in no time.

Your mind feels like it might turn into a frantic mess, but don't lose yourself. Look around.

He couldn't see through the fog. That wasn't just true for Haruhiro; it was true for the enemy, too. It wasn't a one-sided disadvantage. That meant they were on equal terms. His range of vision was extremely limited.

Cool your head.

Kuzaku was keeping the enemies in front under control. That didn't mean he could relax, but he had to believe in his tank.

It wasn't just Haruhiro—Shihoru was also looking around. Yume would occasionally do something considerate, too.

Don't try to do everything alone.

He couldn't do it all, anyway. He'd do his best, of course. He, his comrades, and everyone else would do everything they could.

We don't need to overextend ourselves to kill enemies. Surviving is the key. First, defend. Hang in there. Then, be tenacious. Harass the enemy.

Don't stay in one place, either. Move.

There was no reason they had to fight the enemy straight out.

They could attack enemy groups that Arara, Katsuharu, and the Rocks were already fighting from the side or behind. Once they poked at them a bit, they'd immediately withdraw and target other enemies.

Read the flow. If the Rocks, Arara, and Katsuharu start to push back the enemy and advance, follow immediately. If the flow stagnates, do not, by any means, move up to the front.

Fundamentally, they would stay ready to pull out, and act to disrupt the enemy. They didn't need to think about delivering a direct, crushing blow. In fact, they shouldn't think about that at all.

There were a few times where they struggled with an enemy, and it was all they could do just to protect Shihoru. No matter how scared they became, they didn't panic.

The Rocks had Kuro, who loved to take down enemies with a surprise attack, and was very good at it. Sakanami was the same way. Haruhiro wasn't completely counting on those two to save them, but he didn't think they'd miss the perfect chance when it presented itself.

Everyone was at their most exposed when they went in to press the attack. Even if they knew not to let their guard down, at times like that, openings tended to form naturally. If the enemy showed the slightest opening, Kuro would bring the enemy down with a well-placed shot from that powerful bow of his, or Sakanami would murder them with an ambushing strike so frantic it would seem to be filled with some sort of grudge.

Haruhiro began getting a handle on it. The Rocks didn't do anything that could be called coordination; they were all acting on an individual basis. Rock and Kajita fought on their own, and even Moyugi was wandering around. Tsuga, being the priest, kept an eye on things, going here and there, but Kuro and Sakanami disappeared most of the time so they could ambush enemies.

In Haruhiro's party, everyone acted as one unit. If even one of them was missing, their combat potential fell drastically. They might become completely dysfunctional.

Meanwhile, the Rocks were different. They were each a unit unto themselves. For Moyugi, as their commander, if he included himself and his demon, Moira, he had up to seven units he could move around and plan strategies with.

If Haruhiro's party could increase the number of units they had as well, it would give them more options. It would broaden their range.

Could they do that?

First, there was Merry. She was indispensable. No matter what, they would definitely get her back.

Also...Ranta.

If they had Ranta...

No, Ranta betrayed them. How it happened wasn't clear, but he probably ended up in a situation where he was about to be killed, then got down and performed a kowtow or something to get Forgan to let him join.

Ranta was an enemy. They hadn't encountered him yet, but he may appear before them as an enemy at any moment. The Rocks might have already killed him. If they had, well, that was that.

But had he really betrayed them?

The guy had been with them since they first arrived in Grimgar, so maybe Haruhiro just didn't want to think it was true. But there was still something bothering him about it. What was it?

This was no time to be thinking about Ranta. Although it did show that Haruhiro had a lot of leeway for his thoughts to be drifting like this.

Rock stood as the vanguard and was making steady progress. The enemy's resistance was weak. Haruhiro and his party were moving up while hardly even engaging the enemy.

Even though the fog hadn't thinned, it felt awfully bright. Brilliant, even.

They came to an open area. They were finally through the valley.

"Hahahahahahaha!" Rock let out an excessively cheerful laugh.

When he laughed like that, Haruhiro was no match for him. Rock made it feel like nothing was impossible. If they just stuck with him, everything would work out somehow.

He didn't just provide a push from behind; he dragged everyone along with him. The propelling force created by Rock's very presence was crazy. It had to be some sort of charisma. It felt dangerous, but they had no choice but to press onward.

Haruhiro looked back as he ran. They settled on a system where Haruhiro took point when they moved, and when they encountered enemies, he quickly changed places with Kuzaku. Kuzaku and Yume were both walking with strangely light steps. Only Shihoru, who was sandwiched between the two of them, was looking left and right busily, questioning if this was all right, and if there were any problems.

"Merry should be up ahead!" Haruhiro called out to his comrades. "Keep on your toes, and let's go as far as we can!"

"Meow!"

"'Kay!"

"Right!"

Rock, Arara, Katsuharu. Those three were ahead and to the left of Haruhiro's group.

Was Kajita still fighting with Godo Agaja somewhere? Tsuga was behind Rock and the rest. Moyugi was nowhere to be seen. Were Kuro and Sakanami hiding in the mist?

It wasn't just Haruhiro and his group; none of them were trading blows with the enemy, even though there were still enemies. He could see silhouettes that looked like orcs and undead here and there.

Wait, are we being lured in?

There was a resounding and unsettling howl that likely came from the giant wolf.

There was a hill up ahead. On top of that hill, there were figures: three people, and one large animal. There was a person on top of the animal, too, so make that four people.

Then, at the bottom of the hill, there was a far greater number of enemies.

Rock, then Arara, Katsuharu, and Tsuga all stopped one after another. Haruhiro and his group were forced to stop, too.

Moyugi caught up to them walking at a leisurely pace. His

thin sword was sheathed. He pressed the middle finger of his right hand against the bridge of his glasses.

"Things went just as I planned, I see."

Was that really true? It felt like a blatant lie, but, even if it was the truth, *this* was what he had planned for?

"Dohhhh!" Kajita shouted.

Something big came flying at them from the rear. Well, hey, if it wasn't Kajita-san.

Kajita landed next to Tsuga. Spread-eagled, of course, like before. He didn't look dead, but he wasn't moving.

The giant orc Godo Agaja approached them with his giant katana resting on his shoulder. There were swarms of orc and undead behind him; black wolves, too. There were a bunch of members of other races Haruhiro didn't recognize, as well. Not many of them, but they were there.

No matter how he looked at it, the Rocks, Arara, Katsuharu, and Haruhiro's party were being caught in a pincer attack. What was more, Sakanami and Kuro weren't here, so they were ten people and one pet.

The enemy wasn't just a hundred people, which would already be ten times their number. It wasn't possible to get a clear count with the fog, but there were probably hundreds of them.

The four people and one animal atop the hill were, starting from the right, the great wolf with Onsa on its back, the one-armed, one-eyed, middle-aged human Takasagi, an orc of small build with a black eagle perched on his shoulder, and an undead with four arms, Arnold.

There was a familiar face in the great mass of Forgan members at the base of the hill, too. No, they couldn't see his face, he was wearing his helmet. But there was no way it could be anyone else.

He crossed his arms, puffing out his chest, more self-important than anyone. It seemed he'd already settled in as a member of Forgan.

"Rantaaaa!" Kuzaku walked forward, pointing at Ranta. "How dare you show your face in front of us! I knew you were brazen, but I still can't believe you!"

Ranta shrugged silently. Wasn't he going to argue back?

Haruhiro ground his back teeth. *That's not like you, man, Ranta.*

He was a nasty, arbitrary, nonsensical, stupid, and moronic, but still somehow cunning, strangely confident, ill-mannered, annoying dread knight who was a nuisance just by being there. His personality was also rotten to the core, so he ought to have hurled a bit of verbal abuse their way there. He was a dread knight, after all.

"Murrrgh!" Yume stomped her feet. She was teary-eyed. "Yume hates you, Ranta!"

"Yume..." Shihoru reached out and rubbed Yume's back.

"And?" Takasagi slowly rotated his head. "What is it you people want to do, picking a fight with us? Do you just want to fight? If so, we'll face you. We don't mind a little fighting ourselves. If we're doing this, we'll go all the way. We'll crush you all here. Kill every last one of you."

"I'm not here to fight you." Rock laughed and leveled his sword at Arnold. "Arnold! I want a duel with—"

"No!" Arara jumped forward to stand in front of Rock. "Rock! I am grateful to you for bringing me here, but this, this is one thing I cannot leave to you! Arnold the Bloody Whirlwind! If you are a warrior of honor, face me in a duel!"

Haruhiro saw Katsuharu look down and shake his head. Kajita still hadn't risen.

What about Kuro? Sakanami? He hadn't sensed a nyaa since the black nyaa killed the striped one, either. Had Setora suppressed Forgan's nyaas for them?

If they were going to fight one-on-one, Haruhiro would be glad to let them have at it. For his part, he wanted to get out of here as quickly as possible. He had to find Merry and save her.

Hopefully they could get away with the four of them, but that may be difficult. At the very least, even if Haruhiro had to go it alone, wasn't there some way he could sneak away from here? Forgan were in front of them and behind, but not to the sides. If he timed it right, it might not be impossible. Right?

Timing. The timing was crucial. But even if Haruhiro managed to get away alone, and supposing he somehow was able to rescue Merry, what about their comrades? What would he do about the other three? Was it better to give up on Merry, and to try to get back alive with just the four of them? If he did, he would have to question why they came all this way. But setting aside what they came here for, shouldn't he use the best method, the best path available to him in his current situation? Haruhiro was the party's leader, after all.

How had it come to this? What did that matter? This was just how chance worked. Even without going and looking for trouble themselves, they may still find themselves in a dangerous predicament. Things like that happened all the time. Whining about it would do no good. The question was what to do in the situation they found themselves in. Or, if he could change the situation somehow, to move it in a better direction, even if only slightly. In order to do that, he needed to think, then act.

"For what reason?" the small orc asked in fluent human speech.

This caught Haruhiro a bit by surprise. That was Jumbo. Jumbo, the head of Forgan, huh.

"Woman of the village," Jumbo said. "For what cause do you seek a duel with my companion Arnold?"

"There was a man," Arara said. "I adored him. And he, too, loved me. However, the two of us were torn apart. He was looked down upon in the village. By building his fame as a warrior, he hoped to make the village recognize and accept his love for me."

"There was indeed one who came alone by night to challenge Arnold," said Jumbo.

"Ohhh...Tatsuru-sama..."

"It was over with one swing," Takasagi said with a snort. "I didn't see it, just heard about it later, but Arnold cut that man down more easily than he might swat an irritating fly."

"He never returned," Arara said softly.

"Well, of course not," Takasagi shot back. "If he'd been skilled, some of our undead may have wanted an arm or a leg or two for themselves. Nobody has any use for a weakling's body."

"You dare mock him?!" Arara screamed.

"I'm only telling you the truth. So? You've got a misguided grudge against Arnold, and you're telling me you raised all this hell just to have a duel with him?"

"My grudge is not misguided! The first one to commit an outrageous act of violence was Arnold! It was for that reason Tatsuru-sama went to slay Arnold, the sworn enemy of the village!"

"Oh, yeah, that did happen, huh," Takasagi mused. "Well, Arnold gets thirsty for blood and does weird stuff sometimes. It's like a fit. When it happens, even we can't stop him. He's doing his best to control himself so he doesn't attack our people. We've just got to leave him to it. He doesn't mean anything ill by it, so forgive the guy."

"Y-you think what he did is forgivable?!"

"Well, you've got a point."

That man, Takasagi... It was hard to tell if he was he messing around, or if he was serious. Either way, the fact that Arara was ready to blow her top made her like a toy for Takasagi. He wasn't just handling her; he was toying with her. He couldn't have been treating her more derisively.

"Enough, Arara," Rock said quietly. With just one word, the atmosphere changed drastically.

Rock had his back to Haruhiro, so he couldn't see, but he most likely wasn't smiling. Not one bit. Haruhiro's hair had already begun to prickle, and it was now standing straight up.

"When a person—" Rock took a step forward. Haruhiro got goosebumps. "Whether they're human, or something else, when a *person*—" Rock was angry. "She risked her life to demand you face her in a fair fight, and that's your attitude?"

With each step Rock took forward, Haruhiro's stomach contracted another five millimeters. That was how it felt.

"You're lame, Forgan. They say you've got orcs, and goblins, and even humans, so I thought you'd be a more interesting group. But I misjudged you. You're a bunch of scum."

Most of Forgan probably didn't understand the human language. Even so, could they still understand they'd been insulted? The members of Forgan were suddenly seething with anger and making a fuss.

"Shut up!" Rock bellowed.

With that, he silenced Forgan.

Rock began walking toward the hill. No one could stop him. Not Arara, not anyone.

Gettsu stood on his hind legs and watched Rock go. The Forgan members at the base of the hill seemed paralyzed, unable to move.

"Bring it." Rock stopped a few meters from the hill, beckoning with one hand. "All of you, come at me. I'll send every last one of you flying. You get it? I'm mad. Don't think you're gonna get off lightly after pissing me off. I'm a gentle guy, but, you know, once you make me snap, I don't settle down until things are made right. That happens when either I bite it, or all of you are wiped out. I don't especially like killing, but you guys, I'll kill. Let me see you get serious. I came here for that, anyway. I'm not planning on going back alive. Can't live if you're afraid of dying. If you're always scared, you can't enjoy what there is to enjoy. I'll show you all. The brilliant fire of life that burns inside me, that is. You show me, too. Live, fight, and die here. Entertain me. If you put up a boring fight, I won't let you get away with it. Kill me. If you can, that is. I'm gonna kill all of you. I'll fight, and fight, and kill you.

"Shall we get started? You ready? Who wants to die? Who's gonna entertain me? I'll take any of you. I like guys who entertain me. Friend? Foe? Who cares. Well? Why's no one coming? You don't mean to tell me you're scared, are you? You're all that lame? Show some spirit. Let me see how you live and die!"

"I wan...duel wi...you..."

Was that...a voice?

Arnold jumped down from the hill. It was fluid in a way that didn't let you sense his true weight. The grim reaper had descended; that was what it looked like.

Rock didn't budge as Arnold approached.

There was less than a meter between them now. When that closed to fifty centimeters—no, thirty centimeters—Arnold finally came to a stop.

"This'll be our second time." There was finally a hint of a laugh in Rock's tone. "Let's do it, Arnold. I'm not the same me as I was before, so watch out. I'm in top mental and physical shape, you know."

"I wi...ki...you..."

"Sure. Just try it."

There it was again. They were talking different languages. How did they understand one another?

Takasagi slapped his forehead with his left hand and sighed. "You're actually doing this?"

"U-um..." Arara reached out, her hand hanging in the air. "What about me?"

"I'll be blunt, Arara," Rock said, still facing Arnold. "This man is damn strong. You don't even stand a chance against him alone. Maybe you're fine with losing and getting yourself killed, but I'm not. I'll avenge Tatsuru for you. Leave it to me."

Instead of digging her heels in, Arara hung her head. Haruhiro could only infer, but it might have been that Arara was well aware of the painful difference in ability between herself and Arnold from the beginning. Even if she stood no chance, she might have meant to do as much as she could, then follow after Tatsuru. If that had been her plan, well, it was practically suicide. Perhaps Arara had a change of heart, and it had shaken her resolve to do this or die trying. If she no longer meant to die, she couldn't fight Arnold anymore. Even Haruhiro could tell he was just that dangerous of an opponent.

The black eagle lifted off from Jumbo's shoulder.

It looked like they were about to start. It could happen any moment now.

But wait, this...

Could this be Haruhiro's chance?

Once Rock and Arnold's one-on-one duel began, friend and foe alike would be focused on them. During that time, he would quietly sneak away from here. It might be doable. No, he could do it. He would.

That just left the timing. When should he make his move? Would he consult his comrades? Would they all go? Or just him? Would he go without a word?

Jumbo lowered himself down, sitting on the ground with one knee raised.

The great black eagle rose as they watched, disappearing into the fog.

Everyone held their breath and waited for the moment to come.

Who would make the first move? Either way, weren't they too close to one another?

Haruhiro couldn't decide what to do. Was it safe to move now? Was it too soon?

He looked at Ranta. He was still wearing his helmet, but the visor was up. He seemed to be looking at Rock and Arnold.

If Ranta had completely betrayed them, he might be subtly watching Haruhiro. If he noticed anything, he might report it to Jumbo, or someone else. That would be bad.

Then...they started.

It was Arnold. That undead had four arms. While moving backward, he used two of those arms, one on each side, to unsheathe katanas.

Rock didn't take a single step back. He knocked them away with a clang using his sword.

He charged.

Arnold drew another two katanas, stopping and standing still. Four katanas and one sword collided as if intertwining with each other.

Neither Rock nor Arnold moved, as if both were rooted to their respective spots. They just kept trading blows.

What? How could they do that? Especially Rock? His opponent was a quad wielder, so how could he deflect them all with one sword?

· So fast.

The four katanas and one sword were picking up the pace.

Scary.

This absolutely had to break down sometime, somewhere. If either of them was even a little slow to act, even the slightest bit off, this balance would collapse. And if one of them was going to be too slow, it would be Rock.

Thinking about it normally, there was no way he could keep fending off unceasing attacks from four different directions indefinitely.

But look.

That prediction had been completely off the mark. One of Arnold's katanas broke and went flying.

The moment he went down to three katanas, Arnold moved smoothly to the left. Rock returned his sword to its sheath and drew another.

He closed in and attacked.

Arnold blocked Rock's series of attacks with his three katanas. While defending, he moved further and further to the left, as if trying to divert Rock's momentum.

Suddenly, Rock stood bolt upright and switched swords again. "Looks like my movement is nice and snappy today. How about you, Arnold? Hurry up and get serious."

Haruhiro snapped back to his senses. He'd been watching intently despite himself.

This was unexpected. Wasn't Rock just too damn amazing? Honestly, Haruhiro had thought it'd be a tie at best, or that Arnold would have the upper hand. Rock had said he was in top shape, though, so maybe that was it.

Could he win? Was Rock going to win? Maybe he would make this surprisingly quick and easy?

If he did—what then?

If he said, *Okay, we won, now give us Merry, who you have captive,* would he be able to get them to accept that? That would probably be expecting a little too much. If the rest acted like Rock, challenged them to a duel, and asked for them to return her if they won, it felt like they might let that pass in this atmosphere. But who would fight? Haruhiro? With whom? Ranta had been saying, *That woman belongs to me,* or something like that. So, with Ranta, then?

"KYYYYYYYYYYYYYYYYYYYYYYYYYYYYYYYYYYYY YYY!" Arnold hollered.

Haruhiro's thinking was forcefully interrupted. That dreadful sound. Arnold had his arms spread wide and his back arched backward. It was coming, coming, coming, here…!

Arnold did a spinning jump. It was like he'd turned into a whirlwind.

That was probably Arnold taking this seriously. No way. There was no defending against that. Rock needed to run, no two ways about it.

But, of course, Rock didn't pull back. More than that, he stepped in. There was an incredible cacophony, and Arnold was pushed back.

How had Rock taken Arnold's whirlwind attack? Had he deflected it? Haruhiro couldn't see well enough, so he didn't know. Regardless, he was completely surprised. The chain of surprises continued.

Even once he was pushed away, Arnold kept spinning!

Just like that, he closed in on Rock again.

"Haha!" Rock finally laughed.

It shattered.

One katana shattered.

Rock had pushed Arnold back again, and that wasn't all, he'd smashed another katana.

"I'm coming," Rock said.

He switched swords again, closing in on Arnold. He'd been using his sword with just his right hand up until now, but this time he held it in both hands.

"Oorah, oorah, oorah, oorah, oorah, oorah, oorah, oorah, oorah, oorah, oorah, oorah, oorah, oorah!" he yelled.

It was a combo too fast for the eye to follow. What was more, each and every blow had an awful lot of power.

He was pushing Arnold back. It may have been even more correct to say he was locking Arnold down. Yes, that made sense.

The katanas; Rock's swords were targeting Arnold's katanas. When Arnold began to swing a katana, Rock would slam his sword into it. Arnold couldn't even spin, having far bigger problems.

Rock had two swords, but he only ever used one at a time. However, the length and thickness of the two differed considerably. By switching to whichever of the two was more appropriate, he made it difficult for his opponent to respond. That part was a little unorthodox, but for the rest, it was a frontal attack.

Rock didn't have some especially refined technique. His attacks and defense were both clearly defined. How was he that strong?

He had a small physique, but a high degree of physical ability. If that was correct, it was probably his eyes. Rock had good eyes; his kinetic vision was outstanding.

He wasn't just in good condition. Rock had fought Arnold once before. That time, he'd seen Arnold's movements.

Rock had seen through Arnold.

That was probably why he was in such good shape. Rock had known that if they fought a second time, he was confident he could win. More than that, he might have intended from the beginning to cross blades with Arnold lightly the first time, then settle things definitively the second.

The third katana broke.

One more.

For a moment, Arnold stopped moving. Had he sensed his defeat and become overcome with surprise? Or was it a trap?

Whatever the case, Rock didn't rush things and go in for the kill. With his sword raised aloft in both hands, he let all the muscles in his body relax. In the middle of this intense battle, it wasn't normal that he could let the tension out like that. It showed he had mastery over his own mind and body.

Arnold swung his katana at him. Rock immediately hit it back.

The next moment, Haruhiro doubted his eyes.

Arnold was holding the katana in one of his two right hands. He took a swing at Rock with his two empty left hands. If he did that...

Of course, the inevitable happened. Rock slashed both of Arnold's left arms with his sword. It wasn't hard enough to make them go flying.

One of the arms—

Rock's sword cut off one of Arnold's left arms, and bit deeply into the other. He couldn't sever it.

Arnold may have been sacrificing his left arm in an attempt to rob Rock of his sword. In fact, Arnold's empty right hand reached out for Rock. But before his sword could be stolen, Rock let go of it himself and drew the other.

"If you want it, it's yours."

Rock's sword sent Arnold's katana flying. He dealt a shallow cut to Arnold's shoulder. One of Arnold's right arms was cut up pretty badly.

Arnold staggered backward. For every bit Arnold backed away, Rock moved up.

"Zooah, zooah, zooah, zooah, zooah, zooah, zooah, zooah, zooah, zooah, zooah, zooah, zooah, zooah!" Rock yelled.

It was one-sided.

Arnold ran, desperately trying to escape. He didn't turn his back on Rock, but not out of choice; it was because he couldn't.

"Hey," someone whispered in Haruhiro's ear.

Haruhiro nearly had a heart attack. He wanted to praise himself for not screaming and jumping into the air. No, maybe it wasn't that praiseworthy.

There was someone behind him. They weren't touching him, but they were so close they may as well have been.

To think he wouldn't notice until they got this close. He'd been just that fixated on Rock and Arnold's duel. This when Haruhiro had important things to be doing. He was such a fool.

From the voice, he had an idea who it was.

While still facing forward, Haruhiro said, "Sakanami-san?"

"I am your substitute," said Sakanami. "Let not the light of youth be clouded, for it is a high-density curse. It mustn't be muddied with blood. If you have time to repent, embrace ambition. Your heart will break anyway."

"You're not making any sense, man..."

But Haruhiro did understand what he meant. Sakanami was saying, *Go search for Merry*. He was going to act as Haruhiro's substitute.

My substitute?

"No," Haruhiro whispered. "We don't look particularly alike, Sakanami-san, so if we trade places, it'll be immediately obvious I'm not here."

"We share the same blood."

"We do not. There's no way we're blood relatives."

"Is your mentor Barbara? Does that woman tie you up and make you faint?"

"Oh, because we're both thieves? That's a bit simplistic, don't you think?"

"Can you tell orcs or undead apart?" Sakanami asked.

"Well, not that well, no," Haruhiro confessed.

Haruhiro understood. He had to do it. Rock was chasing Arnold down. He had no confidence in his success, he could make no predictions, but it was still now or never.

What was Ranta doing? He wasn't looking this way. He seemed to be following the fight between Rock and Arnold. Kuzaku, Shihoru, and Yume were the same.

The great black eagle was nowhere to be seen. Maybe it was overthinking things to assume that eagle might be monitoring Haruhiro and the others from above.

Haruhiro nodded slightly. "I'll go."

"We change places on the count of five, eight."

"Why not one, two...?"

"Five, eight."

Holding back his urge to say, *Listen when people talk to you,* Haruhiro turned around and traded places with Sakanami. When he turned, he was surprised by what he saw of Sakanami's back. His posture, the position of his center of gravity, the way he stood... It was all Haruhiro. Was he imitating him? What kind of special talent was that? It was creepy.

Shihoru put her right hand behind her back and made a fist. That was Shihoru for you. She was the only one to notice. She was quietly sending Haruhiro off, saying, *Do your best,* to cheer him on.

Haruhiro nodded.

Stealth, he thought. *The fog. This fog which hangs over Thousand Valley. Become one with the fog.*

First, he went south. There was no one there.

He did his best to pay as little attention to the duel between Rock and Arnold as he could. It would distract him, no matter how he tried not to let it.

Don't rush it.

Float away.

Don't be hasty.

Don't, under any circumstances, let your breathing be disrupted.

My heartbeat is under control.

I can do this.

That was the last thing he thought before panicking.

"AAAAAHHHHHHHHHHHHHHHHHHHHHHHH!" Arnold turned into a whirlwind again. This time, he was low. Folding his body, lowering himself as far as he could, he spun like a top.

"Oh?!" Rock flipped over.

Had Arnold tripped him? Wasn't that kind of bad?

Arnold quickly picked up his katana and went after Rock. Rock jumped up and went to fight back.

Rock's sword and Arnold's katana both broke.

It had turned into a brawl. If they ended up grappling, which of them had the advantage? Haruhiro didn't really know. However, the one thing that was clear was that it was going to be more complicated than a fight with swords and katanas that could easily deal a lethal blow. It was sure to be a real mess.

Don't hesitate, he scolded himself. *Go.*

Move forward.

Turn your heart to ice. Don't feel anything now.

If you see anything that looks humanoid, just avoid it. While making sure you're not spotted, move to the south. Then to the west.

If he searched blindly, he'd never find Merry. From the rough map in his head, he knew the scale of Forgan's encampment, if only vaguely. First, he'd try focusing his attention on the center.

It was like grasping at a cloud. He might be doing something reckless. This might be frivolous of him. Was this really okay? He wasn't making a mistake?

He cast aside all hesitation. Depending on how things went, it might be no use.

Merry.

Merry.

I want to see you.

I want to hear your voice. I want to see your face. I want you to call me Haru. I want to know you're safe as soon as possible. Am I acting out on my feelings here? Yeah, I am. They're my feelings. I can't get rid of them.

It's no good. My heart's getting so heated, it feels like it's going to boil over.

Cool it. Even if I took my feelings out of the equation, I couldn't abandon a comrade. First of all, Merry's our priest, the center of the party. How massively does the absence of a healer limit the party? We learned that in the other world where we couldn't use light magic.

Now, when we finally get back to Grimgar, this happens. Not having Merry is more than just an inconvenience.

I'm going.

To the center of Forgan's encampment.

"Nyaa."

Inhaling sharply, Haruhiro readied his stiletto and the knife with a hand guard despite himself.

He'd heard the meowing of a nyaa. Where? Not far. It was close.

There.

Ahead on the right. There was a gray nyaa sticking its head out from the bushes.

The gray nyaa showed Haruhiro a silent meow. *I'm a friend,* it was saying.

Could he trust it? It was hard to decide.

When the gray nyaa emerged from the bushes, it walked off on all four legs. It went a little way, then turned back to look. It did another silent meow.

Haruhiro bit the corner of his lips.

"You want me to follow you?"

The gray nyaa turned to face forward, then took off at a half-run.

I've got to go, Haruhiro decided.

Intuition, that was all it could be called. But there was, at least, some reasoning behind it.

Forgan's nyaas were being suppressed by Setora's nyaas. That meant it was probably one of Setora's. She knew Haruhiro's objective. That nyaa must have found where she was; it was trying to lead Haruhiro there.

That said, he'd pieced all of this together while following the gray nyaa. He thought it was logical, but he'd only come up with this reasoning after the fact. Intuition had come first.

In the end, it was a good thing he'd gone with his gut. Because the gray nyaa was leading the way, he only had to pay the bare minimum of caution and could focus on moving forward as they crossed two small valleys. Beyond them was a place like a basin that was small, but wide and deep, probably over a hundred meters.

In the corner of it, she was there.

It was Merry.

She was facing downward, sitting on the ground. Was she chained or bound somehow?

Not far from her, was that a human? It was from a race that looked similar to a human—a child...? Was it? There was a creature like that lying down with his head resting on its elbows. Was he guarding Merry? If so, he couldn't be sleeping. Did he have nothing to do, so he was lazing about?

Haruhiro and the gray nyaa were poking their heads up from behind a swell in the ground to see what the situation was, so they were still some distance away. Merry's guard hadn't noticed them yet. From the look of it, there was nothing else moving.

The gray nyaa was looking at Haruhiro. When Haruhiro nodded, the nyaa did another silent meow and ran off.

It still didn't feel real. He felt like his feet weren't touching the ground.

Merry was there. Alive. It should have been fine for him to be happy, but he felt no emotions.

Strange. Was he calm? Was that it? He had to help her. Right. It didn't matter how; he just had to help Merry fast.

Merry was facing toward the north. The childlike guard was to Merry's southeast, maybe two meters away, with his body facing northwest.

From behind; he'd creep up on the guard from behind. He couldn't let the guard get away. He didn't want them making a racket, either. Knock them out? No, that was no good. Had he forgotten the mistake he'd made in Waluandin?

The guard had to die. He'd do it in one blow.

That's not a kid, right? Haruhiro wondered. *He's a guard, so he can't be. He probably just comes from a race that's like that. Besides, even if it were a human child, that wouldn't change what I need to do. I'll kill him.*

I can do it.

Haruhiro carefully crept up to the guard with Stealth. That he might make a noise was a thought that never crossed his mind. What he had to worry about was that the guard would happen to look in his direction. Or that Merry would happen to see him, and that would clue the guard in on his presence.

There was no way to avoid accidents like that. If that happened, he'd finish it quickly. He was prepared. But he was glad it didn't come to that.

Haruhiro had almost reached the childlike guard. The guard was short and fat, had pointy ears, and was humming a happy tune. Haruhiro didn't need to work himself up with a *one, two, go.*

He leaned over the guard and used Spider. He covered the guard's mouth with his left hand, turned him over, stabbed his dagger into the guard's throat with his right hand, then slashed it. The guard struggled, but it was too late. While Haruhiro was using all his strength to hold the guard down, Merry raised her face. When she looked over in his direction, her eyes went wide.

"Haru," she whispered.

Haruhiro didn't know how to respond. For a start, he smiled. That had to be a horribly awkward smile. The guard was still alive, after all, desperately struggling. But naturally, it was all in vain. Finally, the guard stopped moving.

Haruhiro was about to move away from the dead guard, but he thought better of it. Merry was wearing handcuffs. The key; the guard probably had the key.

He hurriedly searched the guard's body. This guy really wasn't a human child. The bridge of his nose was thick, but awfully low, and the shape of his head with the broad, pronounced forehead was a distinctive feature, too. His coarse body hair was like an animal's.

There was a cord around his neck. It was there. The key was hanging from the cord.

Haruhiro rushed to Merry and removed her handcuffs. Neither of them said a word; they had no time for pleasantries. Haruhiro offered Merry his hand and helped her to her feet.

They couldn't return to the village, of course. They'd decided

on a meetup point in advance: that exit. From here, it was to the northeast. It should have been around eight kilometers. He wanted to run, but Merry was exhausted. It was best not to over-exert themselves. They left immediately.

"I had an awful time," Merry said in a low voice, then laughed a little.

Perhaps she meant to reassure Haruhiro by joking around. But he wanted to be the one reassuring her.

"An awful time." Just how awful had it been? What had they done to her? It bothered him. But what reason did he have to ask? What good would come of it? At the very least, now wasn't the time.

"You're okay now," Haruhiro said.

"Yeah."

"I wish I could have come faster, though."

"You were plenty fast. Where are the others?"

"Uh, yeah..."

Honestly, he couldn't say there were no problems, or that she didn't have to worry, because that wasn't necessarily the case. What had happened during Rock and Arnold's showdown? How had it developed from there? How were Shihoru, Yume, and Kuzaku doing? There were too many unknowns, or rather, there were nothing but unknowns. But what of it?

Merry was all right. The rest would work out somehow. They could surely overcome it. They *would* overcome. To do that, he needed to keep his head working, to not relax. Because he didn't let his guard down, he'd be able to detect it.

Haruhiro stopped and raised a hand. Merry immediately stopped, too.

Nearby, there was a hole that was probably not even a meter deep. The two got down inside it and sat there.

He'd heard it.

It was faint, but it was the voice of a nyaa. Were Forgan's nyaas still left? No, probably not. It was Setora's nyaa. Was that a signal? Was it trying to tell Haruhiro something? What?

"Hey!" a voice called.

That, huh. The nyaa was probably trying to tell Haruhiro the owner of that voice was approaching.

"I know you're there, Haruhiro! Get out here, you piece of crap!"

Merry huddled close to him. She was trembling. Her breathing was suddenly ragged.

Haruhiro stuck his head up out of the hole. Was that it? It was coming from the east. He could see silhouettes, not far off. They were obscured by the fog, but they weren't more than fifty meters away.

They weren't alone. Four...no, five people.

Not good. If they were going to run, they had to do it fast. Those guys were getting closer and closer. For every bit closer they got, the odds of escape went down that much.

He'd made the wrong call. What good would hiding do? They should have run immediately. He'd failed.

Should he play decoy so Merry could get away on her own? Merry didn't know the area, so the overwhelming likelihood was that she would get lost. They'd catch her eventually. They had to run away together.

Why was Haruhiro hesitating like this? He knew. Because he thought if it came to this, they probably couldn't escape. At the very least, taking the most obvious approach wouldn't work. Unless something happened, or he made something happen, they wouldn't be able to get away.

For Haruhiro's part, that meant he had to make something happen. He had no idea what, but he'd do something.

"Merry, when I give the signal, run," he said urgently. "With me."

Merry took a short breath.

"Got it."

Even if he told her, *Go by yourself,* there was no way Merry would agree. Either way, they were sticking together. He wouldn't leave Merry alone anymore. Not a chance.

"Get the hell out here, Haruhiro!"

"Stop shouting." Haruhiro didn't just stick his head up, he got out of the hole.

This is the worst, he thought, his heart sinking.

In with the other members of the group that included Ranta was the one-armed, one-eyed, middle-aged man called Takasagi. In addition, there were two orcs, and the thin man with a poor complexion and long ears who seemed to be an elf.

Ranta, Haruhiro thought. *Damn it, Ranta.*

The orcs and the elf might be fine, but why, of all people, did he have to bring Takasagi? That old man was clearly trouble.

Takasagi held his pipe in his mouth and scratched the back of his neck with his left hand. Between him and Haruhiro, who had the sleepier eyes?

When Takasagi came to a stop and pointed to the left and right with his chin, the two orcs went right, and the elf went to the left.

"Hey, Parupirorin." Ranta jaunted right up to him. "Where's Merry?"

"Dunno."

"I'll bet she's here somewhere. Hiding."

Haruhiro didn't answer, gripping the hilt of his stiletto. *Do I do it? Can I fight with him?*

"I see right through you." Ranta lowered his visor and drew RIPer. "Every thought you have."

"Like?"

"From the beginning, you were planning to sneak out and save Merry, weren't you? I waited and waited, but you didn't, so I thought you'd gotten scared."

"Like I'd—"

Damn it.

His hands felt weak. It wasn't just his hands; it was everywhere.

Is this okay?

Ranta.

Is this really okay with you...?

"Takasagi." Ranta leaned forward a little, readying RIPer. "Let me be the one to kill him. I've got to prove my loyalty. You're fine with that, right?"

"Do as you please." Takasagi shrugged. "Let me say, though, I don't particularly doubt you."

"Liar. Well, whatever. I'll make you believe in me soon enough."

Ohhh... Haruhiro thought. *I see.*

So that's it.

Haruhiro drew not just his stiletto, but his knife with the hand guard, too.

Ranta flew at him: Leap Out.

Then, from outside his range—

"Hatred!"

Haruhiro stepped forward and diagonally to the right, dodging it by a hair. Dodging it with room to spare was beyond him. It was a terrifyingly sharp slashing attack, filled with vigor. If he'd never seen it before, he might have been hit; but he had.

More than that, he'd seen Ranta's Hatred with his own eyes, hundreds of times, probably over a thousand by now. He'd been watching it all this time.

But now that it's turned on me, it's this bad?

It hurt. He felt like his nerves were raw and exposed.

Ranta used another Leap Out, trying to get to Haruhiro's side. His specialty was chaining that with a Slice.

I won't let you, thought Haruhiro. *You won't take me down.*

Haruhiro kept on moving to keep Ranta directly in front of him. Move as he might, Ranta was always bouncing around with Leap Out; swinging RIPer; stabbing at him. Haruhiro couldn't catch his breath.

He was fast. Or rather, he was blinding. This was tough.

Haruhiro knew all the cards in Ranta's hand, so he could still deal with it somehow. If he hadn't known Ranta, he'd have already long since taken a wound or two. Until he saw through Ranta, it would be a tough fight. He may be beaten, unable to hold out long enough.

He had to get serious, or he'd be in trouble. No, he was serious, and he was using everything he had to dodge. That wasn't it.

If he didn't seriously intend to defeat Ranta, he may be cut down. He had to take a "kill before you're killed" approach. He couldn't stay passive like this. If he was going to go on the offensive, the sooner the better, while he was still unharmed.

"Nuwah!" Ranta used Leap Out to try to get to Haruhiro's left side.

Haruhiro stepped forward diagonally to the left.

He passed Ranta and turned.

He got there.

Behind him.

He'd quickly get him with Backstab or Spider, and—

"Missing!" Ranta shimmered and vanished.

No, he was using a particular moving style, one that made his opponent, that was to say Haruhiro, hallucinate.

Left. From the left.

He came.

Immediately, Haruhiro caught Ranta's RIPer with his stiletto. He was sure he'd be pushed back with Reject. Before that, Haruhiro jumped back to put distance between them.

Without missing a beat, Ranta closed in. As expected. If he

avoided it any longer, Haruhiro was going to run out of breath first. He'd use Swat.

Swat. Swat. Swat. Swat. Swat. Swat. Swat. Swat. Swat.

Damn it!

Ranta.

Each of his attacks are heavier than I thought.

"Weak! Weak! Weak! Weak, weak! What's wrong?! Why're you so feeble, huh?!"

Ugh. Shut up. You're annoying. You're just Ranta. Damn it, stupid Ranta.

It was compatibility. He knew his personality didn't match Ranta's, but he was an equally bad match for someone to fight. Ranta was the type who fought with agility, variation, and the number of moves he had available. Just like Haruhiro knew Ranta, Ranta knew Haruhiro, too, so it was close to impossible to get behind him in a one-on-one fight. If he couldn't surprise Ranta, couldn't twist Ranta's joints backward, and couldn't move faster, how exactly was he supposed to win?

Maybe I can't win?

Lose, to Ranta?

Haruhiro was a thief. Thieves, unlike dread knights, weren't combat specialists. They were ill-suited for straight-up fights to begin with. Even their equipment was light and thin. That was why it was going this way. Haruhiro was in no way inferior to Ranta. No, it didn't matter who was better or worse. But before worrying that he'd hate to lose to Ranta, or how he didn't want to lose, there was the more practical problem that if he lost, it was all over.

He had to win. He'd have to risk it all. Like he had when he'd defeated the orc at Fire Dragon Mountain. He had to accept that. If Ranta's power was a ten, Haruhiro was a seven, maybe an eight at best. It wasn't as bad as with the orc at Fire Dragon Mountain, but Ranta was stronger than Haruhiro. Even so, there were things he could do. He might end up battered and blue himself, too, but—

This is okay, right? Haruhiro thought. *Ranta, you're okay with this? You know, right? I can't hold back, okay?*

How Haruhiro had beaten down the orc at Fire Dragon Mountain was something Ranta hadn't seen. That meant Ranta hadn't seen Haruhiro giving it absolutely everything he had. Ranta wouldn't be able to deal with that.

Swat.

Swat.

Swat.

Swat.

With each time he used Swat, his senses sharpened.

Ranta took a big swing with RIPer; it was deliberate.

Haruhiro wouldn't go for that bait; not yet. It wasn't time yet. Haruhiro just used Swat.

"Heh!" Ranta laughed and used a light Exhaust. He jumped straight backward to put distance between them. "Man, what are you trying to do? Fine. Bring it. It won't work on me. I'm gonna prove right here that, in the end, you can't beat me!"

"Whatever. Just come at me, Ranta."

"You don't have to tell me!"

Ranta lunged toward Haruhiro with Leap Out. That stance was for Anger. He'd chain from that stab into a combo, but Haruhiro wouldn't let him.

Assault.

Surpassing his limits, Haruhiro moved up with a speed that betrayed Ranta's expectations.

RIPer's sword point grazed Haruhiro's left cheek. Using his knife with the hand guard, Haruhiro used Slap on Ranta's left hand.

Haruhiro slammed the pommel of his stiletto into Ranta's helmeted forehead, sweeping his left leg out from under him with a trip.

Ranta fell on his backside. By that point, Haruhiro was already behind Ranta. He wasn't thinking with his head. Even if he didn't think, his body would move on its own.

He stabbed his stiletto into Ranta's right shoulder.

"Agh!" Ranta groaned and dropped RIPer.

While pulling his stiletto free, Haruhiro wrapped his left arm around Ranta's neck. Even with the visor down, the helmet had holes for him to see through. If he put the stiletto through there—

If he put the stiletto through there—

If he did that—

"Haru!" a voice cried.

Haruhiro pulled back his stiletto.

"No...!"

Merry. She was standing up, and shouting.

"Haruhiro!" Ranta shook free from Haruhiro's left arm. "You—"

"Ur..." One of the orcs crumpled, holding his face.

It was an arrow.

The orc's face had taken an arrow, probably in the eye.

"Huh?!" Takasagi drew his katana, knocking something out of the air.

That something was an arrow. Someone was firing arrows from somewhere.

Haruhiro dashed. Whoever it was, whatever their objective, it didn't matter. For now, something had happened. Thanks to that, a one-in-a-thousand chance had come his way.

Merry was already running, too.

Haruhiro soon caught up with her.

"Dammiiiiit! Haruhiroooo! Merryyyyy!" Ranta's shouts grew more distant by the second.

What about the others? Were they giving chase? Even if they did, Haruhiro would shake them off.

Haruhiro ran, only continuing to sense the presence of Merry beside him. His body felt heavy due to the feeling of lethargy that was a side effect of Assault. What was a little heaviness? It wouldn't kill him.

The next thing he knew, the fog had gotten thicker. Even though he couldn't see the sun, and he'd lost all sense of direction, Haruhiro didn't stop. North. He knew he should be heading roughly north.

They probably didn't have any pursuers. At least, he didn't think any were nearby.

"You owe me, Junior." Shockingly, there was a voice. Haruhiro hadn't been able to count on his own detection abilities.

Although part of that was because he'd been up against a tough opponent.

Haruhiro stopped and looked around the area.

"Kuro-san?"

A tree to the left shook, and there was a rustling of leaves. When he looked up, Kuro was sitting on a branch.

"Moyugi told me to do it, see. He said to go help you out. Feel free to be grateful, okay?"

"Well of course I'm grateful," Haruhiro said. "Earlier, that was you, Kuro-san?"

"Who?" Merry squared off against him while her shoulders heaved with each breath.

"Ohhh—he's in the Day Breakers. Basically, that makes him our ally, or our comrade, you could say."

"I'm the guy who saved your life, yeah? If you want to make it simple."

"I...suppose you are," Haruhiro sighed, shaking his head right away.

This was no good. He felt like he was going to relax. It was too soon to let the tension out now.

"How are Rock and the others?"

"Dunno. Well, I'm sure they're doing fine. It all went according to Moyugi's plan, like always." Kuro put a hand on the branch, hung down from it, and dropped to the ground with an "Oof." Then he yawned and stretched. "All right. Well, later then, Junior."

"Huh? Where are you going?"

"I've worked a little too much today. I'm gonna go get some sleep somewhere. I'm tired, after all. Oh, yeah. You guys were planning to meet up at that cave, right?" Kuro pointed ahead and to the right. "It's thataway. Maybe six kilometers from here. Well, there you have it. Bye."

"Okay..."

Kuro waved to them, then disappeared into the fog. They may have been able to stop him and ask for directions, but Haruhiro didn't feel like it. He didn't just not feel like it; he didn't feel like much of anything.

His hands trembled a little. His feet wouldn't move.

What was he standing around in a daze for? Well, no, he wasn't in a daze.

So what?

"Haru, are you okay?"

He felt Merry's hand on his back.

Haruhiro nodded. Giving her that nod was the best he could manage.

Would Haruhiro have killed Ranta if Merry hadn't stopped him? In the end, he may not have been able to. Or he may have done it.

Had Ranta meant to kill Haruhiro?

It felt like it, but he may have been planning to show mercy at the very end.

Either way, Haruhiro had wounded Ranta with his stiletto. That hadn't been a scratch; it had been a fairly deep wound. If not treated properly, it was entirely possible it would develop into something really bad. It was a serious wound. That wasn't something you gave to a comrade.

Haruhiro wanted to squat down. If he lowered himself down, surely Merry would cheer him up. She'd comfort him; she might even embrace him. Haruhiro wanted those things. To be honest, he wanted them badly. But he couldn't do it.

He didn't want to indulge in Merry's kindness. It wasn't appropriate for Haruhiro to do that; he didn't have the right.

Obviously, he couldn't forgive Ranta. No matter what happened to Ranta, he deserved it. Even so, at least for the moment, he wasn't ready to forgive himself for what he had done with his own hands.

He didn't want to accept that Ranta was no longer their comrade.

I THINK I'LL WRITE about anime. I'd like to have this written down somewhere, so I'll write it here.

I've lived over ten years as a novelist, and taking a quick count, I've put out over eighty volumes, but *Grimgar of Fantasy and Ash* is my first series to be turned into an anime. It might be my first and my last. Honestly, I was half-convinced it was something I wouldn't experience in my lifetime as a novelist. I figured if I could live and die as a novelist, that wouldn't matter to me one bit.

That said, I had imagined it before, if it did happen for me: how I would feel, and what I would think. I was sure I'd be happy and, as it's common to say, I was sure I might think it was a tasty proposition. I might feel gratified that, after XX hard years of struggle, I was finally being recognized, so take that. I haven't exactly walked a flat road to get here, so I figured it might be a moving experience for me, too.

But, really, I was sure it would be a complicated feeling. Novels are, at least in my case, something where I create the main text myself from the ground up. Now that's going out of my hands. Others will be involved. They'll have their interpretations, and it will be expressed in a different way. It's going to become something different.

I might, for instance, have feelings like these about some parts.

Like, What were you thinking?

Or like, No, not like that, it's like this.

Or even, What? You just don't get it. Ugh, you're making

me mad now. Well, there's no helping it, I guess. I mean, I am an adult, after all. I'm writing novels, but I'm still a member of society. It's fine. Yes, yes. Even if I'm not satisfied, I can pretend I am. Well, what does it matter? You're all doing your best. Things are different for everyone, after all. I'm sure this is just how it is. I'll digest it and accept it.

While I can't claim not to have a strong ego, everyone, it's impossible not to have one, at least to some degree. Even if I do have one, I won't let it show, and I'll handle things cleverly. I'm an adult, after all.

Well, once the production of the anime *Grimgar of Fantasy and Ash* began, I was surprised. I didn't fall into that complicated emotional state at all.

In fact, the more I met with Director Ryosuke Nakamura, character designer Mieko Hosoi, the producers, and all the other staff, and the more I saw the scripts, design drawings, setting drawings, and storyboards, the more purely I found myself just looking forward to the anime. I could barely contain myself.

In the first meeting, I recall saying they were free to change anything, in any way, for the sake of the anime adaptation. The most important thing was for it to be interesting as an anime, so I wanted them to not hesitate and do all the things that needed to be done for that.

Director Nakamura immediately rejected this. I recall him saying that, even in the anime, they intended to depict the story of Haruhiro and the others in a way that followed the novel. Rude as this is for me to say, I really got the sense that he had read the novel *Grimgar of Fantasy and Ash*. The structure, the images, seeing various bits and pieces... I thought I could trust him completely, presumptuous as that is of me to say.

However, in fact, it was more than that.

Every time the production moved forward, I found myself captured by a strange feeling. Why did these people know so much about Grimgar? I mean, it was a novel I'd written, you know? I, obviously, understood it entirely. Well, there were some bits that hadn't even been written down, so I understood 120% of it.

What's this? These people understand as much as I do? That's strange. Do things like this happen?

While sitting in on the first recording session, I felt that feeling expand even more. In front of these voice actors who would portray the characters, there was Director Nakamura, who could perfectly put what Grimgar was into clear words better than I could, and who could describe it richly.

I had my chance to greet them, and though I'm an adult, a member of society, I was embarrassed that I could only say silly things. Then, finally, the voice actors performed.

Performed? Acted? No, no, this *was* Haruhiro. Haruhiro was there. Manato was there. Yume, Shihoru, Moguzo, Britney, Barbara-sensei, and Renji were all talking.

There were goblins!

When I heard Nobunaga Shimazaki who plays Manato, Mikako Komatsu who plays Yume, Haruka Terui who plays Shihoru, and Chika Anzai who plays Merry on internet radio and Niconama speaking about it, sometimes with passion, other times with cheer, and other times with tears, I would fall out of my chair laughing, or sometimes cry a little. Especially when it came to Manato, considering he leaves the story early, I, in my amateur estimation, felt it must have been a difficult role.

But Nobunaga really was Manato. Nobunaga even looks the part of Manato. Having written novels for a reasonably long time, this was my first time feeling this way, but I wished Manato could have lived longer. Seeing Nobunaga's Manato, hearing him, I couldn't help myself but think that.

Novelists are isolated. In isolation, there is freedom. In order to truly take hold of that ability to gain freedom, a novelist must be isolated. That's what I think, and that isn't going to change. However, just for the time that I am touching the anime *Grimgar of Fantasy and Ash,* I feel I may not be alone. It gives me the courage to be alone and write novels again.

I've run out of pages.

To Yusuke Kimura, who can fairly be said to have given birth to *Grimgar of Fantasy and Ash,* to Eiri Shirai, to the designers of KOMEWORKS among others, to everyone involved in production and sales of this book, and finally to all of you people now holding this book, I offer my heartfelt appreciation and all my love. Now, I lay down my pen for today.

I hope we will meet again.

—Ao Jyumonji